CONARD COUNTY
WITNESS

BY
RACHEL LEE

MILLS &
BOON

Published in Great Britain 2015
by Mills & Boon, an imprint of Harlequin (UK) Limited,
Eton House, 18-24 Paradise Road, Richmond, Surrey, TW9 1SR

© 2015 Susan Civil Brown

ISBN: 978-0-263-91828-1

18-1215

Printed and bound in Spain
by CPI, Barcelona

Rachel Lee was hooked on writing by the age of twelve and practiced her craft as she moved from place to place all over the United States. This *New York Times* best-selling author now resides in Florida and has the joy of writing full-time.

In honor of combat medics everywhere,
who never count the cost.

Chapter 1

Jess McGregor waited just down the block from Maude's diner at the Conard City bus station. Despite the chill of the late autumn day, he stood outside. His artificial leg was made largely of carbon composite and silicone, but the cold seemed to creep through it, making him ache.

But then, he was getting used to a missing leg that sometimes ached or screamed at him, even though it was gone. Phantom pain didn't feel very much like a phantom.

He waited for his late wife's best friend to arrive. They hadn't seen each other since the funeral five years ago, but they'd talked frequently on the phone since Sara's death, and when he learned that Lacy was afraid for her life, he wanted to make sure she didn't get off the bus in a strange town and not see someone she recognized.

At last, with a heavy chug of a diesel motor and brakes that squealed a little more than they should have, the bus pulled up. The doors opened and he waited with increasing impatience for the woman he was surprisingly eager to see again.

Then there she was, stepping down sideways and holding on to the bar to steady herself.

For an instant, a shaft of old grief speared him, nearly freezing him to the spot. He'd never seen Lacy without Sara, and part of him expected Sara to descend the steps right behind her. Impossible, stupid and the wrong way to feel. With effort, he subdued the pain. Sara was gone forever.

Five years didn't seem to have changed Lacy at all, except her heart-shaped face looked weary. Her long, flaxen hair was exactly as he remembered, gently curling, and her blue eyes, as bright as lasers, found him instantly. The weariness vanished from her face as she smiled and waved.

Even through her coat, he could tell she had lost weight. Not good. She'd been more worried than she had let on. The past couple of years had been hard on her.

Most of the people who climbed off the bus were either met by family or headed straight toward the diner to get some food before continuing their journey.

Lacy Devane strode right toward him. He tried not to limp as he walked toward her, but even after more than three years he had a bit of a hitch in his step. He tried not to do it because it wasn't good for his muscles and joints, but it still appeared from time to time. Especially when it was cold, like today.

"Jess!" She said his name warmly with a big smile and threw her arms around him in a hug. He reciprocated, wrapping her close and catching a whiff of her shampoo. Not since the funeral had he held a woman this close, and it struck him with a hard, unexpected and unwanted shaft of desire.

This would not do.

He stepped back quickly. "Bags?" he asked.

She nodded. "Two suitcases. I can't thank you enough for this invitation, Jess. Probably more than anything, I need to get away from it all and just relax. They keep telling me I'm not at risk anymore."

He snorted quietly. "That's probably hard to believe after all the time you spent under federal protection."

Her eyes danced up to his face, and a smile curved her lips. "That's likely the entire problem. I've been conditioned."

"Well, let's hope so, shall we? Because time will cure that. Do you want to go straight home with me or stop at the diner first? I can feed you at home, if you'd prefer that."

"Home," she said without a moment's hesitation. "I'd prefer the quiet."

And the invisibility, he suspected.

The driver pulled two more bags out of the luggage bins beneath the bus. Lacy headed toward them and he followed. "I'll get them."

He caught her biting her lip and knew she was concerned about his leg. But an artificial leg, while it might not be as good as the original in some ways, was no weaker. Nor was the rest of him. Without difficulty, he lifted both cases.

"Car's up the street a bit. We need to get you out of this cold."

She laughed. "I'm not freezing, but the wind definitely has a bite."

"Beginnings of winter," he responded. Casual, easy.

Except it was beginning to dawn on him that this was going to be neither. He'd met Lacy because he'd married her best friend. Lacy had visited Sara a number of times during their marriage, sometimes when Jess was overseas, sometimes when he was home. He liked her, he was glad Sara had her, and now since Sara's death she'd become a friend to him, too.

Just a friend, he reminded himself as he swung the two suitcases into the back of his SUV. He'd offered to give her a bolt-hole, a place to unwind after the terror she'd lived with for so long now and still couldn't shake even though it was over.

That's all he was doing: what Sara would have wanted him to do. Looking after her best friend.

So why did he keep noticing the way the wind caught her hair and bared the smooth nape of a lovely neck?

Get a grip, Jess. Just get a grip.

Lacy hoped her face hadn't revealed shock when she first saw Jess. The intervening five years hadn't been kind. He definitely looked older than the young man she had last seen at the funeral. Then his face had been muddied with grief, but now it had gained lines and maturity. But then the years hadn't been good to him, first taking Sara from him, then costing him his leg in Afghanistan. She had called often, especially at first, and he'd always tried to sound upbeat. It had been hard for him to do after Sara's passing, but sometimes she wondered how he had managed it at all after he came home from the war with a shattered body.

The lines in his face were attractive, but they spoke of a lot of pain and loss. All the youthful softness had vanished, leaving him with a chiseled face, dark hair and unusual green eyes. He was still tall—that hadn't changed—but she saw the hitch in his step and she suddenly had the worst urge to get him out of that parka and make sure the rest of him was okay.

Had he been a stranger, she might have allowed his sexiness to preoccupy her, but this man had been her best friend's husband. It seemed so out of place to notice such things that she stepped down firmly on her feminine response to his masculinity as he helped her into the car.

As he pulled out of the parking space, she wondered if she might have made a mistake coming here. Oddly, after all the hours they had talked on the phone over the years, now she felt unexpectedly awkward. She had to search for something to say as they drove down narrow streets lined by leafless trees. She seized on the first thing that came to mind.

"It's kind of you to do this," she offered.

"It's what Sara would have wanted."

Well, that was a firm reminder. What Sara would have wanted. She'd at least cherished a small hope that he wasn't doing this entirely out of a sense of obligation. She'd have turned him down. She didn't want to be anyone's duty.

But he seemed to have heard his own words because he qualified them. "I didn't mean to sound like I'm doing this only because of Sara. I've been worried about you. You've been through hell, and you need a break."

The words that emerged from her then shocked them both into silence for the rest of the drive. "Do you ever get a break from hell?"

She wished she could snatch them back, but it was too late. They lay there, poisonous and possibly hurtful. He didn't make a sound in response.

Oh, this was going to go well, she thought. Her visit was open-ended—she had been asked to stay as long as she liked—but at this rate she might be on the road again in a matter of days.

His two-story house was just outside town. It looked like an old farmhouse that had once stood as a solitary sentinel in wide-open spaces framed by distant mountains, but she guessed the town had been steadily, if slowly, reaching out toward it. Now it was less than a mile from the last cluster of dwellings they passed.

Her first impression was that he must have taken good care of it. While maintaining the impression of age, it still looked as fresh as yesterday, with its coat of white paint on the clapboards and straight lines. Against the brown and bare autumn grasses and trees, it stood out like a bright spot. Behind it, the mountains stood guard.

"This is lovely," she said as they pulled up the drive to the wide front porch. A peace offering.

"It keeps me busy." His tone was mild, pleasant. "There's always something that needs attention."

When they stopped, she opened her own door and climbed out. Jess immediately went to get her bags and carried them easily up onto the porch. He seemed to be doing very well with his artificial leg. Amazing man.

As he was unlocking the front door, however, he paused to look down at her gravely. "I get a few breaks from hell. As time passes, I get more of them."

"I shouldn't have said that," she offered quickly. "I'm tired and it just popped out."

One corner of his mouth lifted in a faint smile. "Relax, Lacy. We've walked through the valleys together more than once. Just be you, okay?"

Interesting way of phrasing it, she thought as she

stepped into a foyer that greeted her with polished wood floors and an impressive oak staircase. Walking through the valleys. They'd certainly been through a couple of them on the phone. "This is gorgeous, Jess!"

"This house is a great hobby. Do you want to go straight to your room, or would you rather have a hot drink first? I have tea, coffee and hot chocolate to offer."

"A hot drink sounds wonderful." Reaching for the buttons of her gray wool coat as the house's warmth washed over her, she shrugged it off, revealing a blue mohair sweater and black slacks, and hung it on the coat tree near the door. "From the looks of it, you've been really busy."

"A lot of free time when I'm not working. Kitchen is this way. I'd guess you're not exactly ready to sit yet."

"You've got that right." She traipsed after him, the heels of her boots clattering on the wood. She paused. "Will my boots hurt the floor?"

He glanced over his shoulder, this time really smiling. "That floor has been around a hundred years and it's not meant for basketball. Don't worry about it. Just do whatever feels comfortable."

The kitchen was big, country-style, probably once used to cook for a dozen or more. New appliances had replaced whatever had come before, and a partially finished counter and cabinet construction lined one wall. A round table sat in the center of the space. He hooked his parka over the back of one of the chairs, and she saw his green flannel shirt for the first time. He looked good in it, and the jeans he wore looked like a second skin. The years had changed his face, but evidently he'd maintained his fitness in every respect. His belly was flat, and his shoulders appeared powerful.

"What would you like to drink?" he asked.

She eyed the gleaming espresso machine on the counter. "Espresso? Lots and lots of espresso?"

That drew a laugh from him. "Straight up or latte?"

"Latte, please. Four shots."

"You *are* serious," he joked.

"I've been suffering from a drought ever since I got on that bus. So you're remodeling in here?"

He nodded and turned on the espresso maker. While it heated, he ground coffee beans. "Cabinets and counters weren't so important in the old days, I guess. Not as many cooking gadgets, maybe. I like gadgets."

"High-powered ones, to judge by the espresso maker."

He was putting coffee in the portable filter, but paused long enough to wink at her over his shoulder. "You should see the shed. Tools galore."

Darn, she'd forgotten how charming he could be. Yes, they'd spent countless hours chatting on the phone over the last five years, helping each other through rough times, but it wasn't the same as seeing him in person for the first time since the funeral. She'd never wondered why Sara had fallen for him, but she'd forgotten some of it evidently.

At last, feeling at loose ends, she sat at the table. Then another blunt question burst out of her. "Why wouldn't you let me come visit you in the hospital?"

"Ah, hell," he said quietly. "Hang on for a minute. That answer is going to take my full attention."

He had tall thermal cups for the lattes and soon they were seated at the table together. She waited for him to speak, wondering if she had pressed too far. They were friends, but not in the same way she and Sara had been. In fact, sitting in his house like this, she became acutely aware of all the gaps they had never closed. Places they had never ventured during their conversations.

"I guess," he said finally, "that I didn't want you to see me like that. I didn't even want my parents to see me like that, but they flew in from France and they saw. I'll never forget the expression on my mother's face. If what she saw nearly killed her, her expression nearly killed me. For a while there, I was honestly glad that Sara was gone and didn't have to endure it."

"I'm so sorry, Jess."

"Maybe in a way I was being selfish. I don't know. I just knew I was having enough trouble myself dealing with it all and I didn't want to be worrying about anyone else. So yeah, I guess it was selfishness. I was doped up, I felt like hell, everything hurt, and I just didn't want to deal with anyone else. I needed all my energy for me."

She nodded, feeling her heart squeeze with sympathy. "I get it. I wouldn't call it selfish as much as necessary. You had a lot to cope with, and probably didn't have much left over for trying to put a good face on it for others."

"Well, I suppose I left you wondering why the hell I didn't want a friendly visit. From your perspective it must have seemed cruel."

She lifted her head and gave him a wan smile. "I never thought of you as cruel, but it's nice to know it wasn't something about me. I can't begin to imagine what you were going through."

"It was never about you, Lacy. I just didn't want any friendly or cheerful visits from anyone. I got all the perkiness I could handle from my nurses. All of them excellent by the way, but they were determined not to let me sink into self-pity for even a moment." He paused, his face growing more serious. "Sometimes a self-pity party is useful. I had a few and I always wound up feeling stupid for it, but they helped. Sometimes I was just so damn angry, and I didn't have a thing to take it out on. Safe to say, I was miserable company for a while, and I didn't want to be dumping on the wrong people."

She nodded and sipped her warm coffee. "You make a great latte," she remarked as she set her mug down again. "I think I can understand, Jess. People coming to a hospital want to cheer the patient up. That's okay if the patient is feeling well enough for it. Not so good if it's just added stress."

"Exactly."

"How are your parents doing now?"

"You know they retired to France, right? They've been doing just fine since they hopped the Atlantic to see me getting around on my new leg. But that first visit?" He shook his head. "I'm sure no parent ever wants to see that. It must have shredded my mother's heart."

"Which didn't help you feel any better."

"Absolutely not. For a few days after they went back to France, I hit a low point, thinking it might have been easier on them if all they'd seen was a closed coffin."

Lacy's heart ached uncomfortably. She couldn't imagine it, but at some level she did understand what he was saying. "I'm sure they're glad to still have you."

He flashed an unexpected smile, warm and inviting. "Now they are, for sure." He reached across the table, his palm turned up, and she hesitated only briefly before laying her hand in his. His touch was warm, his skin a little calloused without being rough. A pleasurable shiver ran through her.

He let go of her and leaned back, still smiling. "It's

good to see you, Lacy. Really good. It's been a long time. I wanted to invite you for a visit once I got my new leg under me and settled here, but then you were in that protection thing. It was what, nearly three years? Do you want to tell me about that? It looks like it wasn't easy on you. You've lost weight."

"I have, a little. It wasn't that hard. I think I told you."

He paused, then it was his turn to be surprisingly blunt. "This is weird, sitting across the table from you."

She looked at him. "How so?"

"Like strangers, but not strangers. You've been a voice on the phone for so long. And we usually kept it as light as we could, didn't we?"

She nodded, her gaze drifting down to the dark wooden table. "I know," she said quietly. "So we're barely acquainted. I'm sorry, I shouldn't have come here."

"I didn't say that." His tone sharpened a bit, then quieted again. "It's just different. Maybe after we hang for a few days, we'll cross some of those bridges and be a little more honest with each other."

He was right. Those phone calls hadn't been entirely honest, even when they'd been full of the grief they'd both been trying to contain. As if certain social norms had to be observed no matter what. Politeness. Never really digging into the well of pain and despair that had afflicted them both, first about Sara, then about his wounding and then about her fears.

She sighed, took a deep draft of coffee, then tried for a smile. "Well, let's see if we can get to know each other better. Might as well if I'm going to be here a while."

He nodded. "Definitely. And I want to make it clear again, you're welcome to stay as long as you like. So tell me, Lacy, what was it really like to be a protected witness?"

"Annoying," she admitted. "I had two FBI agents hovering every single minute. At first I was scared. How could I not be? The US Attorney's office told me that someone had picked up intelligence about a threat against me. That I was going to have to be protected until after the trial. Listening to that I felt like ice was running down my spine. That only happens in the movies, you know? But there it was, happening to me. So I wound up being moved and I had my own protection detail. Discovering that your employer is laundering drug money is evidently a dangerous thing to do."

"I should think so! How did you find out?"

"I'm a good accountant. The first thing I noticed was that an awful lot of money was moving through accounts, then dispersing to others. Finally I became curious enough to look closer and I found *all* the accounts were shells. That's when I got scared the first time. A cursory glance wouldn't show anything unusual, but over time..." She shrugged. "Over time, it looked weirder and weirder. So I went to the FBI."

He looked amazed. "Why didn't you just run? Quit?"

"Because it was wrong. I didn't think about consequences, just that it was wrong, and like it or not, I was being made a party to it. So I made copies of some of the most revealing stuff for the FBI, and from there it just snowballed."

"Apparently." He shook his head. "You're a brave woman."

"I don't know about that. I'm here because I'm frightened, even though they keep telling me it's over, that I don't have to worry anymore." But she couldn't help looking toward the windows. The autumn day was beginning to darken.

Almost as if he could read her mind, Jess got up and began to close the dark blue kitchen curtains. They weren't the light, frilly things one usually saw in kitchens, but clearly full of weight and substance.

"These are thermal curtains," he remarked. "The other advantage is that no light passes through them. I'll keep them closed throughout the house until you can relax."

She almost hated herself then. "Jess, you can't live in a cave because I'm scared of the boogeyman!"

He flashed a grin. "It won't be a cave. As we get colder around here, I keep them closed most of the day anyway. I haven't gotten around to installing triple-paned windows yet. The curtains are easier. Don't worry about it. Just call it cozy."

A laugh escaped her, and the sound seemed to brighten his face. "It's been a long time since I heard you laugh."

The remark startled her, but she realized he was right. "It's been a long time since I heard you laugh, too," she replied.

Not since Sara. Before the aneurysm took her so unexpectedly, the three of them had shared a lot of laughter during visits and on the phone. But since Sara...

"There hasn't been a whole lot to laugh about," he said quietly. "Maybe it's time to change that."

But how? she wondered. Life had been slamming them both almost nonstop since Sara died. In the intervening five years, neither of them had experienced much joy in anything. And he'd had it harder than she. Her time in witness protection couldn't in any way measure up to his wounding and recovery. No way.

She suddenly felt almost small, allowing her silly fears to rule her when there was no reason.

"So the FBI keeps telling you you're safe now?"

She looked up, startled out of her internal soul-searching. "Yeah. It's supposed to be over. All the bad guys are behind bars. And I couldn't possibly be a threat to anyone now."

He nodded and came to stand beside her. "Easy for them to say. You're worrying about loose ends, aren't you?"

She nodded. "Loose ends and revenge."

"I don't think that's silly at all. You kept telling me on the phone you were being foolish, but I'm not buying it, Lacy. I'm not saying someone *is* after you, I'm just saying your fear isn't unreasonable. You tangled with some pretty big bad guys, and it hasn't been that long."

"I keep looking over my shoulder," she admitted, trying to repress a shudder. "I've become a nut about checking locks. I had a security system put in my apartment. Sometimes I think I've gone overboard into paranoia."

"Well, no one on earth will find you here. As far as the world is concerned, you and I have had no contact since the funeral. And you bought a bus ticket to Portland, right?"

"Yes." The town where she had gone to college. It would be the logical place for her to go.

"Then you're off the grid," he said cheerfully. "And you're going to stay that way. No accessing your bank accounts, no using credit cards. We can even get you a new cell phone."

She twisted her head, looking up at him. "You're enjoying this!"

He bent, his eyes dancing. "I'm enjoying the challenge. I'm also glad to see you again. And since I think you'll be safe here, why not enjoy it?"

She bit her lip, a maelstrom of unidentifiable emotions sweeping through her, then reluctantly laughed. "You're right. Might as well turn it into a game. It's got to be better than the way I was feeling in Dallas."

He straightened and gave her shoulder a quick squeeze, sending hot honey racing through her veins. The reaction caught her by surprise. *Uh-oh*, she thought. "It'll be a fun game if that's what we choose to make it. Now let's talk about dinner. I have a number of choices for you."

As he opened the fridge and checked the cupboard, tossing out meal ideas, Lacy realized for the first time that this *could* be fun. She was actually beginning to look forward to it. The weight of the past three years seemed to slide from her shoulders. She had an ally now.

Out on the road in front of the house, a man parked for a while, thinking and watching. The woman had arrived with two large suitcases, which seemed to indicate more than a brief visit. The man had brought her to his home, which seemed significant.

Now, unless something changed soon, he had two targets, not one. Damn, he hated it when things didn't go according to his plan. He'd paid dearly for that once, and had come to loathe unexpected complications.

Of course he could deal with it. He had plenty of training in that—not that it always worked, but it worked often enough. However, two targets increased the danger. One person could have an accident or just disappear out here. Two made it more difficult.

And challenging, he thought, a small smile playing over his lips. Drumming his fingers on the steering wheel, he decided he had sat here long enough. No traffic had come by but he didn't want someone to notice a vehicle parked in an unusual place. Didn't want some county mountie stopping to ask if everything was okay.

Putting the car into Drive, he pulled away, thinking. The woman could move on again, removing the second-target problem from the equation. But if she stayed...

He decided he was going to have to keep an eye on those two for a few days, study the pattern of their movements. It was possible he'd only have to take the one he wanted. The other could just be a cipher.

Or, he thought with vicious pleasure, he could just cut loose and find a way to take them both. One was necessary. The other might just be fun.

Sorting through possibilities, he began to think it might be enjoyable. There were certain talents he hadn't been able to use in a long time. The talent for inflicting pain and terror. Yes, it might be a lot of fun. He did, after all, fancy himself to be like a big cat, a lion or tiger. They were patient when they needed to be, and they played with their prey. He could do with a little play.

Deciding that he could enjoy this added fillip put the smile back on his face. He was whistling as he headed down the highway to a roadhouse where no one would even notice him. Too many strangers passing through, too many people with a good reason to keep their mouths shut.

He'd cased it well. He was going to have his revenge and enjoy it, too.

Chapter 2

Jess awoke in the morning, acutely aware that he was not alone in the house. It wasn't some sound that betrayed it, but rather a faint perfume in the air, womanly scents he hadn't shared quarters with since Sara. Amazing how they seemed to make their way through the house.

He rolled over, looked at the clock and saw that it was his usual rising time of six thirty. He'd taken a vacation from the clinic to look after Lacy, but ordinarily he'd rise, shower, dress, scan the news online and be at the clinic by 8:00 a.m. This morning would be different.

No sound indicated that Lacy was up yet. He wasn't surprised. She'd seemed exhausted, and had begun nodding off shortly after dinner, until he'd finally shooed her to her room. Whatever terrors she'd been experiencing, along with a lengthy bus trip, seemed to have drained her.

She'd changed, too, from the relatively carefree woman who had visited him and Sara. He sensed a shell around her now, that she'd been permanently altered by living with so much fear for so long. He understood that to his very core. War and his wound had changed him forever.

He swung himself into a sitting position and reached for his metal crutch. His artificial leg stood poised by the bed, the microprocessor recharging, but first he needed a shower. In fact, converting part of his ground-floor bedroom into a private bath had been his first change to this house. He could crutch into the shower and sit on a bench while he washed. A necessary luxury. Two showerheads were another luxury, not necessary but certainly pleasurable. These days he took all the small pleasures he could find.

When he had dried off sufficiently, he wrapped his stump—not a pretty sight, though the doctors had done their best to neaten it up—applying the silicone sock with the collar that helped keep the leg on, then stepped into the leg. He stamped it five or six times until all the air had been driven out of the socket and the fit felt secure. He often thought he looked like he was part Terminator these days. He had a plastic foot cover for wearing shoes and socks, but the rest of the leg, reaching above his knee, was carbon composite and metal. He wasn't concerned about the cosmetics, simply the ease of maintenance and mobility. It served him well, and except when he was home was always covered by scrubs or jeans.

He pulled on a red sweatshirt and some old jeans, ran a brush quickly through his hair, then made his way down a hallway to the kitchen. He was craving coffee, but he generally did every morning. First things first.

Still no sounds from upstairs, so he figured Lacy was still deep in her dreams. He hoped they were pleasant ones.

It struck him anew how different it felt to actually have her visiting. All those phone conversations had left a distance between them, but he wasn't sure why that surprised him. She was right: they'd spent a whole lot of time trying to be positive, and except for right after Sara's funeral, they hadn't shared much of the heavy stuff. He'd been reluctant to talk about his injury, and maybe she couldn't say much while she was in protection.

That idea that they were strangers, but not really strangers, gripped him. When she had come to visit before, she'd been Sara's friend. And while he had liked her a whole lot, he'd still performed his duties, and made space for the two of them to have their girl time. In short, he'd tried not to intrude unnecessarily on their friendship.

After Sara had died, they'd shared grief in long conversations filled with remembrances. Then he'd returned to his unit in Afghanistan, and conversations had become limited to short letters that passed back and forth. Just before he was wounded, they'd had their one and only Skype conversation.

Afterward, he hadn't talked to her, or much to anyone, for months. As soon as he was able, he'd had the Marines all over him with questions about command decisions made during that last mission. As a combat medic, he didn't have much to offer, although privately he'd thought the CO was a jerk. The CO had changed the mission midstream to one they hadn't planned for, and even a medic knew how dangerous that was. But

Jess hadn't felt qualified to judge, and given all he'd forgotten thanks to his wounding, he didn't really trust his own memory. So he'd kept his mouth pretty much shut.

Then...well then, he'd started his rehab. He'd talked to Lacy only briefly and infrequently during that time. The next thing he knew, he was completing his certification as a physician's assistant, something he'd started while in service, and Lacy was suddenly involved with a legal case that had left her clearly frightened but unable to talk about it.

Five years of phone conversations didn't add up to much, it seemed. Not when he really thought about it. He felt like he knew her but didn't know her at all. A very odd sensation.

He hadn't paid attention to her looks when Sara was alive, and hadn't seen her in real life since the funeral. There was no mistaking, however, the way he was responding to her now. She drew him. Maybe he was finally getting ready to move on with life in important ways. But no one, he was sure, could ever replace Sara, so he put that thought away. It wouldn't be fair to Lacy.

Still, she was quite pretty and if she could just put on those four or five pounds she seemed to have lost, she'd look even better. Heroin chic didn't appeal to him.

But as he sat with his coffee, the toaster, a loaf of bread and a plate of butter in front of him, he wondered about that weight loss. It struck him as a red flag for her level of distress. For the past couple of months, since the trial had ended, he'd been listening to her say how silly she was to still be afraid. The FBI had said so.

Well, you couldn't put someone under protection for the better part of a year and not expect them to have some aftershocks. What's more, he didn't think she was

being at all silly. The Feds thought they'd gotten everyone involved, but how could they be sure? And then there
was the revenge she had mentioned. The huge sums of
money that had been passing through those accounts
might mean someone else was still out there, someone
very angry, someone who held her responsible for their
losses. He wasn't as prepared to dismiss her fears as
the Feds, even if she had already told them everything
she knew.

But she ought to be safe here, he assured himself.
There was no reason anyone should link the two of them,
not when they hadn't seen each other since the funeral.
The phone calls might be like breadcrumbs but probably unavailable to anyone except the phone company
and the government.

"Good morning."

He looked up almost with a start. Only then did he
realize how lost in thought he'd been. He hadn't even
heard her come downstairs, and that disturbed him.
Some gatekeeper he'd make if he lost the basics of staying alert to every noise. He guessed he was rusty, but
that had to end now. Surely he could remember all his
hard-learned skills.

"Good morning. Grab a cup and some coffee. Just
regular this morning. And if you want toast, get a plate,
too. There's jam in the fridge if you like."

He'd already decided that he wasn't going to take care
of her like a guest. He figured that would make her un-
comfortable over the long run.

She was wrapped in a royal-blue fleece robe with
matching slippers on her feet, and her blond hair looked
charmingly tousled, as if she'd only wasted a quick
minute with her brush. "Coffee," she said in a pretend-

zombie voice, holding her arms out in front of her and swaying side to side as she crossed the kitchen.

He laughed. Apparently a good night's sleep had done her wonders. She found herself a mug and a plate, but skipped the offer of jam.

"That bed was so comfortable," she said as she sat with her coffee and plate. "Like sleeping on clouds."

"Or you were just that tired."

Her blue eyes twinkled at him. "That's a definite possibility. I'll test it again tonight and let you know."

"Good idea. I got it in a hurry when you said you'd come, and the selection wasn't exactly breathtaking. I spent about five minutes on each mattress, then realized I didn't have the faintest idea whether you'd prefer hard or soft."

"It was great," she assured him. "The best test is sleeping for ten hours and waking up without any stiffness or sore spots. The mattress passed. Even my bed at home can't do that."

Toast popped up just as he saw a shadow cross her face. He let it ride while he reached for her plate and placed two slices on it. Then he nudged the butter her way.

"Thanks." She busied herself spreading the soft butter thinly on the toast, while he considered how he could get some more calories into her. It wasn't as if he knew what foods she liked, and he'd been reluctant to buy too much until he found out.

"You need to eat more," he said before biting into his own piece of toast.

"Eating hasn't been easy with my stomach always in knots," she confessed. "Are you going all medical on me?"

He half smiled. "Once a medic, always a medic. You know it's not healthy to be underweight. I'm sure you don't need me to tell you that. So if we can unknot your stomach, I suggest you indulge in a little overeating. Not too much, just a little."

"Orders received."

She tried to keep her tone playful, but he heard something else in it, something beneath it that was dark. "Lacy? Talk to me if you can."

"So says the world's biggest clam."

He couldn't deny it. He hadn't always been that way, certainly not before Sara's passing. But he guessed he was now, and stared into the empty years since, years when he'd tried to skim the surface with everyone while facing his demons alone. He'd certainly put this woman at arm's length when it came to the things that mattered most to him. He wondered if he'd been unfair. But at the same time, he'd sensed that opening all that up might spill ugliness all over everyone who cared about him.

"Touché," he said.

She shook her head. "That wasn't fair. You had your reasons."

"And you have yours."

She swallowed another bite of toast and drank some more coffee. "The day the FBI descended on my company with their search warrants, I knew I was in for it. No one there knew I'd told them, but by the time the agents walked out with all those computers and files, it was probably pretty clear it was me. We were all sent home, of course, because no one could work."

"So this effectively cost you your job."

"Mine and a few other people. There was only one

section that was handling these transactions, as it turned out. So everyone else was in the clear."

"Then what?"

She smiled ruefully. Or perhaps bitterly. He couldn't tell. "Nothing for a while. The firm continued to pay me even though I was furloughed, maybe because they didn't want to look bad in the middle of the mess."

"Or maybe because they didn't want any disgruntled employees finding other things to report."

She tilted her head, her blue eyes looking thoughtful. "That might have been it as much as anything. I hadn't thought of that."

She sighed and didn't object when he placed another slice of toast on her plate. Rising, he refreshed both their coffee mugs, then resumed his seat.

He spoke when she remained silent for a while. "So you sat around twiddling your thumbs, wondering if you should find another job?"

"Not exactly. There was little time for thumb twiddling. The FBI and US Attorney kept me pretty busy answering questions about the money trail."

"That's what exposed you to the death threat?"

She nodded and looked down. "That would be my guess. I didn't get details, probably because they were protecting their sources. I just got told to pack up, that there was a credible threat against me, and I was moving to a safe house. After that, the grand jury and the trial. In between, I spent a lot of time with federal forensic accountants, building the information into an unmistakable series of money transfers. They got a number of the people at my company, mostly some higher-ups, and they got the people who were involved in the drug trafficking. All very dull."

"Except the part where you were threatened."

She laughed, a short, humorless sound. "Except that part. Then, all of a sudden the trial was over, everyone was in jail and because of the threat against me, the judge refused to release anyone pending appeal. So I was safe."

He watched her make a nightmare sound mundane, and wondered if either of them would ever get past that. Trivializing all the traumas and fears. It seemed they were a pair. "But not really safe."

She looked at him. "I don't know, Jess. That's the bad part. I don't know. Everyone seems to think I'm past the point of trouble. I have no more information to give, the testifying is all over, the people who might want to hurt me are in prison. But…" She looked away.

"You can't quite believe it."

"No. I can't. I got to watch this whole thing unfold from a front row seat. My God, the tentacles just kept reaching out. When you're dealing with that, how can you be sure you've found everyone? Especially shadowy figures who might be even higher up that no one could find? I don't know. What I do know is that I just don't feel safe anymore. Time will help, I suppose. But nothing is going to help me find another job."

He reared back. "Why?"

"Because obviously I can't be trusted. I revealed privileged information which led to the arrest of some of my former bosses. Who would trust me now?"

"Anybody who wants to run an honest business," he said firmly, but he had to admit he could see her problem. Still, her situation had been unique. Surely some employer ought to see that. "How are you managing? Financially, I mean."

"Well, the Feds took care of my expenses until the trial was over, and I have an inheritance from my parents."

He nodded. He knew her folks had died just after he had married Sara. They'd been sailing to Bermuda on their small boat and had never arrived. The Bermuda Triangle again, except he believed the causes were natural. He'd heard that sudden storms could blow up out there, not to mention rogue waves. And the Gulf Stream itself was fast enough to sweep away wreckage and bodies in no time at all.

"Maybe you should ask the Feds if they need another forensic accountant."

She surprised him with a laugh, her face clearing. "One of them mentioned that possibility to me. At the time, I wasn't looking for a job, obviously, and didn't realize that I'd totally screwed myself by going to the government with that information. But he said he'd be in touch if he heard of an opening. Or I could start my own small firm." She shrugged. "First, I need to stop looking over my shoulder all the time."

There was that, he thought, finishing his toast and getting more coffee. He could make her safe here, off the grid, but what about going home? How much time would pass before she felt truly safe again? Would she ever?

"Jess?" She spoke just as he sat again.

"Hmm?"

"What about you? How are you doing now? Really?"

He hesitated, the urge to say everything was just great taking over again. The two of them had been doing that for a long time now. But she'd just let him know she was facing a problem as big as her fear: finding employment. He preferred riding the surface these days, leaving the depths of his being untouched, but she'd know he wasn't being truthful. On the phone, she'd seemed acutely aware of changes in his tone, even when she had learned not to press him, but now she could see him, face-to-face. Maybe it was time to cross one of those bridges he'd been talking about yesterday.

"Mostly okay," he said. "I run the minor emergency clinic. It's an extension of the community hospital. But I think I told you that. Being a physician's assistant, I can take care of a lot of things on my own, but I'm under a doctor's supervision. I like it."

"Sort of what you trained for."

"Exactly. And I much more enjoy taking care of broken bones or sore throats than war wounds, I can tell you."

"I have absolutely no trouble believing that." She smiled at him over her cup. "I never told you, but I thought you were incredibly brave, being a medic. You strike me as the type who would take risks that others might not be willing to."

"I don't know that that's fair or even true. We were all taking risks. Any one of the guys in my squad would have risked everything to help a wounded buddy. I was just lucky in that I could do more extensive first aid than they could, so I could do more. That's all."

She hesitated visibly. "If you don't want to talk about this, I understand."

"Might as well," he said after a beat. "It's not like the movies anymore. I carried a weapon because of the places we were going into. I had to be prepared to protect my patients or myself. Just like any other soldier. The Red Cross on my pack and shoulders was no protection, but more of a target. In theory, it protected me as long as I didn't shoot offensively. In theory."

She compressed her lips, looking at him from suddenly haunted eyes. "It certainly didn't protect you in the end."

"No." Not much he could say about that. It hadn't protected him, or anyone else, from a glory hound who'd changed the operation in midstream and cost the lives of his buddies and the lives of a lot of innocent civilians. He closed his eyes, allowing himself for one instant to see the little girl he'd been trying to help when the grenade hit too close. He didn't know what happened to that child. Hell, he didn't remember much after that. An air strike had come, they told him; combat search and rescue had pulled out the dead and wounded, but he didn't remember. He just wished he knew what had happened to that little girl.

Ah, hell. Standing, he walked out of the room, letting his leg hitch all it wanted until he stood at the front window. He pulled back the heavy curtain a bit and looked out at a cold gray day. He'd have bet on snow before the day was out. A light one.

A step behind him caused him to turn around. "Jess, you okay?"

He couldn't quite summon a smile. "I will be."

She nodded. "I'm going to head up and take a shower, if that's okay. And don't keep the curtains closed on my account."

Before he could answer, she turned and ran up the stairs.

There were good reasons for skimming the surface. That little girl was one of them. He'd tried to find out about her, but nobody knew. A buddy had been back in the area and asked about the child who had an infected wound and was being helped by a medic before hell had rained on them from the cliffs above. No one knew, or no one wanted to answer. She was a big question mark that would probably remain for the rest of his days.

He turned back to the window, staring blindly out at the winter-dying world. He didn't often open the doors to the past. It was a dangerous place to go, dangerous in a very different way from actually being there.

Unfortunately, by her mere presence here, he suspected Lacy was going to open some of those doors. They had a past together, of sorts, and what else were they going to talk about? The future? Neither of them seemed to have much of one right now.

Swearing softly, he dropped the curtain and decided he'd take Lacy out, show her the little town, go to the grocery and find out what she liked to eat. Take it day by day until she started to settle and feel safe again.

What else could they do?

Lacy scolded herself all the way through her shower, blow-drying her hair and getting dressed. She shouldn't have brought up the war. Some matters were best left alone, and she couldn't imagine his nightmare experiences in combat. Why disturb the ashes by stirring them up? But she'd stirred them and had watched a change come over him, watched him mentally leave the room even before he walked out of it. Going to some faraway place, a bad place he probably wanted to forget.

Man, had she lost all her tact and sensitivity during her time in protection? Basic social skills had repeatedly slipped away from her since Jess had picked her up, and she couldn't blame lack of sleep this morning.

She sat on the edge of her bed to pull on socks and her walking boots, thinking that she needed to rattle herself back into shape. What did she think she was doing here? Hiding out, that was all, and that didn't entitle her to disturb whatever peace Jess had managed to find. Or was she hoping for something else, something she had no right to?

He was sexy, all right. Very. But he was also the husband of her deceased best friend. To see him any other way would dishonor Sara's memory. And if Sara were here, she'd probably be demanding to know when Lacy had become such an emotionally inept idiot. *Leave the man alone.*

Somehow she had to find other things to talk with him about, safe things. Matters that wouldn't stir up painful memories for him.

The problem was, their entire relationship had been founded on Sara. She had brought them together. So they could talk of memories of happier times with her, which would inevitably lead to the sorrow of her sudden loss, or they could talk about the aftermath, the war... God, it seemed hopeless. Everything they had left seemed to rest on pain. How could she get past that?

She found Jess downstairs, looking as if he had shaken off the shadows she had brought back.

"I thought we could go into town," he said. "Conard City is a little place, but it has charm. Then grocery shopping. I didn't do much because I have no idea what you like to eat."

She returned his smile. "Odd, isn't it? We've known each other thirteen years and we don't know the simplest things about each other."

"Well, Sara always took care of the cooking, and I

honestly don't remember if she made any special dishes just for you. It's not like I was home a lot."

"No." Two endless wars, a navy medic assigned to the Marine Corps...no, he hadn't been home a lot. And when he had been, Lacy had kept her visits reasonably brief so as not to impinge on the couple's rare time together. "Well, let's go. I'd like to see the town and maybe we can reach a meeting of palates at the grocery."

He laughed and reached for her coat. "We need to get you a parka. This may be okay for Dallas, but the wind and cold here is going to be a problem."

"I can't," she reminded him. "You told me not to access my bank or credit cards."

He arched a dark brow at her. "Okay then, keep a tally sheet, Ms. CPA, and when you feel safe enough to go home, you can repay me."

She guessed that was fair enough and let him help her into her coat.

"Why did you decide to settle here?" she asked as they drove toward town.

"One of the very few long-range plans Sara and I ever made was to get a place in the country when we retired. This isn't exactly what she was thinking of, but it's fine for me. Anyway, after living all crammed in the kind of housing we could afford around military bases, Sara started longing for open space. She used to say she didn't want neighbors close enough to know every time she flushed the toilet."

Lacy laughed. "I can hear her saying that. Do you see her mother often?"

"Not at all. After the funeral, it was like she didn't want anything to do with me. You?"

Lacy shook her head. "No. I decided it was probably too painful for her."

"Maybe so." He glanced her way. "And you. Losing your parents in the Bermuda Triangle."

A laugh escaped her. "It was a long time ago, Jess. But it sounds like the punch line to a joke, doesn't it?"

"You ever wonder?"

"Constantly. It's not easy to accept that I'll never know what happened. I console myself with the fact that they were doing what they loved. My dad should have been born with webbed feet. Or born in the days of sailing ships. He and mom were fortunate to have enough money to pursue their dreams. It's odd, though."

"What?"

"That sail to Bermuda was something they'd done so many times. I was more worried about their plan to sail around the entire globe the next year. Never occurred to me that something they'd done so often would be what killed them."

"Like driving a car."

"Exactly. When somebody runs to the store, you never imagine they won't come back." She shrugged. "They sailed to the Bahamas several times a year and I thought of it the same way as you would running across town to pick something up. Or they sailed into the South Caribbean. It was hard to keep them on dry land."

"Then I went into the Navy and hardly ever saw water." He spoke with humor, eliciting another laugh from her. "Do you like sailing, too?"

She answered melodramatically. "*I* get seasick."

He laughed. "Motion sickness patches?"

"They only work for me if it's calm. Pitch me around a bit and it's not pretty."

He fell silent while she looked around as they drove through residential streets. People had built close together for the most part, probably for mutual support, because there sure wasn't a lack of land surrounding the town.

Then they hit a street that was wider than the rest, lined with large, gracious houses and tall trees that were probably breathtaking in the spring and summer. Some people around here at one time or another had done very well.

Next came the town center and she was surprised. It didn't look Western, but rather like many old small towns she had seen in the east, with a central courthouse square, the requisite soldier statue out front, and a pretty park surrounding it with paths and stone benches and tables. Inviting. Storefronts surrounded the entire square, but before she could identify more than the one labeled "Sheriff's Office," they turned a corner.

Now she knew where she was. She recognized the bus stop down the street, but Jess pulled them into a space in front of the City Diner.

"Everyone refers to this by the owner's name, Maude. So you won't get confused if someone refers to Maude's diner. The woman is a bear, she seems perpetually in a bad mood, and her daughters take after her both in appearance and manner. Just ignore it. It's local color."

"Gotcha. Why are we stopping?"

"Because you need more than toast for breakfast and so do I. I'm up for steak and eggs right now. Then we can wander around a bit and hit Freitag's for that parka."

Lacy wasn't in any particular rush to get a parka—until she stepped out of the car and the wind hit her. It zipped down the street like a demon on a mission, slicing through her coat like a knife. Her eyes watered and she gasped. "When did it turn so cold?" It hadn't been this cold when they left the house, surely.

"In the last ten minutes," he answered, taking her arm and drawing her to the diner's door. "Ever heard of a clipper?"

"Which kind?"

"Weather. Bet we're getting one. Sudden influx of Arctic air. It can move in fast."

"I need an igloo," she retorted as he opened the door.

Inside she saw a spotlessly clean, if tattered, area of tables and booths, along with a counter and stools. Delicious aromas issued from the kitchen, and the place was half-full. They found a booth by the window unoccupied, but as soon as they sat Lacy wondered if that was wise. She could feel cold coming from that window.

But as she settled, she became aware of the conversation around her. Everyone was talking about the coming change in the weather. Most were older men, probably retired now, and they all seemed to know each other, calling back and forth freely between tables and booths.

"It might take us to twenty or thirty below," said one man.

"But not much snow," answered another. "Still, you don't want to be having car trouble in this. Best eat up fast, George."

Jess spoke to her. "Might be good advice for us, too. We really need to get you something warmer. Soon."

Cups suddenly slammed down on the table in front of them. Lacy almost jumped, then looked up at a large, frowning woman who could have been any age at all past sixty.

"What'll it be, Jess?"

"Steak and eggs for me, the usual. But Lacy hasn't had a chance to look at the menu yet. Could you give us a few, Maude?"

"Don't be taking all morning. Weather's turning bad. Real bad."

"I noticed," Lacy offered with a tentative smile. "It got a lot colder just since we left the house."

Maude grunted and moved on.

"I see what you mean," Lacy told Jess, keeping her voice low. She was glad to see his eyes dance.

"Just one of the entertaining things about living here."

She decided on an omelet and Maude wasted no time collecting the order and heading for the kitchen. A younger clone of her with a name tag that said Mavis filled their coffee cups from a fresh pot.

Lacy noticed that the sky outside was growing increasingly leaden. "Do you think it will snow?" The idea of seeing some real snow excited her.

"We might get a little," Jess answered. "When it turns this cold this fast, though, it's usually just a few inches. These fronts are often dry."

"I bet it's pretty, though."

"But you get snow at home, don't you?"

She nodded. "Not a whole lot, but during December and January we might see it once or twice, and it never lasts long. We're more likely to have ice than snow."

"I've heard Texans say the roads get slipperier there than elsewhere."

"Everything is bigger in Texas," she said drily. "Including the ice. Honestly, I don't know if it's true, or if it's just because people don't know how to drive on it. It's possible, I suppose, given the way the sun bakes the roads most of the year. There might be a lot of oil on them."

"Or maybe because the roads don't really get a chance to get cold, a layer of ice forms on them under the snow."

"I truly don't know. I spent most of my life in Oregon and Miami until I took the job in Texas. When it got icy or snowed, we delayed the opening of business a few hours until the roads cleared. In short, I don't have anything to compare it to."

"If you hang around here for a while, you'll have a comparison."

She returned his smile just as plates were dropped in front of them with a clatter. His steak and eggs looked perfectly done, as did her omelet. It looked so light she thought it might deflate if she put her fork in it. A tall stack of toast arrived and was set between them like the Leaning Tower of Pisa.

"Dig in," he said. "You're about to find out why everyone puts up with Maude."

The omelet was incredible, amazingly fluffy without being dry. She closed her eyes with pleasure as it almost seemed to melt in her mouth. "All sins are forgiven," she said after she swallowed.

Jess cracked a laugh. "Exactly." He glanced out the window again. "Let's not take too long, though. We need to get you a jacket quickly. Then we'll see if you're warm enough to continue to the grocery."

It seemed almost heretical to hurry, but she did. It was clear others around them were as concerned about the incoming weather, and the place began to empty out before she was half done with her omelet.

"I'm full," she said regretfully. "And it won't keep well."

"If you're ready, let's go. We need to get some food in that house. Really need. If the weather turns seriously bad, we'd better be prepared."

She pulled on her own coat while he paid the bill, then he drove them around the corner and a little way down the main street.

"Ordinarily I'd walk this distance," he remarked. "But today's not the day for it."

She agreed. Just her brief exposure had left her feeling chilled, and her eyes were watering again.

One step into Freitag's Mercantile made her want to stay and browse forever, though. It reminded her of older times with its jammed racks and shelves, piled tables and creaky wooden floors. Jess was a man on a mission, however. He led her straight back to the parkas, eyed her and pulled a small one off the rack. Electric blue.

"Try this."

It was puffy with fiberfill, and the hood had gray fur around it. When fully zipped up, she was peeking out a tunnel. "Wow," she said from the depths.

"You'll understand the need when it gets really cold." Reaching out, he unzipped it a bit and pushed the hood back. "Now for some insulated underclothes."

"You're kidding."

"Nope. Long johns for sure. Layers are good unless you're planning to spend much time outside. Then we'll need to take some added steps."

He pointed to a rack of silky thermal undergarments. "Shirts and pants both. You might even find you like lounging around in them. Then for some decent gloves or mittens."

She emerged from the store wearing her new parka and was immediately grateful for it. The difference was remarkable. Jess tossed her coat into the back along with her bags of thermal underwear and they climbed quickly into his SUV. "The market," he said. "And I don't like the look of the sky to the northwest. When we get to the grocery parking lot, you can get a full view. Ugly would be a good word for it."

"So we need to keep hurrying?"

"Double-time."

"I can do that." Deciding this was fun, probably because she didn't *have* to go anywhere, she leaned back and prepared to enjoy her first experience of a clipper. Well, that, and Jess's company.

Neither of them noticed the car that followed at a distance to the grocery parking lot. It settled into a space away from the front door, near the street, and eyes followed them as they climbed out and went inside.

The new jacket was a sign, the hunter thought. This was no short visit; she wouldn't be gone in a few days. He, too, had heard the weather warnings, and decided the extreme cold would work against him. The tinny radio station said it should warm up to safer temperatures in a few days. Safer to operate then, when he wouldn't be risking his own life in temperatures well below zero.

He could wait. He'd waited a long time already. He could afford a few more days, or even a few weeks, if that seemed best.

He'd learned to bide his time, not to leap too quickly at opportunities. Which made him ever so much more effective, he figured.

More time to gather intelligence. More time to see if the woman showed any signs of moving on. More time to pick his place and means. More time to play with his prey.

More time. He savored the idea. With each additional

day, he could build his strategy, make it better. Make it more foolproof. And he could terrorize them even longer.

Yes, he liked that very much. Whistling again, he ignored the stiffening wind even when it rocked his car a bit, and waited for the two to emerge from the grocery.

Chapter 3

"Go put your thermals on," Jess said as they piled out of the car. "I'll bring in the groceries."

She might have argued out of sheer politeness, but it seemed to have grown even colder, and the wind cut through her jeans. She grabbed the bag from Freitag's and headed inside, running upstairs to hurry so she could help Jess with the ton of groceries he'd bought. It seemed like a lot to her, but she usually shopped for one, and didn't know the size of Jess's appetite. Besides, apparently he didn't want to get caught short if the weather turned really bad and stayed that way.

Finding a small pair of scissors in her travel sewing kit, she used them to cut off all the tags and then climbed into her new underwear. Man, it was silky on her skin, but in no time at all she could feel how it was capturing her body's heat. By the time she pulled on her yellow sweater and jeans again, she felt comfortably warm.

Downstairs, though, she found Jess bringing in the last of the canvas bags of groceries. He had the table and counters full of them.

"Let me help," she said.

"I can do it," he assured her.

She hesitated, wondering if his leg made him demand independence, or if he was just being gentlemanly. This could be a minefield. Finally, she said tentatively, "It would be nice if I knew where everything was."

He paused, cans in his large hands, then smiled. "You're right. I'm just used to doing everything myself. Help is welcome."

Well, they'd skated over that one, she thought with relief. If any skating had been involved. How would she know? On the phone he cracked jokes about his artificial leg, but maybe it wasn't so funny in real life. She hoped he'd talk about it at some point so she knew what the safe topics were. More important, she wanted to know how he really felt about it.

"You're not worried about the power going out?" she asked as she stacked meat and frozen vegetables in the freezer.

"Hardly. The back porch makes a great freezer this time of year."

She laughed quietly. "I didn't think of that. Duh."

When they'd finished stashing supplies for an army, Jess folded the canvas bags neatly—military training, she supposed—and placed them on a shelf by the side door. "Let's go check the weather," he suggested.

A glance out the window seemed enough. Everything about the day appeared inhospitable, from the darkening sky to the tumbleweeds that blew past so fast she could only imagine the strength of the wind that was driving them.

In the front room, Jess turned on the TV. The image was a little snowy, but the weather report came across loud and clear. A fast-moving Arctic air mass was pushing south toward Denver, bringing temperatures as low as thirty below in some areas with wind gusts up to fifty miles an hour at the frontal boundary. Residents were advised to stay indoors if at all possible and to try to avoid travel, as a car breakdown could prove deadly. Only two or three inches of snow were expected, but would be accompanied by whiteout conditions, bringing visibility to near zero. The meteorologist moved on to talk about how rare a polar outbreak was this early in the year, explaining it was being caused by a Pacific typhoon that was pushing the jet stream northward with a resultant dip as it tried to swing south again.

Lacy had paid scant attention to the weather in Dallas unless there was a severe storm or tornado warning, but she'd never really wondered about the mechanics of it all. This global view fascinated her.

"You look excited," Jess remarked.

She glanced away from the TV and saw him smiling at her.

"I've never been through this before," she answered, "and thirty below sounds more like a movie title to me. Now it's for real. Can I actually step out into it?"

"Briefly, when the wind calms a bit. Right now, any exposed skin would be in danger of frostbite faster than you could believe."

She nodded, accepting his greater expertise. "What about heat?"

He pointed to a cast-iron woodstove in one corner. "I've got plenty of wood stacked out back. Would you like a fire?"

Instantly she became enchanted. "Oh yes! I know a lot of people in Dallas and Florida have fireplaces, but they only get used once or twice a year."

"This gets a lot more use," he answered. "If the power goes out I can cook on the propane stove, but running a heater is impossible without a blower. Even so, I prefer using the woodstove. Then I can be as warm as I want."

"Is that a problem?"

She thought he hesitated, then his green eyes met hers forthrightly. "I have an artificial leg, Lacy. And while it's insulated somewhat from me, it feels like it gets icy and the cold creeps up inside me. I can't tell you if that's my imagination or what."

She shook her head. "Does it matter? If you feel cold, you feel cold. Just the idea of it after what I felt outside earlier makes me want to shiver."

He surprised her with a smile that crinkled the corners of his eyes. Dang, he was attractive. More attractive, she thought, than when he'd been younger. "Don't be surprised if I don't always put it on. Some days it annoys me and I just crutch around."

She sat on the edge of a burgundy recliner sofa. "Don't mind me. Just be comfortable, Jess. Like you told me. But why does it annoy you?"

He bent to pull some logs out from near the woodstove and bent to put them in the firebox. "Why does it annoy me? Let me count the ways." Shaved tinder followed, and a couple of twisted newspapers, then a handful of what looked like dryer lint. With the strike of a long match, the lint caught fast and he soon had flames dancing around the logs. Satisfied, he closed the door and she realized it had a window on it, so she could see the fire. She really liked that.

"Count the ways," she reminded him as he settled in a padded rocker across from her.

"As long as you don't think I'm ungrateful for the prosthesis. But it's not part of me. I feel it hanging on my thigh like a weight. A lot of the time I don't notice, but sometimes I do. I can't feel anything with it, so walking has to be purely out of habit. I can be thrown by stepping on an uneven surface, although I'm getting better at it. I'm supposed to walk as evenly as possible so I don't damage my back or other joints, but I don't always succeed, and sometimes by the end of a day I feel the aches and pains. Then there's the itching and pain."

"Itching and pain?" She suspected he didn't mean what was left of his leg.

"You might not believe it, but a metal leg can itch like the devil or hurt like hell. It's called phantom pain, but it's real to me." He tilted his head. "The itching drives me crazier."

"Can they do anything to help? Will it get better?"

"They can't help, although sometimes I take aspirin for the placebo effect on the pain. The itching? Forget it. I could scratch a hole in my pants and never get to it. They offered opioids, but I don't want to be doped up, not in my job. Nerve stimulation didn't help."

"I'm sorry, Jess," she said, her chest squeezing with sympathy for him. "That's awful."

He shook his head again. "There are far worse things and I know it. Mostly I get around just fine. I'm lucky to be mobile, lucky to be able to work. But yeah, occasionally I just leave it in the corner. Sometimes I feel freer and can move faster without it." He shrugged one shoulder. "Probably my mood on a given day, more than anything."

She looked down at her hands, twisted her fingers together and murmured, "I bet that's only half of it."

"Meaning?"

She shrugged and summoned a smile. "You've been unfailingly Pollyanna about this since you started taking my phone calls again. You still are. It could be worse, of course. Most things could. But promise me something?"

"If I can."

"If there's anything I can do, let me know. After all, you're taking care of me, sheltering me from my fears. Seems only fair that if I can help you in some way, you tell me."

"I guess that's fair."

When she looked up, he was smiling again. "What?" she asked.

"I was just thinking that we're both very independent people. Life seems to have made us that way, for different reasons. Anyway…" Whatever he had been about to say was cut off when she heard the window behind the curtain rattle loudly.

"Here we go," he said. "Full force Arctic gale. Prepare to hunker down. I'm going to make coffee. Want another latte?"

"That sounds wonderful, if you don't mind."

"Of course not."

This time she noticed that he used his arms and then only one leg to lever himself out of the chair. As he crossed the room, she could see that swinging his artificial leg forward wasn't exactly the same as the way he moved with his natural leg. He might be trying to walk as if he had two real legs and doing a good job of it, but apparently there was no real substitute for nature.

The thought of the phantom pain and itching bothered her, too. She'd had an occasional itch she couldn't locate and knew how that had maddened her. What if you knew you'd never find it or never know how long it would go on? And how bad was the pain? He'd mentioned it, so it had to be more than an occasional twinge.

She resisted the urge to go help make the lattes. Maybe she was wrong, but she sensed in him a need to prove he was as capable as ever, despite the loss of his leg. A mother hen was probably the last thing he wanted.

The wind rattled the windows again, and then she heard it keen around the corner of the house. She was tempted to peek out, then decided against it. The heat from the woodstove had begun to fill the room and she was feeling supremely comfortable on the sofa. She had seen the effects of wind before, and a glance out the window would hardly let her know more about what sub-zero temperatures felt like. Whatever temperature she had tasted earlier had told her she was a Southern girl. Remembering how the cold had made her eyes tear up and the way it had whipped through her coat as if she wasn't even wearing one was probably all the lesson she needed.

Then she noticed a photo album on the table beneath the flat-screen TV. She wondered if she could look at it.

It might be a mistake, since she suspected it would be full of pictures of Jess and Sara, and she didn't want to open that can of worms unless he brought it up.

They had both grieved Sara's passing, although in different ways, she supposed. She'd lost her best friend since childhood, but he had lost his wife, his lover, his friend and the whole future they had planned together. If there were scales to weigh grief, his might well be heavier than hers. Not that it was something she wanted to compare as if it were a contest. She just didn't want to cause him pain by bringing it up, unless he wanted to discuss it.

It was easy to remember Sara, though. Easy to recall childhood days when the Florida summers had seemed full of endless freedom, and how they had occupied one another with games, or just by walking and talking together about anything and everything. When each of them had started dating in high school, they'd sometimes gone their separate ways, only to come back together again when the relationships broke up. Then had come college, where they'd headed in different directions. That's where Sara had met Jess. He was at her university's medical center taking trauma training for the Navy. Instant, total love.

Lacy figured it had taken her six months to stop being jealous and start being happy for Sara. Childish maybe, but real. Then the wedding, and longer separations were filled in with visits. When Jess had been at home, Lacy had come to like him bunches and stopped seeing him as competition. Somehow the three of them had knitted a friendship.

And then, in one horrible instant, Sara was gone. She'd been dead for several hours before she was found. Her aorta had ruptured silently during the early morning hours, killing her before her carpool had arrived to pick her up for work and had become concerned enough to call the police.

Just like that, as if a hand had reached out and squeezed the life from her.

All that laughter and life, lost. Lacy closed her eyes tightly, letting the grief wash over her again, then popped them open as she heard Jess's approach. His gait had evened out a bit, so she guessed he was working on it.

She smiled as he entered the room with two tall thermal mugs. "Thank you," she said as she took hers.

"My pleasure. I think I need to turn down that stove some." He set his cup on the table beside the rocker and went to fiddle with what she assumed must be a damper.

"I think it's cool that I can see the fire," she said. "Very cool."

"Best of both worlds," he answered. "A fireplace that doesn't waste heat."

He returned to the rocker. "Leave your bedroom door open, and that heat will climb the stairs and keep you warm all night. That's why I haven't done anything to close the foyer off."

"Do you burn it all the time?"

"When it gets really cold, yes."

She looked over her mug. "Today seems to be the day. Did you know this weather was coming?"

"Honestly, no. It seemed too early in the year to be worrying about extremes, and I think I told you I don't follow the weather that closely."

"But winter's coming and it must be more important up here than it is for me."

He laughed. "I usually get informed by my patients if something's coming up, but I took the last two days off."

She nodded, sipping the latte and settling more comfortably on the couch. With her boots off, she didn't hesitate to curl her legs under her. "When do you go back to work?"

"I'm on vacation. For which my boss is extremely grateful."

Surprised, she nearly gaped at him. "Why would he be grateful?"

"Because I have four weeks of vacation built up. He's of the opinion that I'm setting a bad example, and at some point some bean counter is going to be knocking on his door asking why I never use any of my time."

"Do you like your job that much?"

"I love it. But there's no place I want to go, so I reserve vacation for when I want to spend some extra time on projects around the house. I'll probably work some more on the kitchen in the next few weeks."

She looked around the room again, realization slamming her. He was building a memorial to Sara. The house in the country she'd wanted, and probably all the remodeling to make it a place she would have liked.

All of a sudden feeling like an interloper, Lacy looked down, staring at her mug as if it fascinated her. She was in Sara's house with Sara's husband. All that was missing was Sara.

God. She had the worst urge to get up and leave. Why had he asked her here? Friendship, yes, but something more? She couldn't imagine what. All she knew was that she suddenly felt as if she were in a mausoleum.

She tried to shake the feeling. Five years had passed. Surely Jess wasn't still devoting himself to fulfilling Sara's dreams. He didn't seem like that kind of a man, but then how well did she know him? Even if he were, what difference did it make? It was up to him how he spent his life.

For some reason, she shivered a bit and once again had that creeping sensation that some threat stalked her. "Oh, for heaven's sake," she said aloud.

Jess looked startled. "What?"

"Here I am, sitting perfectly safe in the middle of no-where in your house with you right here, and I just had that feeling again."

"That you're somehow threatened?"

"Yes." Annoyed with herself, she uncurled her legs, put her mug down and started pacing the warm room. "This is nuts! Nothing with any brains is going to be moving in the cold out there, and even so, how would anyone know where I am? It's not as if I left notes for my friends or a trail of some kind. I mentioned a few times that I was thinking of going to Portland to visit some old college friends, but that's it. I think I told only two people. Not even the FBI cared where I was going. Free as a bird. Maybe I need some therapy."

"At the very least, no one would have known you were getting off that bus out here."

"Exactly. But every so often it washes over me, this icy foreboding, as if something bad is about to happen. It's crazy."

He put his own cup aside and levered himself out of the chair. He crossed to her and touched her shoulder. The calm that touch induced surprised her, but then she felt a trickle of desire. Oh, heck, not that, too. Wrong guy, wrong time, wrong place. What was the matter with her?

"I don't think you're crazy," he said quietly. "I wouldn't have asked you to come here if I thought all you needed was a therapist. Maybe it's conditioning, like you said. That's hard to break. But maybe some-thing you're not even aware of put you on high alert. Speaking as someone who has been in combat, I never dismiss those feelings. So run with it. Pay attention to it. Maybe it's not real, but what if it is?"

After a moment, she nodded. His touch comforted

her with surprising ease, but she still couldn't quite escape the feeling.

He astonished her by unexpectedly drawing her into the circle of his arms, wrapping her in strength as he pressed her against his hard chest. "The thing is, you're not alone, Lacy. I may be crippled, but I can still protect you if you need it. Only time will tell if your feelings bear out."

She rested her cheek against his sweatshirt, soaking up his heat, his masculinity, and suddenly feeling very feminine and very safe. "Jess?"

"Yeah?"

"Please don't call yourself a cripple. I've met people far more crippled than you, and their bodies were normal." She felt him stiffen and feared she might have offended him. Then he surprised her with a laugh.

"You're right. Okay, no more of that." He let go of her, stepping back one pace, looking down into her face. "You going to be all right?"

She nodded, even though she regretted losing his embrace. Never before had a man's hug made her feel quite like that, all quivering expectation, and so meltingly safe. She wanted it back, and had absolutely no right to it. And not just because he was Sara's husband, but because at some point she'd need to rebuild a normal life, fears notwithstanding. To do that, she'd need to leave this small town. That wouldn't be fair to either of them. Jess had lost enough already.

God, she had never imagined how awkward this might become, or how quickly. But how could she have? Never before had she felt the least sexual response to Jess, and now, for the very first time, she seemed to be swamped by it. Had she changed that much? Had he?

She'd always been aware that he was an attractive man, but these feelings for him had never plagued her before. Where were they coming from?

"Want to check the weather again?"

She took her courage in her hands, considering that the last tendrils of fear still clung to her, nibbling around the edges of her wakening desire. Anything was better than standing here wondering if she'd lost her entire mind, not just parts of it. Maybe a good dose of open space and frigid air would be a tonic to all her emotions. "Can we step outside? I want to see what it feels like."

Turning, he took two steps and pulled the curtain back a bit. "The wind seems to have quieted. Okay, get your parka and gloves. You can have a couple of minutes to feel like a snowman."

Despite the internal ice she couldn't quite shake, and maybe because of the growing heat in her own center, she smiled and hurried into the hall, where she jammed her feet into her boots and pulled on the parka. She zipped it only to her neck, leaving the snorkel open, but pulled up the hood.

Jess grinned at her eagerness. "I've never before seen anyone so eager to freeze."

"It's a whole new experience for me. Of course I want to try it."

"Portland has a milder climate, too, doesn't it?"

"I don't remember any clippers."

Soon he was wearing his outer gear and gloves, ready to go. It was then that she hesitated.

"Jess? I could step out alone. Your leg…"

"It's impermeable, despite what my mind insists. A few minutes won't be a problem, but no longer than that. And if the wind kicks up, we come straight back in, got it?"

She promised, and they stepped through the door. Despite the warmth of her clothing, her face instantly felt as if it were hardening. Jess reached out and with deft fingers sealed her snorkel, then his own.

"No foolishness," he said, his voice muffled.

Even as bundled up as she was, it wasn't long before she could feel that even thermal underwear wasn't enough protection against this cold. The skin of her thighs began to grow numb, and she realized it would be foolish to ignore it.

"Let's go," she said. "I had my taste."

He was just opening the front door for her when she saw it. "Jess?"

He looked as she pointed one gloved hand to an envelope under a small rock. Gravel was scattered all over the porch, maybe from the wind, but an envelope? "Weird," he said. "I do have a mailbox at the road. Maybe one of the neighbors left me something."

Bending, he scooped it up and hurried her inside. The envelope landed on a side table, forgotten as Lacy began to shiver.

"Okay," she said, fumbling as she pulled off her gloves and tried to manipulate the zipper, "that was *too* cold. It goes right to the bone in no time at all."

He brushed her hands aside and dealt with the zipper until she could shrug off her parka. "Isn't it warm enough?"

"The parka is. My legs weren't. Wow."

He shook his head smiling. "Now you know. Let's go look at the weather so you can later brag how cold it was. Then I'm getting another hot drink into you."

He headed for the kitchen while she waited for the local weather. *Thirty* below? She turned and followed Jess hurriedly. "It's thirty below. Really. I should be a polar bear."

"Are you thawing yet? Go stand beside the stove."

"I'll survive," she answered. "That's the first time I felt my skin go numb that fast, though. Amazing."

"For this weather, you need more than long johns. When it's like this, people who can should stay inside."

"Was that why the guys were hurrying at the diner?"

"You don't want to have your car break down on some isolated road during this. Cell phones can be sketchy out there, and while your car makes a good windbreak, you can't run it for long at one time, so you wind up bundled in blankets, using candles to heat something to drink, and hoping like mad that someone will report you didn't get home in time for help to come. I don't recommend it. I've seen a few patients in the emergency room after incidents like that."

She nodded understanding. "But the whole winter isn't like this?"

"Not usually. Although, who can say anymore?"

Jess was amused by her reaction to the cold. She'd wanted to test it, and then was frank in her assessment. But she'd enjoyed it. It was nice to see that pinched look gone from her face as she settled again in the living room, this time with a mug of hot chocolate, and plenty of heat from the stove to warm her up.

She chattered for a while about ice storms in Portland, explaining that while she had thought *they* were bad, they didn't hold a candle to this. He nodded and listened, enjoying the animation of her face, the most he had seen yet. Her entire body got into the act as she described coming down one hill outside Portland and her car spinning complete circles again and again until she reached the bottom. "Thank goodness nobody else was on the road."

"What did you do when you reached bottom?"

"Inched my way to the nearest motel and spent the night. Fortunately, there was one right up the street. But I've never forgotten that awful loss of control. Being out of control is terrifying."

"I know." He answered pleasantly enough, but maybe something had come through in his tone.

Her animation faded, and her brow creased faintly. "I guess you do," she said quietly. "I can't imagine."

He gentled his voice. "Don't try, Lacy. Please don't try."

"But I want to understand."

"Innocence is a beautiful thing. Treasure it. It certainly won't do anyone any good if you wade into that hell even a few small steps. Anyway, you went through your own kind of hell. It seems life doesn't leave anyone utterly untouched."

He watched her expression turn thoughtful, and wished he could bring back her earlier animation. At least she wasn't looking tense at the moment. Small triumph. He enjoyed seeing her curled on the couch in her jeans and yellow sweater, her blond hair all mussed by the parka's hood. Curls had begun to show, and he wondered if they were natural. He liked them, and wondered why her hair had appeared so straight earlier.

Maybe she'd made a practice of trying to look businesslike, and for a woman that would mean minimizing her attractions. She certainly had plenty of them. He felt his body stirring in response and turned to the fire, a much safer object for his attention.

He realized with relief that he was getting past expecting to hear Sara's voice answer her, or see Sara come around the corner at any moment. That was one side effect of seeing Lacy that he hadn't anticipated: the link between the two of them in his mind. He was glad to feel it breaking, because much as he missed Sara, he wanted to get to know Lacy Devane, apart from his late wife. A person unto herself.

In the corner, the TV still played, muted. But the weather was running along the bottom of the screen and he sat forward a little as he realized the predictions were worsening.

"What?" he heard Lacy ask.

"The weather's getting worse."

"How can it possibly get worse? Isn't thirty below bad enough?"

He looked at her. "That's not all of it. About three inches of snow, and more wind. Lots of wind. We're going to whiteout, and that little bit of snow is going to seem like a huge blizzard. It won't settle until the wind dies down."

"Then I'm glad we went shopping."

He turned a little toward her. "You understand how deadly this weather is, Lacy? I can't emphasize enough. You could get lost in the whiteout only a few feet from the house. You could freeze to death in very short order. So no going out, not even to see what it's like, okay?"

She nodded then flashed a grin. "I guess my boogeyman won't be able to get me today."

That surprised a laugh from him, and any remaining tension blew away as if a fresh wind had entered the house. "He'd freeze to death climbing the porch steps… if he could find them."

"I like the sound of that. Kudos to the clipper."

He chuckled again. "So what would you like to do since we're cut off from the world? Play a game? Watch a movie?"

"What about working on that kitchen of yours? Is it possible?"

"Not today, unfortunately. Tools are out in the shed."

He enjoyed her widening eyes. "Won't they freeze? The lubricants, I mean?"

"I have a heater out there. Never goes below forty degrees." Tools hardly held his attention with Lacy sitting across from him. Parts of his mind, body and heart seemed to be waking from a long sleep. Not good. She'd come here for protection, not harassment. Besides, Sara stood between them, a ghost as real as their memories of her. He wouldn't want to dishonor her memory by dishonoring her friend.

Then another thought struck him: that shed was heated. A great place for someone to hide out during this weather. He shifted uneasily, wondering if he'd been too quick to dismiss Lacy's fears as being the result of having been threatened for so long.

What if she was right? He'd admitted the possibility but…for someone to follow her here? It seemed so unlikely. If anyone really did want to get to her, wouldn't they simply look for her getting off the bus in Portland?

But when she didn't get off…

He sprang from his chair as quickly as he could, given his leg. He needed to check that shed, make sure it was still locked. He could use the cold as an excuse, say he was going to check the heater.

Damn, he felt like an idiot, holding out a helping hand, assuring her that her fears were reasonable, then acting as if they weren't. What the hell was wrong with him?

"Jess?"

He looked at her, hoping his face didn't reveal his sudden uneasiness. "You just made me think. I checked the heater this fall when it started getting cold but given these temps, maybe I'd better check it again before the whiteout hits. It'll only take a minute." He pulled back the curtain. Still fairly calm.

"Didn't you just warn me about the cold?"

"Yeah, but I have the gear for it. Never know when I might be called in to work for an emergency. So I'll dress. Like I said, it'll only take a few minutes."

She half smiled. "Then bring back some tools. I could do with hammering some nails or something."

"If you're that eager, I guess we could work on the backsplash. But let me check that heater."

He pulled on his windproof snow pants, his thermal-lined boots and his parka, zipping up the snorkel against the hood. Thick gloves with liners protected his hands, at least until he tried to unlock the shed. A few seconds of exposure through the liners would be necessary to open the shed, but with his inner gloves on he should be okay for the time it took. He made sure the key was in an accessible pocket, then headed out the back door. He could feel Lacy's eyes on him through the window beside the door as he limped his way to the shed.

Because he was limping again. No amount of trying to walk normally seemed to be working right now. Maybe he should be using his cane. Too late.

Inside his winter gear, his body warmth acted like a

heater. Except for his artificial leg. No heat there, and he once again seemed to feel the cold creeping upward to his thigh. Imagination, he told himself. His brain expected the cold and created it.

Sometimes he felt that losing his leg was a kind of universal justice. He'd volunteered, he'd gone into a war zone, and when he remembered it, he sometimes didn't think being there as a medic in any way excused his participation. Not always. But he lived with nightmares he didn't share with anyone, and rightly or wrongly, a collective guilt sometimes weighed on him.

Wrongly, he decided. He knew what he'd done, how many lives he had saved, how many civilians he had helped with everything from vaccinations to wound treatment and antibiotics. He'd been trying to do good. Too bad it had been in the middle of hell.

He reached the shed without falling, yanked off his glove and reached for the key. The heavy-duty padlock was untouched, but he opened it anyway. Might as well check the heat and pick up a few tools. Leaving the key in the lock, he pulled the bar back and opened the door. Warm. The heater was working, operating on a buried propane tank just like the heater and the stove in his house.

Out here, though, he used radiant heat from water that circulated in pipes from a heated reservoir. Safer than having an open flame, more reliable than electricity. When the water heated up enough, it moved through the pipes. He picked up some grouting tools, smiled faintly at the hammer because Lacy had mentioned wanting to pound something, and wondered what he could give her to pound on. Nothing at the moment. The tiles, grout and glue were all in the house already.

Satisfied that everything was okay, he stepped out into the cold, noticing that the wind was starting to pick up again. A threat all by itself, it didn't need any snow to make it dangerous. That would probably come later.

He locked up, tested the latch, then hobbled back to the house, feeling utterly graceless. One of these days he was going to have to look into a better leg, one that would allow him to really run again. Dang things cost too much, but it might be worth it. He missed a full-out lope.

He had to steady himself on the back porch rail to climb the steps, then he was back inside. Lacy waited anxiously.

"I'm fine," he said as he dumped the tools on the unfinished counter. Yeah, he was fine, although his leg didn't feel like it. He wondered if the cold had stiffened the knee joint a bit.

He shed his parka as he hobbled to the front room, then dropped into the rocker. Lacy grabbed his parka and gloves and carried them to the hall.

When she returned, he was still waiting for the heat from the woodstove to thaw him out. Thaw his pretend leg out. Boy, that sounded weird.

She approached almost tentatively and touched his shoulder lightly. She might as well have touched him with a brand. He felt it in every cell of his being, the wonderful, nearly forgotten, flare of desire. A different kind of heat.

"Are you all right?" she asked.

"Fine," he repeated. "I think my leg stiffened a bit. The artificial one. It'll be okay as soon as it warms up."

She hesitated beside him, and he could feel her need

to do something for him. "Maybe I should get your crutch?"

He shook his head. "It'll thaw. Dang, it's nasty out there, and the snow hasn't even started. But the heater's working just fine."

"Well that's good."

He tilted his head back and looked up at her. "You don't need to hover, Lacy. I know you're concerned, but it'll be all better in just a minute."

"Sure."

She almost seemed to shrink back to the couch and he felt just awful when he realized how she must have heard that bit about hovering. People didn't usually say that in a complimentary way. It was too late to rephrase it now, though.

He sat there, feeling about an inch tall, and wondering how he could fix things. Finally he decided to just address it straight up.

"Lacy, I didn't mean anything critical with that comment. Poor choice of words. I just didn't want you to worry needlessly about me."

She offered a wan smile. "Sure."

This was going well, he thought. Facing once again how much they were still strangers when one thoughtless thing could have that much impact. Finally it just burst out of him. "Do I need to walk on eggshells?"

Oh, that got a blazing spark from her blue eyes. "No," she answered tautly.

"Good, because if I have to watch every word I say, neither of us is going to be comfortable. I wasn't being critical of you. I repeat. No criticism intended. Yes, I'm frustrated at the way my leg stiffened up, yes, it was a poor choice of words, but no criticism."

"Okay." But then her face softened a bit.

Relief washed through him. Good. They'd get through this. Time to move on. "I brought in the tools I needed for grouting the tile, but first we'll have to glue them into place on the wall. How dirty do you want to get?"

He was pleased to see a more natural smile come to her face. "I get to play with mud?"

"I couldn't have expressed it better. Did you bring any grungies with you?"

"You mean clothes I don't mind ruining? Sure."

"Then go put them on while I continue to thaw this leg. Then we'll have some fun."

As soon as she went upstairs, he pulled off his snow pants and dumped them on the floor. Sitting again, he felt his leg through the fabric of his jeans. Practically an ice cube still. Amazing how fast that composite had cooled down. But the heat from the stove was beginning to penetrate, and when he bent the knee joint he could feel it moving more smoothly. Right as rain in just a few minutes.

The things you didn't think to ask about when rehab handed you your brand new leg. After a couple of years, he was beginning to understand why so many amputees had a collection of different legs, and spent thousands to get them. His leg was suitable enough for most of what he did, but with time he became increasingly aware that it could be better. He guessed that in the end it wasn't just enough to be able to walk and maybe run short distances.

Shaking his head a little at himself, he bent to unlace his boots. The plastic covering for his foot and ankle was purely cosmetic, a concession to looking as normal as possible to patients he met for the first time. He could have done without it. A sock concealed it right now, and he dropped the cuff of his jeans to cover it so Lacy wouldn't see the gear above it.

A small vanity, but one he still seemed to need.

Hey, I'm just a guy like any other guy. Except he didn't always feel like one. He figured he'd know he had truly accepted his amputation when the day came that he was willing to let the world see that he was indeed different now. When he was willing to flash that leg without worrying about how someone might react to it.

Or maybe he was afraid of seeing pity. He sure as hell didn't want any of that.

The window glass behind him rattled again, noisily. The wind was returning. He scanned the TV screen again and saw they were showing the front beginning to reach them. The entire area was colored in to show expected snow. A frigid afternoon and night ahead of them.

Rising, he walked around, found he had completely thawed out aside from a persistent sensation of cold from a leg that didn't exist. Sometimes it amused him, these phantom sensations. The mind was a devious thing.

Heading for the kitchen, he spied the envelope forgotten on the hall table. Grabbing it, he noted that nothing at all was written on the outside. Disturbed by that, he tore it open and pulled out a single piece of cheap paper. The words block-printed on it chilled him to his soul.

I found you. The game begins.

Chapter 4

They spent the rest of the day placing the tiles on the wall for the backsplash behind the range and the sink. Jess had already measured everything, and after watching for a little while, Lacy figured out how to apply the glue and use the spacers. Every so often she asked Jess to check her work and he approved.

"I think you have a knack for this," he said. "Good eye."

"I like the tiles you chose, too." They were large, made of coppery steel with a pattern embossed on them. They looked pleasantly old-fashioned.

"I thought about doing them on the ceiling, too, but then decided that was overkill."

She looked up. "It could be pretty."

"Or it could be overwhelming. I still haven't settled on the right countertops. Every kind has advantages and disadvantages."

A thought suddenly struck her. "Shouldn't the countertops have come before the backsplash?"

Jess shook his head. "I've measured carefully, but whichever way I do it, I'm going to probably be cutting some tin to fit in small spaces." He shrugged and grinned. "The nice thing about doing it myself is that if I mess up, nobody knows but me. And I've got all the time in the world to fix it."

She laughed, liking his easy approach to the project. Clearly he'd already done a lot to the house. She thought of long hours alone, when he'd kept his hands busy working around here so he wouldn't notice what was missing. Sara would always be missing. She smothered a sigh, and closed her eyes briefly.

He washed his hands at the sink. "Coffee, latte or hot chocolate? And we haven't eaten since breakfast. Getting hungry?"

"Starting to," she admitted. "Coffee sounds great."

"If lasagna sounds good, I have some left over in the freezer. When I cook, I make extra so I don't have to do it every night."

"Good idea, and lasagna sounds wonderful." Rising, she washed her own hands and started a pot of coffee while he pulled the lasagna out of the freezer. In serving-size plastic containers, they just needed to be microwaved. Instead he set them on a pan of warm water.

"I'm going to heat them slowly in the oven, if you can wait. Otherwise we'd eat in shifts."

"Either is fine by me." She'd enjoyed working in the kitchen and during that whole time she hadn't spared one thought for her fears. In fact, being here seemed to be steadily driving them into the background. She wondered if that was because she wasn't alone anymore, or if it was the cold weather, or a combination of both. Her friends certainly hadn't been able to babysit her the way Jess was doing.

He wouldn't be able to do it indefinitely, though. Sooner or later he'd have to go back to work, and then she'd be all alone in this relatively isolated house.

The windows had begun to rattle incessantly, and she had the worst urge to look out, but all of a sudden realized she didn't want to pull back the curtains.

So the fear hadn't entirely left her. It had just given her a vacation.

Man. She sat at the table again when they had fresh mugs of coffee, and studied its scarred surface. What was wrong with her? Nobody could know where she was. So why couldn't she go look out to see if it had started snowing yet?

The warm water loosened the lasagna in the containers, and soon Jess was popping it into the oven in a glass dish. "It'll take a while," he said. "Let's move to the other room. The glue fumes aren't toxic, but they're not that pleasant, either."

She took his advice, although her nose seemed to have become deadened to the odor, then wondered why he didn't follow immediately. Ten minutes later she found out as he presented her with a plate of cheese and crackers.

"I hope you like sharp cheddar," he said as he put his own plate and mug on the side table.

"Love it," she answered. Then he did what she had been unable to do. He opened the curtains to look out.

"Come see," he said. "It must have been snowing while we worked. We have full whiteout right now."

She put her plate on the end table and went to stand

beside him at the window. The stove was no longer putting out as much heat, so she could feel the warmth radiating from Jess. The man was practically a heater all by himself, she thought with mild amusement. And he heated her in more than one way.

She felt a silly, pointless giggle coming on, but suppressed it because she might have to explain it. Bending, she stepped under his arm to peer around the curtain he held open and all thoughts of giggling vanished in wonder.

"Oh, wow," she breathed. She couldn't even see the porch railing, except for an occasional glimpse as a swirl of snow moved past and revealed it. The world outside had turned totally white, the snow erasing everything beyond a few feet. She would have expected the day to be dark, but all that snow caught every shard of light and while it wasn't bright, it certainly wasn't dark, either. It was like being inside an extreme snow globe.

"And that," he said, "is why every living creature is staying safely at home today. Beautiful but deadly."

"I wouldn't want to be out there," she agreed.

"If you were, it likely wouldn't be a problem for long. Not at these temps."

Bending, he opened the stove door and stirred around the fire a bit, then he twisted and put another log on. "I'm starting to feel drafts wend their way in. Are you?"

She hadn't been paying attention but nodded anyway. Branded in her mind's eye was his tight backside as he bent. She hoped she didn't sound breathless and tried to distract herself. "Can you cook on that stove?"

"Absolutely. It won't be haute cuisine, but it'll be tasty. And I even have a percolator to make coffee."

Very self-reliant, she thought. Far different from what

she was used to. Her world had consisted of things that turned on when you needed them and stores right around the corner. She'd grown up in Florida with Sara next door, but when hurricanes were on the way, both families evacuated to relative comfort. There'd been tornadoes in Texas, but none had affected her directly. As for Portland, it had a benign climate for the most part, and she had given scant thought to the volcano that loomed over the town in the distance.

She glanced toward the window again as she heard the glass shudder. The wind evidently was still howling, and sometimes she heard a faint rattle against the glass. Snow? The curtains muffled the sound as much as they muffled the light and cold.

"Are you okay?" All of a sudden, Jess bent in front of her. He didn't squat and she wondered how much that added to his back's discomfort.

"I'm fine," she answered, summoning a smile.

"You looked awfully far away." Straightening, he returned to the rocker and sat.

"I was thinking about how I never had to deal with anything like this."

He arched a brow. "Tornadoes?"

"Not directly. Although when the sky changed a certain way, turning a kind of inky black, and the pillow clouds seemed to touch the tops of buildings, I got edgy. Once I even watched as a tornado tried to form. It was fantastic. Amazing. But they don't last long, Jess. Not usually. A few minutes and they've moved on. Not like this."

"This certainly won't blow the house away. We're safe as long as we stay inside."

"I believe you." She offered another smile. "Some

friends drove me down to see where a tornado had nearly wiped a small town from the map. I've never forgotten the way it ripped a path across fields, leaving only bare dirt. And one house was shifted half off its foundation and still stood. After that I never ignored a warning."

"I wouldn't, either." He drummed his fingers on the arm of his chair. "You're still not relaxing."

She stiffened. "What do you mean?"

"I'm not sure. But we're making conversation like two people who hardly know each other. You can talk about Sara, if you want. She's not off-limits, and we both loved her. The point is, nothing's off-limits, okay?"

If she hadn't been unwittingly tense before, she became so now. "Am I doing something wrong?"

"No." He shook his head, looking faintly rueful. "It's just that I keep feeling there's this big wall between us, and both of us are afraid of taking it down. And I don't know why. Strangers, but not strangers. I get it. But we still know each other better than to be discussing the weather all the time."

She couldn't deny that. "We both have pasts we don't seem to want to talk about."

"You're right. But maybe that's exactly what we need to talk about." He pointed. "Why don't you get the photo album from under the TV? Sara put plenty of pictures of the two of you in there from before I came along. There's a lot more, as well. You can fill in gaps for me and I can fill in gaps for you."

Part of her wanted to pull back, to avoid opening those doors, but another part of her yearned to swing them wide to fresh air and sunlight. Sara was the link between them, the tie that had held them together all these years. Ignoring her might not be saving them a bit of trouble or pain.

At last she rose and went to get the thick, heavy album. "I thought everything was on computers these days," she remarked.

"Sara said a photo album wouldn't crash."

Despite her trepidation, a small laugh escaped Lacy. "That's Sara, all right."

Jess rose and limped over to sit by her on the couch. "She was right in another way. I love the heft of that album. I love knowing it's packed with good memories. I love being able to touch the pages and the pictures, if I'm careful. Anyway, be prepared. It starts when you were both toddlers in Jacksonville."

"No, really?"

"Yeah, and diaperless, too."

"Oh, Sara," she said wistfully. "You would do that to me, wouldn't you?"

"She did," Jess agreed. "I don't know how many photos you might have, but she seemed to keep them all."

Sara hoarded things. No question. But only some items. "She told me once that photos were like our footprints in life. She was always taking them."

"More than I wanted to be in, that's for sure," he said wryly. "Cell phones only made my life more miserable. In the early days I could see her get out the camera and prepare myself. Later I never knew when that omnipresent phone was going to click."

That drew a deep laugh from her. "Camera shy?"

"Wait until you see some of them. Who wants to be recorded for posterity in the midst of a pratfall?"

She giggled again. "No video, though?"

He shook his head. "She said that recording things

on video would mean she was watching life through a lens, not living it."

"I never thought of it that way."

"Are you a picture taker?"

She shook her head. "Never felt the urge."

He waved to the album. "Then Sara did it for you."

The amount of trepidation that filled her as she reached to flip the cover open surprised her. Sara. A great gaping hole in her life, her mementos tucked in these pages. The girl she had grown up with, the woman who had remained her best friend, was gone. Living with that hadn't been easy. How many times over the last few years had she just wanted to hear Sara's voice on the phone one more time? How many times had she started to dial her out of a need for that friendly, understanding voice?

With her fingertips just touching the corner of the album cover, she realized that her grief over Sara had never really eased or gone away. It had become familiar, and with the passage of time she had papered over the hole in her life, like putting wallpaper over a damaged wall. The hole was still there, but hidden.

"Lacy? You don't have to if you don't want to."

"I know." Of course she knew. Jess wasn't trying to make her miserable; he was trying to bring something into the open, something they shared, something that had hurt them both. So they could talk about it, about Sara. "Do you look at it?"

"All the time. It's what I have left, memories. They were good memories. I don't want to forget them."

He was right about that, too. Steadying herself, she flipped open the cover. The first picture to greet her eyes was of herself and Sara, completely nude, all of two, standing beside a colorful kiddie pool in the backyard. She couldn't tell for sure whose backyard it was, but she remembered the photo. "I have a copy of this one, too," she murmured.

"The start of a lifelong friendship."

"Yes." She flipped a page and there were more pictures of them sitting in the pool, playing with little toys, laughing. Another page of the two of them in cheery sunsuits walking down a sidewalk with their hands entwined. With each page turn, they grew a little older until she reached pictures of moments she dimly remembered. The two of them sitting on the grass, playing with dolls, an experience that had ended up with Lacy in tears.

She pointed. "Right after that, a bee stung me. I remember shrieking, and Sara calling for her mom, and getting mad at the stupid bees." She gave a small broken laugh. "Stupid bees. Her mom explained the bee wasn't being stupid, but Sara insisted on it."

"She was always opinionated. And she never told me that story. Thank you."

Feeling overwhelmed, Lacy leaned back on the couch and closed her eyes for a few minutes. "Life was so simple then. Dolls and stupid bees. Tea parties on the screened lanai. The boy down the block who bullied us until she and I ganged up on him."

"Did you really?"

She opened her eyes and saw his dancing gaze. "Yeah, we really did. I got put in time-out for endless hours for hitting him, but he never bothered us again."

He laughed. "Tough stuff, lady."

"Sometimes." But the memory had brought the smile back to her face. "We were like the Two Musketeers.

There was never a third one. At least, not until you came along."

"Not even boyfriends?"

She waved a hand. "In high school they didn't last long. Like trying on clothes only to find out they didn't fit."

He seemed to be waiting, so she sat up and flipped a few more pages. The awkward stage of teeth falling out and growing in bigger. Braces. School events. Sunday-best dresses, and muddy shorts and tops. Finally she closed the album. "I can't do more right now."

"Sara said you were a badminton champ."

The tightness inside Lacy eased again. "I'll have you know I beat every single person in my sixth-grade class at our class picnic. My moment of glory."

"You must have left some bruised egos." A laugh trembled in his voice.

"I don't know. I was just having fun." She twisted her head to look at him. "I didn't want to go to the picnic. Sara was my only friend. Did she tell you I was painfully shy?"

He shook his head. "I never would have guessed."

"Well, I was, and maybe still am. Totally introverted."

"Hence the CPA?"

She gave it a moment's thought. "Maybe so. Numbers are very predictable, and most of the time no one bothers you when you're working with them. I love numbers. There's always a correct answer."

"I never thought of them that way."

"Oh, I do. They're not like people. I think of them as solid and enduring and always behaving in the same ways."

Now it was his turn to look pensive. She rose and carried the album back to its place on the shelf beneath the TV. The screen was still on, the sound muted, weather warnings traipsing across the bottom in endless cycles.

"Numbers," she said, "don't lie. When they do, it's because some *person* did something wrong. Sometimes they can be inexact for lack of information, but they never lie."

She turned and saw that he was watching her. What was he thinking? That she sounded like some kind of nut? Maybe she did.

"And numbers provided you with a glowing trail leading to wrongdoing," he said after a moment.

"Yes, they did."

"Amazing." Then he stood up, smiling slightly. "I'll bet that lasagna is ready to eat. Still hungry?"

Her stomach rumbled an answer. His smile widened and he held out his hand. Stepping forward, she took it and went to the kitchen to eat with him.

Outside the weather continued to rage, like an omen.

Chapter 5

Lacy retired early again. Jess wondered if he'd pushed her too far with that photo album, but he was glad he had. He'd learned more about Lacy in a short hour than he'd learned about her in all the time he'd known her.

Shy? Sara her only real friend? Strange that Sara had never mentioned that. Sara had been naturally outgoing, building a circle wherever they went. But no one, he realized in retrospect, had ever been as close to her as Lacy. The two of them had been as thick as thieves and on the phone constantly.

Then there was that thing about numbers. Lacy liked numbers because they were reliable and didn't lie? It was possible that was just a natural inclination, but it was equally possible that it had grown out of something deeper. Something that was a really important key to who she was.

It spoke of an inherent distrust of people, so totally

out of tune with her relationship with Sara. The past few years could have hardly added to her trust.

He sighed, then remembered the envelope he'd found earlier. He'd pushed it out of his mind because he hadn't wanted to frighten Lacy any more than she already was. Nor was it something he could take to the sheriff. Just a statement that might be a threat, or could even be a prank. It wasn't as if none of his younger neighbors ever got up to any hijinks. Sometimes he even saw the results in his little minor emergency center.

It was little enough to go on, but enough to concern him. He found it difficult to believe that the people Lacy continued to fear could have found her so rapidly, unless they had ridden the bus with her, and that seemed totally unrealistic. If so, they could have removed her from the picture at any stop along the route from Dallas. Why wait for her to disembark here, then leave that stupid note like a red flag only a few hours later?

Inevitably he thought of a cat toying with a mouse. Except a cat wasn't playing, merely tiring its prey until it was safe to eat. This was uglier, whether someone's lousy idea of a joke or for real.

Of only one thing was he fairly certain: anyone would stay inside during weather like this. When he peeked out from time to time, it was clear they were still in a state of whiteout. The wind hadn't quit, much to his surprise, and a couple of inches of snow couldn't seem to settle anywhere, but blew endlessly, blindingly. People around here who needed to get out to barns to tend livestock were probably moving with ropes wrapped around them, or sticking to rope lines they'd put up earlier to guide them.

Yeah, there was GPS these days, but it didn't always

work well during a storm, and besides, with this wind and these temperatures, any exposed skin would freeze fast. Way fast.

Even a man with a deadly mission would have hunkered down somewhere safe.

He could reasonably assume nothing would happen until the weather changed, but it wouldn't do to let his guard down too far. He spread the folded paper, which had been tucked in his jeans pocket and burning at the back of his mind all day, and read those block-printed words again. "I found you. The game begins."

What the hell did that mean? It wasn't a direct threat, unless someone didn't want to be found. Indirectly, it threatened nothing at all. He could just imagine the sheriff looking at it and feeling pretty much as Jess did. Was this a stalking? One note wasn't a crime of any kind. Who was being stalked? Had this even come to the right house?

After all, sometimes the college and high school kids staged treasure hunts based on following GPS coordinates. *The game is on?* It might be as simple as that, although there were no coordinates on the note. Just a message that might have blown onto his porch.

Remembering that a small stone had been lying on top of it, it would seem deliberate. But that might even have been an accident. As hard as the wind was blowing, the envelope could have been pushed under a stone that was already there. His front porch wasn't exactly the cleanest place in the world. All summer and fall he'd been using it to store tools and supplies overnight, then he'd had that truckload of gravel spread on the drive and graded out and…

Yeah, there were lots of small stones on his porch.

He could rationalize it as much as he wanted. What he couldn't safely do was ignore it.

Lacy felt afraid. Maybe she had good reason. He was the last person to deny that you could sense it if you were being watched. Some atavistic instinct that remained in human beings. Eyes were on you.

Sighing, he shoved it into his pocket. At least he'd had to take combat training with the Marines when he was attached as a medic. Not even a Red Cross was barred against that, not with the Marines. He could handle himself, even with an artificial leg.

What might have gotten soft over the years was his alertness to threats. Rising, ignoring the way his nonexistent leg had decided to hurt as if it were full of knives, he got himself some more coffee. Too early to sleep. Only that storm outside would make it possible for him to sleep at all. He could also still set his internal alarm clock to wake him every hour to check on things.

He thought about sleeping on the couch, then wondered if Lacy would be disturbed by it. It wasn't as if his bedroom wasn't on this floor. If she found him there, he could just blame it on the phantom pain…a phantom that felt real enough right now.

He popped three ibuprofens with scant hope they'd help much. Any nerves they could work on weren't the nonexistent ones in his leg. Pain was a perception. How many times had that been drilled into him? It was the brain's interpretation of a signal. Or, in his case, remembered signals. Anxiety increased the perception of pain. He'd long ago conquered the anxiety, but the likelihood that his phantom pain would eventually vanish was disappearing with the passage of time. The longer he continued to experience it, the more likely it was to become permanent.

Going to his bedroom, he pulled off his jeans and removed his leg. Enough. He didn't need it tonight, not remotely, given how bad the weather was. After pulling on sweatpants and pinning up the empty leg portion, he reached for his crutch and swung his way out to the living room couch.

He paused in the foyer, hearing the sound of light steps, and looked up the stairs. Lacy was descending, wearing a blue fleece jogging suit and big fuzzy slippers that somehow touched him. The child in her peeking out.

"Something wrong?" he asked. At least this time he didn't feel an internal lurch because Sara wasn't right behind her.

He waited, seeing her pause as she took in his missing leg. Then she astonished him with a smile. "Decided to get comfortable?" she asked as she came down the rest of the way.

"Yeah," he answered, leaving the pain out of it. "You?"

"I slept a little, then the wind woke me. It feels so restless tonight. Or at least I do. Can I make some coffee?"

"Sure. I don't think I left much." He held up the mug he carried in his free hand.

"Don't let me keep you up."

"You aren't. I was about to go settle for a bit in the living room."

"Want some fresh coffee?"

"Might as well. Thanks."

He watched her as she walked away, then settled himself lengthwise on the couch so that his good leg was on the outside. It made it easier for him to move quickly.

Funny, he hadn't thought about that in a while. That note had changed things, whether he wanted it to or not.

He appreciated her reaction to seeing him without his leg. After a moment of surprise, she'd ignored it. Nor was she acting at all troubled by it. Of course, she might feel differently if she saw the scars. He'd had plenty of time to get used to them, but he knew they were ugly.

The TV continued to run warnings, now predicting two days of this cold and continued high winds. They might as well be shut off from the world.

Good. That note, now that he had looked at it again, continued to trouble him. Found who? He didn't think anyone was looking for him, so that left Lacy, and the idea that she might actually be stalked by someone who intended her harm made his gut twist.

He might not know her that well, but she'd been important to Sara. Extremely important, and that made her important to him in ways beyond the casual friendship that had grown between them over the years. Sara had been the apex of a triad, with two people who loved her dearly. She had brought them together, had sealed them with the bond of her love.

For Sara, if nothing else, he was going to make sure nothing bad happened to Lacy. Not if he could prevent it. The image of himself as a knight in armor wasn't quite making it, not with less than half of one leg. He could have laughed at himself.

But he didn't because he'd seen guys in far worse condition perform feats beyond imagining. Amazing what a human being could be capable of when it was necessary.

He hoped it wouldn't become necessary, though. Lacy had dealt with enough fear. She needed to feel safe again, and if someone struck out at her here, he wondered if she would ever feel safe again anywhere.

That thing she had said about numbers kept dancing through his mind, too, convincing him Lacy harbored a secret of her own, a reason to distrust. He had to be very careful not to give her a reason to distrust him.

So of course he'd hidden that note from her. If she found out about that…

Smothering a groan, he let his head fall back against the arm of the couch. *Great way to start, Jess*, he scolded himself. Nobody built trust by hiding things.

Too late now. With his eyes closed, he wondered how he'd deal with it if she found out, hoping like hell she'd never learn.

"Here you go."

He raised his head and saw Lacy standing over him, mugs in hand. He pushed himself up and reached for one, cradling its warmth in both hands. She went to sit in the rocking chair.

"I can see why you like this chair," she remarked with a smile and sipped her coffee.

Easy to get out of, but he didn't say that. It was comfortable enough. He could rise from it with his arms and one leg, which mattered to him sometimes. Right now, getting off the couch would require the crutch propped nearby.

He'd adapted, but sometimes he hated the adjustments he was constantly making. Another round of self-pity? Sour amusement filled him. Bad time for that.

The storm outside grew noisier for a few minutes, penetrating even the thick curtains with its fury, then settled again. He realized he was staring at Lacy, enjoying the sight of her so near. Far from feeling like opening an old wound, it felt right and good. Plus, she was some serious eye candy, and it had been a while since he'd been interested in even scanning the possibilities. That part of him had seemed to die with Sara…until Lacy arrived. Great time to discover he still had a man's desires. Lacy probably thought of him like a brother.

"I like your house," she said, evidently seeking a topic of conversation. "It's snug and friendly, and not too big."

"There was an extra wing when I bought it, probably an addition to house a passel of kids. I don't know. Regardless, it was in such bad shape I had it razed. I like it the way it is now."

She nodded, sipping her coffee. "Me, too. Cozy."

"I need to do a lot of work upstairs yet. Sorry about that."

She gaped and then laughed quietly. "Sorry for what? It's fine. I like the old bathtub, and the shower works."

"I suppose." He'd concentrated his efforts down here because it was where he lived, but he was regretting that a bit now. Lacy was upstairs looking at ancient wallpaper, outdated lighting fixtures and some drywall that bowed a bit, as if it had gotten wet once upon a time. But working upstairs would create additional problems for him, too. He'd need some help because of the damn stairs.

Rather than look at her, which was beginning to turn into a contest of wills between his sense of what was right and Lacy's desirability, he stared into his mug and at the TV screen. Damn, not since Sara had a woman awakened his hungers the way this one was. It would be so nice if he could just go for it, but Lacy was afraid, and Sara stood invisibly between them. A past neither of them could forget. Or even wanted to.

"I always wanted to fix up a house," she said. "Are you enjoying it?"

"For the most part. It's a great hobby."

"I was never sure that I knew enough or could learn enough to do it. And it's a huge commitment."

"Huge," he agreed, wondering if that was another clue to her. "But I've got plenty of time."

"I used to think I would," she answered. "I even looked around at a few places in Dallas. Now it's a pipe dream."

"Only temporarily. And you can practice on this place if you want."

She brightened. "I did enjoy putting up those tiles this afternoon. And they're so pretty."

"You seem to have a knack for it." He waited, wondering where this was going, or if she was just filling dead air with casual conversation. Funny, before she'd arrived he'd thought he knew her. Now he had more questions than ever.

She spoke again. "Was this something Sara wanted to do, too? Remodel a house? I don't recall her ever mentioning it."

He paused, surprised by the question, finally answering truthfully. "I don't know. We never talked about it. Seems odd, doesn't it, that in eight years we never plotted the future in any detail?" A shadow moved through him. "Hell."

"What?"

"She wasn't sure there'd be a future for us."

Lacy's eyes widened. "How can you say that?"

"Because. Because I was gone so much. Because there was always a chance I might not come back. We had only vague ideas about the future, as if neither of us wanted to plan for something that might never happen."

"Oh my God," Lacy breathed. Her entire face saddened, and for long minutes neither of them said anything. Then she added, "She never talked to me about fears like that."

"But how often did she mention 'someday'?"

Lacy closed her eyes, clearly searching her memory. "Not often," she finally admitted in a small voice. "Once in a while she'd talk about things she wanted to do when you came home, but never any farther down the road than that."

He nodded, absorbing the blow. Sara had been afraid. The whole damn time she'd been afraid to plan because she'd feared she'd lose him. The tables had turned, though, and he'd lost her instead.

He saw Lacy shiver. "Cold?"

"No. I was just thinking…" She shook her head quickly. "Never mind."

"Just say it."

She shook her head and for a minute he thought she was going to be stubborn. He hated it when someone started a thought and then just left it dangling. He doubted anything could be as bad as leaving him to wonder if she knew something about Sara that he didn't.

"It was just a crazy thought," Lacy said finally. "Just that it's like maybe the two of you had some kind of premonition. Given your job, though, it's probably likely that neither of you wanted to tempt fate." She gave a little laugh. "That was one superstition my mother managed to pass on to me. Don't tempt fate. Knock on wood."

He smiled almost in spite of himself. "Sara knocked on wood."

"We both did. It's a silly superstition, but a hard one to overcome."

He'd run into plenty of superstitions, some utterly new to him, when he'd been with combat units. Some were personal to an individual, others were cultural, but nearly everyone possessed a "lucky" object of one kind or another. But this was different. Thinking about how he and Sara had skipped all the talk of "someday" left him wondering if he'd failed her in some important way. How would he know? He'd only been part of one couple.

"Sara was strong," Lacy said unexpectedly. "Really strong. She took your absences in stride. She missed you, I know she did, but she didn't focus on it, Jess. She had a great ability to exist in the moment. Maybe that's part of the reason you never made long-range plans. She was very much a here-and-now kind of person. Maybe that's why she managed your absences so well."

He lifted one corner of his mouth. She was right about how Sara had lived very much in the moment. It was one of the things he had loved about the woman. He could come home on leave and the days wouldn't be shadowed by his eventual departure. Not for her, anyway. She seized the moment and enjoyed it.

"I wish I could be more like her," Lacy remarked.

"There's nothing wrong with the way you are," he objected.

"Sure, there is. Can you imagine Sara spending all these months looking over her shoulder? Not her style at all."

He couldn't deny it. "And maybe that wouldn't have been wise," he said after a beat. "I'm not going to argue that there's no reason for you to be concerned. And since you are, we'll deal with it. There's an instinct I learned never to ignore when I was overseas. The feeling of being watched or stalked. You've got that feeling. Nothing could make me ignore it."

"But was it always right?"

"How often does it have to be right to be valid?" Damn, that note was practically burning a hole in his brain, but he didn't want to tell her about it. Without something else to go on, it was useless and pointless. But maybe he was getting soft. He'd wondered that earlier today. Maybe he should wonder harder.

"Interesting way to put it. More coffee?"

His smile widened a bit. "You planning to sleep tonight at all?"

She flushed, and he instantly felt bad. She asked, "Am I keeping you awake? I can go back upstairs."

"That isn't what I meant at all." With his arms he turned himself on the couch so that he was sitting upright. "I just wondered if you wanted to stay awake. You were so tired earlier. But I'm not ready to close my eyes by a long shot. It's nice to have company. Usually I'd be sitting here, listening to the wind."

She tilted her head a little, studying him. "Do you have trouble sleeping? Or is something bothering you tonight?"

That drew a laugh out of him. "That's what I was going to ask you. Okay, me first. Usually I sleep well enough. Tonight, I'm hurting."

"Phantom pain?"

"None other. Now what about you?"

She paused as if considering the question. "I used to sleep well. Not so much since this whole crime blew up. I tend to wake up a lot and wander around. I lost count of the nights I played Solitaire. I think I drove my agents nuts with it. It was as if they were always worried I'd try to slip their cordon, so they never relaxed when I was stirring."

"Would you have?"

She shook her head. "I'm more cautious than that. Anyway, uninterrupted nights are rare. And tonight the storm seems to be making me edgy. It's noisier upstairs."

He hadn't thought of that, but he could believe it. Upstairs there were no nearby trees or shrubs to slow the wind. "Maybe you should try to sleep down here. The couch isn't bad."

"If I get sleepy. Right now I feel wired." She rose from the rocker and walked around the room slowly, carrying her coffee. With each of her movements, fleece moved against her, delineating her curves, reminding him she was all woman. Hell.

She spoke again. "It's amazing how fast life can change, leaving you permanently altered. Sara, your wounding, the announcement that someone wanted to kill me…" She faced him, standing in front of the stove. "There's no way back, Jess."

"No," he agreed. No way at all. If he'd had a magic wand…well, he didn't. Time flowed in only one direction for mortals. Of that much he was sure. For a long time he'd have given anything in the world to have Sara back. But with time he'd accepted one thing: she was probably better off without him. If he'd thought his mother had been ripped up by his injuries, he hated to think of how Sara would have responded. And worse, he wouldn't have been able to send her back to France during the time he had been so antisocial. He didn't want to imagine how much hurt he might have inflicted on her with his rage and self-pity. His refusal to talk. He hadn't been a nice person for a long while there. He'd just wanted to be left alone.

Look at how he'd turned Lacy away. Wouldn't let her visit, wouldn't take her phone calls for the longest time. If he had treated Sara that way... He shuddered to think.

Lacy had forgiven him, but she hadn't been vulnerable to the kinds of scars he could have inflicted on his wife. There was a mercy in that, painful as it was to face it.

Lacy sighed and started to walk back to the rocker. Impulse seized him and he patted the couch beside him. "Wanna sit here? It's softer."

She hardly hesitated, but settled on the cushion beside him. He could feel her warmth, detect her lovely scents, and for a few minutes pretend he was just an ordinary guy. Maybe not fair to her, but she'd never know.

She leaned forward, with her elbows on her knees, her cup cradled in both hands. A strangely closed posture when she had been willing to come so close.

He finally spoke. "Wanna talk more about why you've been so on edge? I get that it's hard to shake the idea that you've been threatened, but has something else been going on?"

"You mean have I seen something? Nothing I could report. I mean, I kept seeing this one guy around, but you know how that is. If you start watching, you see the same faces pretty often even on a busy street. People who commute along the same route, people who go to work in the same or nearby buildings, people who use the same grocery store. I called the FBI, and they reassured me. They're certain that they unraveled the whole operation. They'd know, wouldn't they?"

He answered cautiously. "You'd think."

"Yeah." She sighed and at last leaned back. "I've become a paranoid nut. I need to get over it. Then I need to find a job, maybe some other place besides Dallas. A place where I won't have a history. I'm assuming, of course, that my former employer wouldn't dare give me a bad recommendation."

"Doing so, under the circumstances, might be grounds to sue them. Isn't there whistleblower protection?"

"Not for this kind of thing. It's all right. I'll find work again, I'm sure. Or maybe open my own accounting practice, although going back to small business accounting doesn't really appeal to me." She turned, giving him a rueful smile. "I was working with the big boys, lots of money, lots of accounts. Auditing books for local government agencies and big corporations. Having my own business would probably be mostly dull by comparison."

"But safer."

"Unquestionably." At last she relaxed enough to laugh briefly. "I'm not without options. I just need to remember how to relax."

Impulsively, he stretched out his arm and drew her closer to his side. She didn't stiffen, but leaned into him as if she needed the human contact as much as he did. For a while they just sat, listening to their own thoughts, to the occasional burst of wind, to the muffled crackling of the fire in the stove.

After a while he asked, "Did you leave a boyfriend behind?"

"I was dating someone at the firm. Casually. He bailed the minute I became tainted. I can't blame him. It must have seemed as if I had the plague."

"I'd blame him," Jess said. "Most definitely. People who run from trouble aren't good bets."

"Well, it *was* just casual. I shouldn't have dated him anyway. Dating in the workplace can create problems. But you know, we were all workaholics. Come tax season, we were up to our eyebrows, working round the clock. Then there was the second tax season for all the delayed filers. And a lot of companies had different fiscal years. So we had our lists of clients, and when we weren't working with them we helped others."

"Is that how you found out about the transfers?"

She nodded. "I was helping one of the partners. He needed more time to play golf with clients, and I was promised that if I kept on being a good girl I'd make partner someday. So I took on the additional work with a smile."

"Then *kaboom*."

"Yeah, *kaboom*. I spent days, weeks, trying to find a way around what I suspected, until there was no way out."

"So did he think you were too stupid to see it?"

"Either that, or he thought I wanted to be the first female partner badly enough to keep my mouth shut."

"Big misjudgment." He gave her a gentle squeeze. "You should be proud of yourself."

"It's not like I didn't have a horse in this race. I could have gotten into trouble, too."

He shook his head. "Don't put yourself down. You reported wrongdoing to the Feds. I think an awful lot of people would have just found another job."

"Maybe."

He was touched when she rested her head against his shoulder. He also felt like a bit of a sham for not sharing that note with her, but still couldn't imagine what earthly good it could do.

Besides, he was losing track of everything except the woman who was leaning against his side. He could smell her shampoo, a delicate scent like flowers, and despite her recent bath, her womanly scents were beginning to emerge somehow. They filled his head with dreams of taking her to his bed and loving her until she forgot everything else.

Shock rippled through him, but not enough to completely erase his desire for her. Man, she'd probably have nightmares if she saw the stump of his leg. It would inevitably destroy the mood. Then there was Sara, a woman they had both loved. He'd feel as if he was cheating on her, and he suspected Lacy might as well, ridiculous as that might be. Loyalties evidently didn't go to the grave.

He sighed and reached down with his free hand to rub his stump, as if it could free him from the pain he had never felt when he was hit, pain that his body evidently refused to forget.

"Can I help?"

"Naw." Oh yeah, she could. With a few touches she could probably carry him to a place where nothing but the two of them could exist. But afterward... Hell, he feared the guilt that might follow. He could ruin a perfectly good friendship by getting out of line with this woman.

He and Sara had once had a serious discussion about the possibility he might not return from one of his deployments. Just once, but he remembered telling her to move on with life, that he'd never forgive himself if she buried herself with him.

She'd cocked a brow in that humorous way of hers and asked, "Do you really think I'm the type to do that?"

"Just promise me," he'd said.

It was one of those rare occasions where she'd grown utterly serious. "I'll promise if you'll promise me the same thing."

Of course he'd promised. It had never occurred to him he might be the lone survivor. But that didn't mean he wouldn't feel guilty anyway. Maybe he had some more demons to get past.

He realized that Lacy had unexpectedly dozed off against him. Smiling into the empty night, he removed the mug from her loosening grip and put it on the side table. He guessed she felt safe with him, but he wasn't at all sure that was a good idea.

That note. It hung over him like a sword. What the hell did it mean? He stared into the fire, uneasiness joining the pain that crept along his nerve endings and the desire that wouldn't stop humming quietly.

Chapter 6

The hunter waited. He waited impatiently. He didn't think of himself as a killer, any more than a tiger did. No, this was purely self-defense. By the time the worst of the storm passed, he was crawling with the need for action, like the predator he sometimes fancied himself. Unfortunately, lessening snow and wind didn't drive the temperatures up by much. A battery-operated radio warned him of the dangers outside.

He'd found an unoccupied house off the beaten path, not too far from his target. It was sturdy and windproof enough that he'd been able to weather the worst of the clipper with a kerosene heater. And of course he had the proper gear. If the military had taught him nothing else, it was how important proper gear was.

Right now he would have very much liked to be able to drop a rocket-propelled grenade on McGregor's house, but that was foolish thinking and he knew it. Besides, the guy had the devil's own luck, having already survived an RPG attack. The hunter—yes, he preferred to think of himself as a hunter, just like a tiger—had great belief in luck. McGregor should be dead. He wasn't. Hence a problem.

Then there was the woman. Where the hell had she come from, and why was she there? He'd been watching for a while, and McGregor had never shown any romantic interest in a woman. As a widower, he was apparently still grieving, which served him right.

The hunter didn't approve of military people getting married. Spouses at home could be a distraction. What's more, few of the enlisted men in the lower ranks could afford to support a family. It had annoyed him how much time they'd wasted on those Skype calls home when they were at a base, reinforcing the idea they needed to survive.

A true soldier didn't think of such things. A true soldier didn't allow distractions. He had one purpose and one only: to win. To kill. To be killed, if necessary.

The woman surprised him, though. If anyone in the area knew a thing about her, they weren't talking. Which, in itself, wasn't surprising. It was a small community and he was a stranger who spent most of his time trying to avoid attention. He'd prefer it if, when he left here, nobody remembered him at all. Hell, he didn't even eat at the diner, but occasionally at the truck stop on the edge of town where people came and went with dizzying regularity.

He'd planned well, he thought as he heated instant coffee over the kerosene heater. He didn't stay anywhere he could be traced, he didn't shop locally, he had a stack of MREs to eat, purchased at a military outlet long before he'd gotten here. Self-sufficient. Leaving no trail.

But that still left the problem ahead of him. Jess McGregor would be easy to take out alone. If he always had that woman with him, the possibilities that something would go wrong multiplied enormously.

However, the woman could supply him with some fun after he knocked out McGregor. That was another thing he'd learned in the military: the unparalleled pleasure of dominating a woman, taking what he wanted over her screams and protests. Not that he'd had the opportunity often. Those damn savages over there were seldom alone, and for his part he seldom got out of reach of his own unit. But once in a while…

He smiled, then sipped his coffee, which was almost hot enough to burn his tongue. Yeah, that woman could be of some use before he dealt with her, too. It might even be interesting to take a blonde. He'd never done that before. Blond hair, pale skin.

For a while, he forgot about his larger plan, indulging in some fantasy about the woman. Different, for certain.

But while the storm had passed, at least for now, the weather hadn't warmed enough. If he was going to be outside, he'd have to stay on the move or risk frostbite. Simply lying in wait to watch could be dangerous.

So he sat on the bare floor, hunkered by his heater, and tried to pull thoughts together into a plan. But no plan would be guaranteed until he gleaned enough intelligence.

Somehow he had to find out what was going on with those two. If she was only there for a few days, he could wait and dismiss his fantasies of what he'd like to do to her.

Success depended on self-control. He could control himself as long as necessary. He had years of practice at that.

In the meantime, he wondered just how unnerved he'd made McGregor with that note. Hell, the guy probably didn't even know which of them it was directed at.

Savoring the notion of McGregor's concern, he made another cup of coffee. Oh, this was going to be good. Payback for years of worry at last.

Waking to silence the next morning seemed almost eerie to Lacy. Curious to see what the day was like, she pulled her robe on over her flannel nightgown, pushed her feet into slippers and went over to the window to draw back the heavy curtains.

Blinding sunlight greeted her, so strong she narrowed her eyes and blinked. The world had turned mostly white, although scrub still poked up everywhere, indicating the snowfall was measured in inches. Here and there, she saw a windswept dune of snow that had caught on some obstacle.

Part of her was thrilled to be done with the storm. She wasn't used to being stuck in one place, unable to just hop into a car or a bus and go wherever she liked. Cabin fever after only two days? She could have laughed at herself. And it was such a cozy cabin to be in.

She washed quickly in the bathroom, then headed downstairs. A fire crackled in the woodstove, looking freshly fed, and warmth surrounded her. Following the aroma of coffee, she found Jess in the kitchen with a book and a mug of coffee.

"What a bright day out there," she remarked.

He looked up with a smile. "Blinding. I hope you brought sunglasses."

"Always have them in my purse." She got her own coffee, then joined him at the table. "Did you sleep last night, eventually?" She almost colored as she remembered the way she had snuggled into his side. She vaguely remembered finally dozing against his shoulder in the circle of his arm, feeling so safe and secure, until finally he'd wakened her and said with obvious reluctance, "I have to move."

She'd hardly opened her eyes as she climbed the stairs to change for bed, and was sure she couldn't even remember the moment her head hit the pillow.

"Yeah," he answered, still smiling pleasantly. "The pain went away."

"But they can't do anything about it? Really?"

He shrugged. "They tried. They can't do any more than that. It might get better with time."

"I hope so." She decided a change of subject might be in order, especially when he tempted her more than a fresh cup of coffee. "It seemed eerie to wake to silence this morning. I hadn't realized how accustomed I was getting to the sound of the wind."

"Well, don't get used to the quiet. We usually have some wind stirring around here, although not like yesterday."

Almost as if to verify his comment, the window rattled. She laughed quietly. "I guess not."

"It's still deadly cold out there, though," he warned her.

"Was there much snow?"

"TV said just a couple of inches. Most of it probably blew right off the roads and settled in gullies, so if you decide you want to get out later, we can probably get safely to town. Maybe find you some really good snow pants, something that'll keep the wind out."

"Am I going to be here that long?"

The question caused a new kind of silence in the house. Jess regarded her steadily. "Ready to move on?" he asked casually.

"I didn't mean that." All of sudden she felt awful. "Honestly. But how long do you want to put up with me?"

"As long as it takes, and longer if you like." He pushed his book aside and surprised her by holding his hand out across the table.

After a moment's hesitation, she rested her hand in his and felt his gentle grip. Sara's husband. In that instant the little hang-up didn't seem quite so important.

"I'm enjoying your company," he said. "What's more, I'm beginning to realize how little I really know about you. So I'm fascinated. You're an intriguing woman, Lacy. You don't share a whole lot, do you?"

"Meaning?"

"You shared your fears with me, some of the details of what you got involved in, but little more. All these years and I feel like I've barely scraped the surface of Lacy Devane. Odd, don't you think?"

She bridled a bit, but didn't remove her hand from his. His touch was welcome, comforting, stirring her in ways she didn't dare think about. He looked so good sitting there in a black sweater that appeared to have seen many years of wear. It stretched across shoulders that must now be broader than when he'd bought it, clung to his chest muscles. Green eyes staring thoughtfully at her as if nothing else existed.

Being the total focus of this man was oddly exhilarating.

"You didn't tell me much, either," she answered, feeling a bit defensive.

He laughed, squeezed her fingers and let go. "Like I said, I'm enjoying having you here. Most of the time, I rattle around in this place like a mad carpenter, talking to myself."

"You have friends, surely!"

"Of course. But most of them work, too, and have families. And I put in long days at the clinic. By choice, because I love what I do, and there's a crying need in this county for readily accessible medical care that can't wait for an appointment. But lest you wonder, yeah, I have friends and we get together for poker games or a few beers at Mahoney's. Sometimes we have barbecues, but I think that'll have to wait a few months now. I'm not a hermit. But it's nice not to be alone in this house, so you're welcome to share it with me for as long as you like."

She nodded, missing his touch more than she should have. "I get it. I didn't mean anything by that. I worked long hours, too, and for the last year and a half of that mess I couldn't even talk to my friends. They weren't allowed to know where I was. When I got out of protective custody...well, they'd moved on. We couldn't quite pick up the pieces somehow."

"Not like it was with you and Sara."

"Never like that."

"You two were as thick as thieves. You get close, really close to your buddies in the military, but it's not the same as someone you've known your whole life."

"How so?"

He rose, and she saw he was wearing his leg today under fleece pants. "There's a deep bond, but it's built on the present. Not on years and years of knowing someone. Everything is mission-focused, task-focused. You'd lay down your life for a guy you only met a few months ago. Weird, but true. But what you and Sara had..." He returned with his full cup, his smile a little off. "You knew her in ways I never could, Lacy."

"I could say the same about you."

At that he laughed. "True." He sat facing her again and his smile looked more natural. "So, okay, I'm interested in getting to know you. What you like and dislike, where you've been. Where you'd like to go someday. Something more than watching you and Sara giggle together, and hearing about this mess you just got out of. Surely there's another Lacy, too. Just let me know what's off-limits."

"What's off-limits with you?"

His face shadowed. "The war. Let's just put that off the table unless there's a damn good reason to bring it up. Hell does exist on earth, but there's no reason to open those doors."

She bit her lip, hesitating, then blurted, "Do you have anyone at all to talk to about it?"

"Other vets," he said simply. "They get it."

And she never would. Those tours abroad had to have played a large part in the man he had become, but she was wise enough to realize that she had no way to truly understand. Sometimes even the best imagination had to fail, and unless you walked in someone else's shoes, all the empathy in the world would fall short.

Nor did she have any desire to unsettle him by prying into things he didn't want to talk about. Whatever peace he had needed to make with that part of his life, he seemed to have made it, or to be making it.

"Okay," she said, feeling a need to reassure him. "Off the table. Not that I wanted to stir things up for you."

The wall was there, though. It would have been there for Sara, too. Things he wanted to spare her. Experiences no one should ever have. Parts of him could never be shared except with someone who had been there. That saddened her.

"So what about the perky nurses in the hospital?" she asked, trying to ease away from the untouchable stuff.

"Oh my God," he groaned and made her laugh by putting his head in his hands. "I don't know if they put them on joy juice or what."

"Seriously?"

He lifted his head. "Well, there was one battle-ax who'd rap the end of my bed with her clipboard and tell me to stop feeling sorry for myself or she'd take me upstairs and introduce me to guys with *real* problems."

Lacy drew a breath. "Really? She said that?"

"Of course she did. Life teaches you sooner or later that no matter how bad you think you have it, someone else has it worse. Sometimes it's just hard to remember. But most of the nurses, male and female, were all perky beyond belief." He paused, then added, "It was a bitch of a job for them. Amazing how they clung to those good spirits. They rotated a lot, so maybe that helped."

Lacy just sat and listened, unable to think of a single thing to say that wouldn't sound stupid or trite.

He shook his head. "They dealt with the detritus of war. A lot of them had even served in field hospitals. Maybe dealing with us was cheerful by comparison. I don't know."

"Well, you were right at the front. Maybe you do know." Then she realized she'd gone where she had promised not to go. "Sorry. I'm getting hungry. Want me to make something?"

She pushed back from the table and stood, adding one last thing, "Don't refer to yourself as detritus. Please."

He let it pass, apparently willing to move on. "What are you in the mood for? We've got eggs, toast, some frozen hash browns, mix for pancakes and some honest-to-goodness real maple syrup."

She paused halfway to the fridge. "*Real* maple syrup?"

That settled the issue for both of them. She pulled out the pancake mix after he told her where to look, found a skillet and heated it while she mixed. "Do you like them full size or dollar size?"

"Big ones for me."

A while later, a big stack of flapjacks sat on the table between them. She only wanted one for herself, but he didn't hesitate to take three. The maple syrup was exquisite enough that she closed her eyes to savor it. There was nothing quite like it.

"I see a happy Lacy," he remarked.

She opened her eyes as she swallowed. "After this, I think I'll do without pancakes unless I can have real maple syrup. The difference is wonderful."

"Liquid gold," he agreed.

"And almost as expensive."

He laughed. "There are some things in life worth paying for. This is one."

As she enjoyed her breakfast, however, she realized that the familiar uneasiness was building in her again. Keeping her eyes on her plate, she wondered if she had become one of Pavlov's dogs, trained to salivate at the sound of a bell. Why couldn't she shake the fear? She'd been under protection for a long time, true, but surrounded by agents, she had been as safe as anyone could be. So why did fear still haunt her?

"Penny for your thoughts?" Jess asked.

She shook her head a little, wishing she could shake away the discomfort. "I'm trying to figure out how I could be sitting here with you having a wonderful breakfast and still feel as if I need to look over my shoulder. This is nuts, Jess. Maybe I slipped a cog."

"I don't think you're crazy," he said firmly. "You know about post-traumatic stress, right?"

"A bit."

"Have you considered that you might be experiencing it? You had a frightening shock—I mean, it's not everyday someone has the FBI telling them that they've been targeted by a killer, right?"

"Right."

"Then you had your whole life upended, and how could you brush aside the threat when they took it seriously enough to put you in protection? So you spent more than a year living with a very real threat you couldn't even begin to forget. I'd be surprised if that hadn't changed you."

She nodded slowly, accepting his assessment. Maybe he was right. She'd lived with that threat for a long time. Simply having someone say it was over might not be enough. But he was certainly making her feel better about her reaction to all this. Nowhere near as silly as she had been telling herself.

"You said you weren't allowed to call your friends."

She looked up. "No. Well, only a couple of times. They had me use a special phone, like when they let me call you. You got more calls than my friends did, but they seemed more nervous about me making local calls of any kind. I don't know why."

"Maybe they feared one of your friends would figure out where you were somehow. Me on the other hand... In the boonies, unable to imagine where they might have stashed you because I don't know Dallas."

She blew a breath and put her fork down, reaching up to push hair back from her face. "You're right."

"Plus," he continued, "they probably had a complete background on me. Unlike your friends, most of my life is filed with the federal government."

For some reason, that drew a laugh from her. "You got a file, huh?"

"Big one. They know damn near everything about me from the day I turned eighteen."

"Does that bother you?"

"Why would it? I chose to put on that uniform. Admittedly, the record is probably a little sketchy since I got here, but my life's an open book. Ask any of my neighbors."

That made her laugh again. "I've heard that about small towns."

"It's true." He took some more pancakes. "You should eat another one, too. Five pounds, right?"

"Six or so."

"So an extra flapjack won't kill you." All of a sudden he paused and cleared his throat. "Officially, however, as a PA, I should be advising you against all those empty calories. Pure sugar, fat and processed flour. Oh, man."

"And it tastes so good." She felt her fears easing away, and an urge to giggle overcoming her.

"Which is why I indulge sometimes. Just don't tell my patients on me." He winked and continued to eat.

Settling down again, she did take another pancake, although she doubted she'd be able to finish it. The syrup was so rich and sweet it nearly made her toes curl.

His comment about post-traumatic stress made a lot of sense to her, though. While she hadn't thought of all that had happened as being terribly traumatic, maybe it had been, more so than she had realized.

Another thought struck her as she was helping wash up. "I've become rusty."

That caused Jess to pause as he put a plate in the dishwasher. "Rusty?"

"After all that time being cooped up with those agents I hardly knew, I got in the habit of keeping my thoughts to myself. They were essentially strangers. What was I going to talk to them about? Certainly not anything that really mattered."

He put the last plate in the dishwasher and closed the door. When he straightened, he leaned against the counter with one hip and took the pan she had just washed, drying it with a towel. "That makes sense. And you said you were shy to begin with."

"Shy and a bit of an introvert. Part of why Sara and I were such good friends was because…well, this is going to sound odd, but I've been thinking about it since we lost her. It was as if she was the other part of me, Jess. She was all the things I couldn't be naturally, but she carried me along with her. I met people I might never have met, did things I might never have done."

He twisted, hanging the pan from the pot rack on the one otherwise bare wall. "Must've been hard on you when you went to separate colleges. When we got married."

She hoped her flush didn't show. She never wanted him to guess how much she had resented him when he first entered Sara's life. "Hard, but not that hard." She sighed and wiped the counter with a sponge. "I learned a lot from her. I got better at reaching out, making friends, going out."

"But then all the old habits slammed back into place when you were in protective custody."

"The old inclinations, anyway. But yes. I went back to being an introvert. When I talked, it was when we were working on the case. All business. The rest of the time..." She shrugged, rinsed the sponge and put in on the dish beside the stainless-steel sink. "I guess I reverted to type."

He refilled their coffee mugs from the fresh pot he'd made before they started clearing the table. "If you're an introvert, you must find it hard to have me around all the time."

Startled, she looked at him. "No, not at all. It's comfortable being with you."

"It might have been comfortable resuming your other friendships," he said. "Or not."

She got caught on that statement. "Maybe it was my fault."

"Did I say that?"

"No...it's just that..." She wondered where she was going with this. He motioned with his head toward the living room and she went. He sat on the rocker again, so she perched on the end of the couch. Coffee mug on the side table, because even though its bitterness was easing the overwhelming sweetness of breakfast, she was beginning to feel overloaded on something.

"Just what?" he prompted.

"I'm not sure. You're right. If I'd been willing to make the effort, I could have resumed some of those friend-ships."

"Only some?"

"Only some," she repeated. "You have to remember what I did. I didn't just kill my job prospects, but some of the people I thought of as friends figured I'd com-mitted a major act of disloyalty. They didn't want me to call them, even when I was still in protection. The few who didn't run… Maybe I didn't want to make the effort anymore. Or maybe I was afraid I'd bring trouble their way. Remember, I can't believe I'm safe even now. And what if my actions affected them somehow?"

He sat rocking for a while, saying nothing, appar-ently thinking over what she'd said. Hardly surprising, because it wasn't exactly making sense to her, either. She could understand why some of the people whose work was associated with hers, either through the firm she'd been part of or because they had the same careers as CPAs, might have felt it best to avoid her. But what about the others? Had she really feared she might bring them trouble through this probably imaginary feeling that she might still be in danger?

Or had something else driven her to put distance between herself and her remaining friends? Since this whole mess had begun, she'd been reacting to events as they unfolded, and once she'd made the decision to go to the US Attorney with what she had, she'd stopped thinking about anything else. Everything had been put on hold from that point.

But it was over now. Was fear alone guiding her? Or was there a bigger issue at the heart of all this?

"Tell me," Jess said finally, "how you feel about what you did."

She lifted her brows. "How do you mean?"

"Well, you took a dangerous leap, you blew the whistle on your firm, your bosses, maybe some of your co-workers. I don't know all the details, because you haven't really told me, and while I tried to follow it in press reports online, they weren't exactly overflowing with details."

"Not the kind of details people want to read about," she said wryly.

He half smiled. "Admittedly. The ins and outs of accounting would probably put half the world to sleep. So all I got was an outline, and you evidently couldn't say all that much. But what none of this is telling me is how you, Lacy Devane, really feel about what you did. Do you have doubts? Were you right? Were you the hero of the story?"

At that she gaped. "I'm no hero."

"Interesting." He leaned forward and put his elbows on his thighs. "Lacy Devane single-handedly takes down a money-laundering operation which, as a by-product, evidently takes down a big drug operation, and she doesn't feel like a hero? Why not?"

The question drew her up short. She'd done the right thing. She'd paid a heavy price, too. Maybe she wasn't a hero, but he was right about one thing—she'd taken a very dangerous step that put her life at risk. How did she feel about that? Maybe it was time she sorted that out.

"I did what I had to do," she answered.

"Funny, every hero I've ever heard says exactly the

same thing. But that's not what I'm asking. I'm asking how you *feel* about it. And that's what you're afraid to share, isn't it? Numbers are ever so much consistent and reliable than messy feelings."

Hearing a version of her own words come back at her stung. She stood up, not liking this conversation, wanting to walk away from it. But once on her feet, she remained frozen, nearly glaring at Jess. She felt as if he wanted to take a can opener to places inside nobody had a right to go.

"Sorry," he said after a minute. "I'm pushing you and I don't have the right."

"Why?" she demanded.

"Because I want to know you. The real Lacy. Sara loved you. I saw how much fun you two had together, but there was more than fun to your relationship. There had to be. And right now you don't have anyone to re-place Sara in your life. Hell, neither do I."

"I don't want to be Sara's stand-in!"

"Neither do I. But maybe, between us, we can build real friendship. And I do mean *real*. Or we can bump along the way we are as strangers-but-not-strangers, keeping all our little secrets, and then once you're safe you can move on and we'll go back to monthly phone calls that consist of little more than *Hi, how are you?*"

She realized her heart had begun to pound, indicating that something in what he was saying unnerved her. Maybe threatened her. And damn him, he sat there in that rocking chair, reminding her by his simple presence that he was attractively male and off-limits. Sara put him off-limits. So, maybe, did her own hang-ups. What a mess!

"What do you want from me, Jess?"

"I told you. To get to really know you."

"What I am is what you see."

He snorted, but didn't push it. Slowly she resumed her seat, trying to brush away cobwebs of desire that had ensnared her, that had nothing to do with this clash they were having. So out of place that they startled her. But he kept having that effect on her. Each time she saw him, she felt that breathless recognition that she wanted this man.

She couldn't have him, though. That theoretically made her safe. But safe from what? Along with the miasma of hunger that seemed to surround her right now, questions were buzzing, questions about herself. He hadn't asked anything out of line. He'd simply asked what she needed to ask herself.

The problem was, she had plenty of excuses not to answer those questions. Reacting, always reacting, and if she tried to face up to what was inside her, well…she could always distract herself with the case, with her fears, with the way friends had abandoned her, with the way her future seemed to have blown away like dead leaves because of what she had done.

It occurred to her that she was lacking in the self-knowledge department. She saw herself as a reflection of those around her, not as independent. But who was really independent?

She gave herself an internal shake and warned herself not to turn this into a philosophy lesson. He was asking for real stuff, not roundabout evasions or answers to universal questions.

Just start with one question, she advised herself. How *did* she feel about what she had done?

The answer emerged, slowly and painfully, and for

once she shared it with him. "I feel awful about what I did."

He nodded and reached for his mug. "Why?" The question wasn't accusatory.

"Because it wasn't pure."

"Pure?" A crease formed on his brow.

She made a harsh sound. "Altruism? Doesn't exist. I wasn't being altruistic. I saw what was going on. I figured it out. And I was aware that I was in it up to my neck. No plausible deniability would cover me. But once I figured it out, even claims of stupidity weren't enough. So I did the only thing I could do. I meant that, you know. And in the process I took down some people I liked. I don't feel good about it. Not at all. For the rest of my life, I'm going to wonder how many innocent people got caught in that snare, people who really didn't know what was happening. Maybe they didn't get convicted, but they sure as hell lost their jobs and future prospects."

"Ugly."

"Yes, it was ugly. I loathe myself for it."

Presently he said, "Like war."

The silence that filled the room then was almost heavy, suffocating. He was comparing their experiences and she knew it, but she figured his own must have been a million times worse.

"Collateral damage," he said after a few minutes. "Such a clean, clinical word for destruction of lives and property. It's not intentional, but it *is* inevitable."

"I'm sorry, Jess."

He shook his head. "No need. I was just trying to let you know that I understand."

"Probably better than anyone."

A crooked smile. "Maybe. Maybe not."

He rocked for a while, finishing his coffee. "You up for a trip to town if I warm the car first?"

She leaped at the opportunity. Enough soul-searching for one morning. "Love it."

"Good. We'll get you some proper pants for weather like this, and I want to stop in and say hi to the sheriff."

"Why?"

"Because he needs to know about you. Amazing man, our sheriff. I just want to tell him why you're here. He'll keep an eye out, and if your fears are well-grounded, you're going to need more eyes than mine."

Chapter 7

The icy day held the beauty of absolutely clear air. Even the distant mountains appeared almost magnified as their contours showed sharply and glistened brightly where snow had settled.

Jess was glad to see Lacy put on sunglasses as soon as they stepped outside. He hoped they were strong enough. The car had been warming for fifteen minutes, and as she slipped inside a blast of hot air escaped.

Warm enough, he thought as he climbed in beside her. He still felt guilty about not showing her the note in his pocket, but he was going to share it with the sheriff if he could get a minute alone with the man. He just couldn't see any point in scaring Lacy needlessly. Her feeling that someone might be keeping an eye on her in Dallas was not one he was willing to ignore. On the other hand, how would someone have followed her here so quickly?

So he'd put Gage Dalton's head on the question. The

man knew law enforcement and threats of this kind better than he ever would, and not just because he was sheriff. Before coming to Conard County, he'd been with the DEA. He'd be far more capable of assessing whether a threat to Lacy still remained, and whether that note made any sense at all.

Lacy held his attention all the way into town, however. One moment, she seemed totally absorbed by the winter beauty around her, the next nervous and scanning rapidly as if she feared someone's approach. Man, he felt bad for her. He couldn't imagine how she'd clung to her equanimity after so many months of feeling like this. At least when he'd come home from Afghanistan each time, he had known he was as safe as anyone else. Couldn't always quite believe it, but after a few days he had always settled down. Lacy wasn't getting that break.

For her, every day must be something like the way he'd felt when he walked into a new village in Afghanistan for the first time, and anyone could be friend or foe. All well and good to try to make them friends, but you never knew. They seemed grateful enough for the clinics he often held, dealing with illnesses and injuries, and even doling out vaccinations for the kids when he had the supplies. Winning hearts and minds. He wasn't sure they'd ever won much of either.

But he still remembered the skin-crawling feeling of wondering which wall, which door, which rooftop might harbor a deadly threat. People who came to him for medical attention were often putting their own lives at risk, depending on who might be watching. And sometimes no one at all came to him, a sure signal they were in enemy territory.

Lacy had no signals to assure her she might be safe,

even here. He stifled a sigh, hoping they could find a way to get her past this. That note provided little reassurance.

Stupid. He'd thought just bringing her here would make her safe, would make her feel safe. Apparently she'd forgotten how to trust in her own safety, and now he wasn't so sure himself.

He glanced her way again, and saw her leaning toward the window, as if enjoying the snow-laden trees that lined the street.

"It looks so Christmasy," she said. "Like a postcard."

"Yeah, it does." And she looked better than the winter's charms. His body insisted on stirring every time he saw her, and no amount of mental warning and self-checks could prevent a very masculine response to her. Damn, under any other circumstances he'd be trying to date her, dreaming about eventually making love to her.

But not under these circumstances. It would be a betrayal worse than that note he'd kept secret. She'd come to him for safety, not a fling, not a romance. She'd come to him as Sara's husband, and he needed to remember that. What's more, he'd invited her, promising safety. He hated to think he might not be able to provide it, but at the time it had seemed like a good idea. Get her away from Dallas, get her off the grid. At least then she could relax for a while.

Except she wasn't relaxing and now he was wondering what he might have waded into. Money laundering indicated some very high-level operation. Big bucks, nasty people. He wondered if Gage would just automatically agree that the FBI's assessment was the best, or if he'd poke around a bit.

He went straight to the sheriff's office and parked on the side street facing the courthouse square.

"Will he be in?" Lacy asked.

"Probably. He swears his entire job has devolved to handling paperwork and politics."

A little laugh escaped her. "Probably."

He set the parking brake and turned off the ignition. "Do you want to talk to him?"

She looked down for a moment. "Not really," she admitted. "Every time I say this out loud, I start to feel silly."

"So I'll have a word with him for you." Which would make it easier for him to share that damn note. "Okay?"

"Thanks. I mean, if he really wants to talk with me, I will, but…you know what?" All of a sudden her voice grew tight.

"What?"

"The agents made me feel like a fool for even thinking someone might be after me."

He drummed his fingers on the steering wheel for a moment. "Bad on them. You'd just helped them solve a major case. Helped bring the bad guys to justice. Stuck your neck out. A little courtesy seems like the least they could do."

"Oh, they were courteous. It was the *way* they did it."

He nodded. "Got it. Well, Gage is a pretty good guy, but you can wait out front unless he needs to see you."

"Thanks."

Inside the sheriff's office, everything looked the same as it always did. He sometimes thought it was an unchanging tableau, especially with old Velma sitting at the dispatch desk and still puffing away at her cigarettes under the no-smoking sign. A couple of deputies were engaged at various desks. A line of battered chairs stood along the window front. Lacy hesitated only a moment before sitting in one.

Velma waved him back through a cloud of smoke and he headed for Gage's office. The sheriff sat behind a desk that was buried in files, papers and a computer, any one of which looked in danger of being accidentally pushed to the floor.

Gage himself was a tall man with dark but slowly graying hair and a burn scar that covered nearly one side of his face. From a car bomb back in his DEA days, Jess had heard. It was a story people around here never seemed to tire of telling. Hell's Own Archangel, they'd nicknamed him when he'd first arrived here. The opinion had apparently changed considerably over the years.

Gage leaned forward without rising and shook Jess's hand. "What can I do for you?"

"Evaluate my thinking, assess a situation."

Gage smiled crookedly. "Do I look like a psychiatrist?"

Jess flashed a grin. "You look like a lawman with a lot of experience. I have none."

"So shoot."

Jess took the chair facing the desk and arranged his bum leg for maximum comfort. It had been a short walk from the heated car to the front door, but the joint felt stiff and cranky. He pushed the awareness aside. "I have a friend visiting."

"I heard."

Jess rolled his eyes, making Gage chuckle.

"What can I say?" Gage asked. "The confirmed widower suddenly brings a lovely young lady to stay. You think the grapevine hasn't been working? Even a storm can't stop those phone calls. So tell me."

"She's Lacy Devane, my late wife's oldest friend. They go all the way back to childhood."

Gage nodded. "So you've known her a long time, too."

"Thirteen years."

"Friendly visit?"

"Not quite."

Gage nodded and reached for a legal pad and pen. "So now we get to the law enforcement stuff. What's up?"

"Lacy turned in some of her former bosses to the Feds in Dallas. Seems they were money laundering for a drug operation."

Gage sat bolt upright. "I remember that case. She's the one who reported it?"

"And worked with forensic accountants on developing the case. And testified both to the grand jury and in court. And was in protective custody until the trial was over."

Gage whistled quietly. "Quite a brave woman."

"Well, that's the thing, Gage. She's not feeling very brave right now." Jess moved his leg again, then leaned forward until his arms were folded on a narrow strip of bare desk. "The Feds assured her the threat was over, that they'd mopped up everyone who was involved, and now that the convictions have come down, she's safe."

Gage frowned faintly. "She doesn't believe it."

"I figure it's kind of hard after being in protection for so long. Her whole life upended because there was a credible threat against her. Living in a safe house with agents around all the time. How do you shake that off?"

"It wouldn't be easy," Gage said slowly. "Not easy at all. But she got assurances?"

"Apparently so. But she still feels like she's being watched. Stalked. I don't know exactly. What I do know is that she was turning into a wreck, always looking over her shoulder. So I suggested she come visit me. We made a plan. She bought a bus ticket to Portland, told her friends—the ones that are left, anyway—that she was going back to visit some old friends from college, and then she got off the bus here. She hasn't been using credit cards or debit cards since she left Dallas, at my insistence."

"Good thinking." Gage rapped his pen on the desk a few times. "What's your gut feeling?"

"That I can't ignore her gut feeling."

After a beat, Gage spoke again, quietly. "I ignored a gut feeling once, to my everlasting sorrow. Logic said my cover hadn't been blown. My gut was turning sour. I should have listened."

"The bomb?"

"It cost me my family. Anyway, I don't want to go back over that, except to say I pay attention to my gut. Her gut is screaming, and I guess you have the same attitude."

"War does that."

"Yeah, I imagine it would. Okay, I can rattle some old contacts, call a few favors. Since this was drug money, you can believe DEA fingerprints are all over the case. I should be able to learn something. Anything else?"

Shifting onto one hip, Jess pulled the folded and crumpled paper from his pocket. "Found this on my porch, just before the storm really got going. Less than a day after I picked up Lacy at the bus."

Gage opened and smoothed it out, staring at it while Jess's internal clock ticked impatiently. Lacy was out there waiting for him, probably wondering what the heck was happening.

Then Gage shocked him, putting a cold spear right through him. "Jess. You wouldn't have any enemies, would you? From before?"

"Jess? Jess?"

He'd been far away in a place he never wanted to go again, explosions inside his head, screams filling his ears, curses erupting around him, a child falling... He blinked.

Lacy bent over him. Gage stood to one side. "Jess," he said. "Come back."

"Yeah," he mumbled. His mouth felt dry as dust. He realized he was gripping the arms of a chair so tightly that his hands ached. *Come back.* Gage's office. Lacy looking worried. Here. Now. Not back then.

Gage pried one of his hands open and pressed a bottle into it. Lacy urged it up to his mouth, and next thing he was drinking as if he hadn't wet his mouth in a week. The last drop went down his throat and he tossed the bottle. He didn't care where it landed.

No one really touched him, except for Lacy gently bringing that bottle to his mouth. Then she pulled back, squatted and waited, looking at him with fear. Fear? Worry. He closed his eyes, reaching for the present. He definitely didn't want to be touched right now. Not yet. He might react the wrong way.

That thought, as much as anything, firmly centered him in the now. He opened his eyes again, forced himself to mutter, "I'm okay."

Gage studied him a moment, then nodded. He pulled a chair over for Lacy and urged her to sit beside Jess. Then everything was silent except for phones ringing in the outer office and the occasional sound of Velma's cough.

They left him alone, but after a couple of minutes he felt he had to say something. "It hasn't hit me like that in a long time."

Gage nodded. Lacy asked, "What?"

"Flashback," Gage answered for him. "Just let him be. He's going to be okay."

"But what happened?" Lacy asked Gage.

"Guess I said exactly the wrong thing," Gage answered.

Jess couldn't deny it, but neither was he sure what had triggered the flashback. A quiet conversation. A simple question. What the hell?

Gage limped out of the office and yelled down the hall. "One of you run across the way to Maude's. I want coffee, three lattes and three pieces of pie. Make it fast."

Gage then returned to his seat. "You need some calories, my man. That'll take it out of you fast."

Jess managed a short nod. "I didn't do anything?"

"You didn't do a damn thing. You just snapped back to some place you don't want to go like a switch flipped. But you didn't do anything. You just froze up, wouldn't respond."

"Great," he muttered. Reluctantly he looked at Lacy. He'd never wanted her to see him like this, but now they had another problem. "Some protector I'll be."

She edged closer and tentatively touched his forearm. At least he didn't flinch. He was indeed coming back. "I don't want a protector. What I needed was not to be alone with my fears. You're providing that, Jess, and I can't tell you how grateful I am."

She smiled then, the sincerest, most open smile he had seen from her since her arrival. It warmed him to his very core.

"About the protection thing," Gage said. "We'll discuss that after we get him warmed up and full of calories. Adrenaline does the damnedest things."

"He's damp," Lacy said.

"I know," Gage responded.

"Fear and rage can do that," Jess said. But he wasn't afraid to look at Lacy as he said it. She'd just seen something worse than his stump and she was still there, still touching him, still smiling at him.

Flashbacks hadn't troubled him in years. He was still shocked that Gage's question had snapped him back in time like that. He needed to think about that. But later, when he was sure his mind was his own again.

A deputy eased through the door with a big brown bag. "Thanks, Lou. Close the door on your way out."

Then Gage opened the bag and doled out coffee and foam containers that held lemon pie. Rich, calorie-laden.

"Eat, drink and be merry," Gage said, resuming his seat with a faint grimace. "And I'm not kidding, Jess."

Jess knew he wasn't. He'd been in borderline shock from that memory. He was professional enough to recognize the symptoms in himself.

The latte was hot, almost too hot to drink, but he guzzled it anyway. A coldness seemed to have seeped into his bones.

"Eat my pie, too," Lacy said, pushing it toward him. "I'm still on sugar overload from breakfast."

Gage looked at Lacy, removing Jess from the center

of attention for the moment, and he was grateful for it. Soon he'd have enough energy to feel embarrassed for losing it. Then he'd have to start wondering why he had.

"So Jess has explained your situation to me," Gage said. "Did he tell you I'm former DEA?"

She nodded.

"It was a while ago, but I still keep up my contacts. I read about the case you were involved in. Call it professional interest. Anyway, since it was drug money that was being laundered, I'm sure DEA was involved, even if you never saw it or knew it. So I'll call a few people and get their assessment of your situation." He tilted his head. "The FBI is good, but DEA undoubtedly handled all the operations against the drug people. Which means they might have a better assessment of your situation than the FBI."

"Thank you. I'm so grateful. Sometimes I just think I'm losing it."

"Don't tell yourself that," Gage said gently. "Drug operations have lots of heads and even more tails. Seldom are they totally contained. So there might still be remnants of this group out there. The question is whether they'd have any reason to want to get you."

Lacy hesitated. "Would they? For revenge?"

"It's always possible. Some of these guys have a lot on the line when it comes to scaring people into not giving them trouble. On the other hand, you were a high-profile witness, and if anything happens to you, everyone is going to know which way to look. So I'll find out what I can."

Jess saw Lacy smile crookedly. "Maybe I'm more trouble than I'm worth to them."

"Very possible. But I don't think you're losing your

mind or silly to be concerned about it, okay? I'd be concerned in your shoes. So let's get some real information if we can."

"I am so grateful. To both of you."

Jess didn't feel as if he deserved much gratitude just then. Gage's question plagued him on two levels. First, it had precipitated a flashback for some reason. Secondly, what if he did have an old enemy coming back to haunt him?

He might have put Lacy in even more danger. The possibility made his insides curdle.

Lacy was more shocked than she wanted to let on. She'd gone racing back to the sheriff's office when she had heard him insistently calling Jess's name. What she had seen had shaken her to the core. He'd been as rigid as stone, so pale he'd had no color at all. Occasional tremors had run through him, but he made no sound, and was utterly unresponsive. It was like a seizure, but not, not really.

Memory could do this to someone? She never would have imagined. She'd had minor flashbacks, but she'd always been aware, as some moment of memory had gripped her, of the world around her. In an instant she could return to the moment she had learned Sara was dead, to the minute she realized that she was caught in a spider's web of deceit and illegality, to the moment when the FBI had told her she was being put in protective custody. The moment when she had been told her parents were missing at sea.

Those memories could rise up and transport her back to the very instant, the feelings, the shock and horror. But not the way Jess had apparently gone back to some time and place in his memory. For several minutes he had simply been elsewhere, as if only his body remained in the present.

She was glad that he was able to eat both pieces of the lemon pie, and when he finished his coffee she passed him hers. Her stomach had knotted up too much to be able to eat or drink much of anything.

Thank God Sara hadn't had to see this. Or maybe she had sometimes when he'd been home on leave. She'd never mentioned it, but much as the two of them had shared, Sara had never shared details about Jess except for the lighthearted and romantic. If there had been any darkness in their years together, Sara had remained firmly mum.

She worried, too, about what had set it off. Her situation? Or something else? He said it had been years since he'd done that. Something must have happened.

Gage had mentioned a question, but she didn't dare ask about it. She didn't want Jess to have any more trouble.

Ten minutes later, Jess stood. "We need to get Lacy some pants to protect her legs from this cold. And some decent boots."

She looked up at him. "That can wait."

He shook his head. "I'm fine now. And the last thing I want is for you to get frostbite because we didn't take reasonable precautions. It's too cold out there right now, and while it'll warm up again, this isn't the last of it for the winter." He smiled crookedly. "That is, unless you've decided to move on quickly."

She jumped to her feet. "No way," she said firmly. "Your invitation was open-ended, and I'm holding you to it."

She meant it, too, and hoped he could read her determination. What had happened had scared her only for his well-being. Apparently they both could use a friend. If there was anything she could do for him, she intended to do it. Anything.

After they left the sheriff's offices, the wind snatched her breath. "When is this warm-up promised?" she asked.

He laughed, sounding more like himself, and ushered her hurriedly into the car. "Let's get those clothes and boots."

But just before she climbed in, Lacy felt the back of her neck prickle. Helplessly, she looked quickly around, trying to see who was watching, but saw nothing, except a man in a car some distance away with a map held up and spread out.

She was imagining things again. Would this never stop?

The hunter watched from just half a block away. He held a map up to shield his face as an extra precaution. He wished he could find out what business they'd had with the sheriff. That little note of his? Nothing useful in that. Any decent lawman would laugh Jess out of the office for being concerned about it, and Jess must know that. So what had they been there about?

Too damn cold, he thought again, although he prided himself on being able to withstand the elements. Still, it was too cold to risk taking any action, that woman seemed to be stapled to McGregor's side, and he doubted he could park far enough away and safely make the trek to the house in the dark without running into trouble from this damn cold wind. Even if he did, when he arrived he'd be so bundled that his motion would be restricted, putting him at a disadvantage.

Besides, he hadn't finished planning, and the woman had thrown a wrench into the works.

He cussed under his breath and pulled the ski mask back into place. At least around here, today, wearing one wouldn't draw any attention. Not that there were many people about on this frigid day. Even the locals had evidently decided it would be safer to stay inside. Then, using the cold as an excuse to keep his head down, he walked to the corner and looked around. He saw McGregor's vehicle at the department store.

But his leg and hip were aching again. He hadn't come through that final operation unscathed himself. The cold penetrated until with each step he felt every shattered bone and torn muscle he had all over again. You never healed. Never.

But once he was done with Jess McGregor he could head back to warm, sunny climes and resume his career.

The pain had advantages, though. It reminded him of why he was here and why he wanted to silence the man. A wounded vet shouldn't have been treated the way he'd been treated, questioned as if he had done something criminal when he hadn't. Three men had survived, three men who could remember that day, and while none of them had said much about it, questions had been raised. He needed to put it to bed for good, to ensure no witnesses ever came forward to ruin him.

But they'd put the hunter through hell and could do it again if anyone opened his yap. So far no one had really said much, and McGregor had never known the full story. He was just a medic, and what would a medic know? He was going to learn it now. Learn it in a way he'd carry with him to the grave the hunter planned to put him in. He was going to savor every moment of the man's shock when he learned the truth. He was even going to enjoy the moment when McGregor admitted he'd been no judge of the situation. And then he was going to kill him. Should've been dead, anyway, four years ago.

But there was still that damn woman. She'd have to be dealt with, too, if she didn't leave soon. The hunter had learned patience, but it wasn't infinite. While he savored the fantasies of how he could use her, he wasn't going to let her interfere with his primary goal.

Take out McGregor. Everything else was secondary.

First he had to play out his little cat-and-mouse game. It might even make the woman leave.

But it at last occurred to him how he could hide himself in that house and gather more intelligence.

Chapter 8

Jess seemed withdrawn when they got back to the house. He'd bought her the snow pants and boots he'd insisted she would need, and Lacy figured she was well prepped for an Arctic climate. She hardly cared at this point. The house was plenty warm, especially after he added some more wood to the stove. It was cozy indoors, and right now she felt almost safe. Even the feeling that someone was watching had vanished the instant they entered the store.

No, she was worried about Jess. Something had happened to him at the sheriff's office, and clearly it still troubled him. He didn't mention it, though, and she didn't know whether to pursue it. He was so right that they were still strangers in many ways. She didn't want to tread where she wasn't welcome, but she wanted to help in some way. The haunted look in his green eyes disturbed her as much as her own fears ever had.

She went to the kitchen to make cocoa, figuring he

probably still needed some calories, and brought him a mug. Once again he was seated on the rocking chair, this time rocking back and forth slowly but steadily. Working something out in his head, she guessed. Maybe she should just sit quietly.

Eventually, he was the one who broke the silence. "Lacy?"

"Yes?"

"What did you mean about numbers never lying, always being reliable?"

"Well, they are, aren't they? An equation will come out the same every time you run it. Add up numbers and the total is always the same. If something is out of whack, it's because someone did something wrong."

His gaze turned to her. "You trust them more than people?"

The question startled her. What was he driving at? "Most of the time, yes. They're predictable."

"And they don't lie. That's what you said."

She nodded, wishing he knew where he was taking this. "I guess I like things neat and tidy."

"Why?"

Taken aback, she hardly knew how to answer.

"Did something happen to you? Or were you always into numbers?"

In that moment it all became clear to her. He thought her love of numbers had its roots in something sinister. Some bad experience. She opened her mouth to deny it, but something held the words back. Finally all she could mumble was, "I don't know."

He smiled faintly. "I didn't think you would. Just like I don't know what kicked me into that episode this morning."

"It was pretty bad," she admitted.

"Yeah, it's been years since I had one like that. Where everything just receded as if I were caught in another place and time."

She hesitated, then asked, "Do you think me being around is a problem?" Because she was a huge reminder of Sara. Funny she hadn't thought of that when she'd agreed to come racing out here for her own protection. Not a thought of what it might awaken in him in terms of grief and loss. She'd been selfish.

"You weren't even in the room," he said quietly. "No, it was something Gage said, and I'm not sure why it hit me that way."

"What did he say?" She desperately wanted to know, wanted to listen and maybe help. Sara's ghost might still stand between them, possibly in ways she hadn't even begun to imagine, but there was no escaping the fact that in a very short time she was coming to care about Jess in a different way. Jess apart from being Sara's husband. Jess the man.

He sighed and stopped rocking. After a few beats, he turned in the rocking chair so that he was facing her more directly. "I haven't been entirely straight with you. So maybe you were right to trust numbers more than people."

She stiffened. Her heart slammed in her chest, then leaped to high speed. All of a sudden she couldn't seem to get enough air. "Jess?" Her voice came out reedy.

"Remember when we stepped out so you could see how the cold was? That envelope on the porch?"

She'd forgotten it, thinking it was his personal business, dismissing it entirely. Only now did she recall how it had been under that piece of gravel. Her mouth began to dry out and unease crept along her nerves like a million ants. "Jess?" she said again.

"It was an anonymous note. All it said was *I found you. The game's on.*"

She couldn't breathe. She absolutely could not find air. But then anger hit her so hard that she erupted from the sofa. She could breathe again, breathe well enough to raise her voice.

"Why didn't you tell me?" In the quiet house, her voice sounded way too loud but she didn't care. A sense of betrayal began to darken her heart. "I trusted you!"

"I know." His eyes remained fixed to her as she began to pace. He didn't speak, didn't defend himself, didn't try to soften what he had done. He had kept critical information from her and right now if he'd tried to explain or apologize she would have erupted like a volcano.

No words could take back what he'd done. For all she knew, some killer was out there stalking her right now, and he hadn't told her? Had even taken her to town as if nothing was going on?

Then it struck her. He'd gone to the sheriff's office. He hadn't treated the note as if it didn't matter; he just hadn't told her. Which infuriated her, but then some objective little voice in her brain asked the all-important question: What difference would it have made?

They had been caught in the midst of a storm, and it was still so cold out there that exposure was dangerous. She was safer with Jess than she would have been at home in Dallas by herself. And how could anyone have found her here that fast?

At last she faced him, putting her hands on her hips. He was still watching her, an almost preternatural stillness about him. When she spoke, her voice had leveled out. "Explain what you were thinking. Please."

"Somebody would have had to ride that bus with you to locate you so fast."

She couldn't deny it, but she wasn't satisfied even though her anger ebbed a little. "So?"

"So if someone were after you, how many opportunities did they have on your way here from Dallas? How many little towns did you stop in? How many times did you get off the bus to eat or get coffee? Any one of those stops was an opportunity. Why wait until you were here with me and then announce himself with a note?"

"That still doesn't explain why you didn't tell me." Although, in a way, it did. Even she had to admit it. Why get her stirred up over something so vague? "So you just dismissed it?"

"Hardly. Where did we go this morning?"

The sheriff. The balloon of her anger began losing air. Slowly, very slowly, she perched on the edge of the couch again. "Talk to me, Jess. I want to be able to trust you."

"I'm not sure you should. I may have dragged you into danger."

"What?" The second blow in just a few minutes hit her hard, but not as hard as the first. Apparently she still had enough adrenaline in her system to fortify her. Besides, there was something else. Something in the way he looked, something about that flashback he'd had. Was he trying to tell her *he* was the one at risk?

God, what a coil. Helpless, frustrated, upset and worried now about him as well, all she could do was wish he'd lay it all out in one piece like a list. He hadn't dismissed the note as unimportant. No, he'd gone to the sheriff with it. Okay. He hadn't told her about it because he couldn't see upsetting her needlessly. She could even understand that now. Why set her on edge without a good reason? Would it have made any difference if they had discussed this last night? Not really.

"Just don't hide things from me again," she said finally. "And will you just tell me what's going on?"

"The truth is, I don't know what's going on. The envelope might have wound up there by accident. The wind was blowing hard enough to push the gravel on my driveway around. That thing could have landed there. It makes no sense by itself. If you weren't worried about someone being after you, it would have ended up in the trash and been forgotten."

Also true. She sat there wondering vaguely if she was going to have a total meltdown when the last of the adrenaline washed out of her, or if she would just calm down. At least to as calm a state as she could achieve since she'd become involved with drug dealings. "How is it you may have put me in more danger?"

"I don't know. Honest to God, I don't know."

Now frustration was replacing the waning anger. "For heaven's sake, Jess, this is no time to clam up. Just talk. Ramble if necessary. This has something to do with that flashback, doesn't it? Well, talk to me!"

He wiped a hand over his face. "You already know most of it. I took that note to the sheriff. It's vague enough that by itself it's no threat, but he could understand why you're concerned. He told you that, right? He's going to look into it."

"I got that. But something else happened."

"Yeah." He paused. "He asked me if *I* had any enemies."

She sucked in a short, sharp breath. "That's what hit you?"

"Like a ton of bricks," he admitted. "Bam, I was back in Afghanistan. Nothing about what I remembered gave me any clue as to why, but it must mean something. And if the sheriff was right, that if I have an enemy, then you couldn't have come to any place less safe for you on the planet. So maybe you should get back on that bus."

The word left her lips before it even formed in her mind. "No."

Now his voice grew tight. "This is no time to be foolishly brave."

She answered just as tautly. "And this is no time to hightail it. We don't know what's going on, if anything is. If you could take on my fears, then maybe I can help just by being here. One person alone is a much easier target."

He stared at her for several beats, then a crooked, humorless smile touched his lips. "The buddy system."

"Exactly." Maybe she was losing her mind. She'd fled Dallas seeking safety, and now that she might have planted herself in a truly dangerous situation, she was going to dig in her heels?

She told herself it was the least she owed to Sara's memory, but that was a delusion and she knew it. This had gone beyond Sara, to something that had grown in her for Jess. He'd opened his house and life to her to give her sanctuary, and now she owed him something, as well.

Besides, while she had left Dallas because she'd been offered a break from looking over her shoulder constantly, the simple fact was that she had a stubborn streak too wide for her own good. If she hadn't, she would

have found a way to take herself out of the center of
the case the Feds had built against her own employer.
She could have refused to testify. She'd certainly given
them enough on paper that they could have continued
without her.

But she'd gotten her back up. She'd been mad at being
taken advantage of. She didn't like people who played
games with the books. She had become determined to
take the bad guys down no matter what it cost.

Brilliant, Watson, she said to herself now. Brilliant.
And here she was possibly taking another huge risk because Jess might have been threatened. Although she
couldn't imagine why.

"What do you think, Jess?" she asked quietly. "Do
you have that kind of enemy? One who would hunt you
down?"

"I damn well may," he said bluntly. "Three tours in
Afghanistan while wearing a uniform? I'd be surprised
if I didn't have a whole bunch of enemies, in general
and personally."

"But you were a medic!"

"So? To some people I was also an invader." Moving
as if he had stiffened up, he rose from the rocker. "I'm
gonna make coffee. You want some?"

Breakfast suddenly seemed like a long time ago.
"Please," she said.

"I'll understand if you want to leave," he said as he
started for the kitchen. "You have no reason to trust
me now, and I may have dragged you into some serious trouble."

"We don't know that," she said, jumping up to follow.
"Like you said, it might not even have been intended for
this house. Besides, for all I came running to you for

safety, did you ever consider that I might have brought my trouble to your door?"

As she spoke the words, Lacy realized they were true. For the very first time, she looked beyond her own fears and acknowledged that if she was in danger, she might have put Jess in danger. The thought pierced her so hard she almost cried out. How could she have been so blind?

"Maybe the trouble is mine," she repeated. "What if I brought it here?"

"I'm not banking on it. Not now."

He was probably right, she thought as she watched him move around the half-finished kitchen to make coffee. Not when it had caused him to have a flashback, even if it hadn't offered any useful information. The question had triggered some kind of reaction in him, a big one.

She dared to ask a question. "Do you remember much about right after you came home?"

He shook his head. "Not really. It's all a haze basically. One day blended into another. I was full of all kinds of meds for pain, to prevent infection. A number of surgeries. No, I don't remember much."

"Probably just as well."

"Maybe." He paused. "But maybe I need to try to remember some of it. That last mission we were on... well, it wasn't our planned target. I don't know why we diverted but I always blamed it on our CO."

"Your commander? Why?"

"The guy was a glory hound. Everyone knew it. Nobody really trusted him. But it wasn't our job to question, just to do what we were told."

"And it ended badly?"

"Obviously. But it wasn't the only mission that ended badly. Not unique in the least."

She let it go, and watched him gradually relax a bit. Clearly he didn't want to revisit this, and she didn't want to make him. Besides, he wanted her to leave because he feared *he* was the one threatened. And if she added to that the very real possibility that the only danger here might have come with her, she had a very good reason to just move on. To protect him.

But what if it wasn't about her at all? Now they knew even less than they had before, and she realized she couldn't just get on the bus and walk away, leaving him alone to face whatever was coming. The same stubbornness that had made her go to the US Attorney was reviving in her. Long forgotten, but as strong as ever.

If there was something he needed to know, she suspected it would work its way to the surface again, maybe this time without throwing him into another flashback. And if she was the source of the possible trouble, she might not protect him just by leaving. Whoever might be after her could consider him a threat, too. What might she have told him?

Damn, she wanted to bang her head on the wall. This just kept getting more convoluted.

Instead, she walked over to him as he leaned against the counter and slipped an arm around his waist. Intimate, but not too intimate. After a moment, he draped his arm around her shoulders, accepting the contact.

The relief that filled her was nearly heady. She knew she wanted him; desire kept flaring in her like a blossom that couldn't quite make it, mainly because she wouldn't let it. Sara, long gone, remained both an invisible link and an invisible wall between them. Looking at this man as Sara's husband was both important and necessary to her peace of mind.

But this, this moment of shared comfort and closeness, seemed even more important right now.

"Forgive me?" he asked.

"Yeah. You're not a number."

She felt him tense, then was amazed to hear laughter roll out of him.

"No," he agreed, "I'm not a number."

Then, depriving her of breath, he turned until he could brush a soft kiss on her lips. "You're a beautiful woman, Lacy. Sure you don't want to run?"

She met his gaze and realized that he looked more unguarded and youthful in that instant than he had since she'd first met him. Nothing could have hidden her smile. "Absolutely not, Jess. Absolutely not."

Night fell quickly with the shortening days. She and Jess had whiled away some hours playing cards, then they had cooked a meal of chicken scampi. Afterward, it was back to the living room, where he started pacing.

She could hear the wind had picked up again, and the TV in the corner was warning people to stay home. Windchills could kill in a matter of minutes.

"I'm not used to this," Jess announced as he limped back and forth. "I work about fifty hours a week. Then I come home exhausted enough to fall asleep in front of the TV. I spend weekends working around the house if I don't have something planned with friends."

"Cabin fever?" she asked wryly. "I'm not used to this, either. Not even those months in protection got rid of a sense of claustrophobia."

He glanced at her, and some warmth seemed to dance

through his gaze. "Prisoners under our own house arrest. We could risk a run to the movies. Or we could hit a roadhouse. I couldn't dance with you, but I'm sure plenty of others would be more than willing."

Two things struck her, the first that he said he couldn't dance with her, the other that he was willing to go out into the world and face whatever risks might be lurking.

Maybe nothing was lurking, but in that moment she caught a glimpse of the man who had repeatedly gone off to war. Jess wasn't afraid. Oh, he might get afraid when things started popping, but he didn't live his life in fear. Maybe she should follow his example, if she could. Maybe she needed to stop being afraid as a matter of course. Once, she hadn't been this bad. Once, her main misery had been fear of meeting new people. She'd even managed to get that under control.

"Got any friends you could invite over for a card game?" she asked.

He glanced at the clock. "Weeknight. School. Kids. Wives. Nah."

She almost laughed. "That was succinct."

He smiled crookedly. "Well rehearsed."

So he was a lonely man a lot of the time. She felt stupid for not having considered that, but why wouldn't he be? He'd lost Sara. Nothing could ever fill that hole in his life.

"I think I'm going to take a walk around outside before it gets any colder," he announced.

"But the windchill…" She let her objection trail off. He was used to this. If he thought it was safe… "I'll come with you unless you'd rather be alone."

One corner of his mouth lifted. "Wanna try out the new pants and boots?"

"Yes." It was as good an excuse as any, and truthfully, she was having her own touch of cabin fever. She wanted to be outside, to get cold enough to be glad to be inside again. To look at the heavens and see stars if she could. In a city you saw only a few, but she'd discovered a place like this revealed more stars than you could count, unless there was cloud cover. She glanced at the TV again, but they said nothing about cloudiness, just extreme cold.

So she hurried to put on all the outer gear he'd bought for her, including the lace-up boots with a felt liner. By the time she finished, she was getting hot.

Jess was grinning, standing by the door, all ready to go.

"Sorry," she said through the snorkel as she zipped it the rest of the way.

"It's new to you. Let's go before you melt. I know I'm ready for some cold."

She bet he was.

They stepped out the side door onto a small porch. Lacy felt so hot that she barely noticed a bit of cold air making it to her nose, and that went away as soon she exhaled. The genius of the snorkel hood came home to her.

Jess held out a gloved hand and together they descended two steps. The wind had kept them swept clean, although some snow had gathered in the corners of the porch against the wall.

The air was so dry that the snow whispered beneath her feet. With each step she kicked up powdery clouds that blew away on the strengthening breeze. When she looked back, she realized the wind had erased their footprints. As if they had never come this way.

It was an amazingly dark night. The snow seemed to

glow a little as if catching light from somewhere, but everything else disappeared into the inkiness. They were halfway around the house before she caught sight of a pinpoint of light in the distance.

"That'd be the Halko place," Jess said. "They have a security light they keep on all the time."

"Security for what?"

"Not getting lost."

Made sense, she thought. The light from Jess's house was totally damped by the heavy curtains he'd put up. Barely a sliver escaped anywhere.

But the stars she had been hoping for never materialized. Apparently there were clouds up there, riding the seas of night. It felt good to be out and walking, though, and she was tempted to ask if there was anywhere they could safely walk to, just to lengthen the time out, but even she could see that might be dangerous. A gust of wind caught her unexpectedly and she staggered. Jess steadied her quickly.

"That's the shed," he said, gesturing. "Wait here while I make sure the heater is still working?"

"Can't I come?"

"Stay against the house. The wind is already enough to almost blow you away."

She wished she could argue, but instead she stood alone at the side of the house and watched him nearly disappear into the night.

All alone in the dark, everything else seemed to sweep away. All alone, unable to betray herself to anyone else, she could confront a wish that Jess hadn't belonged to Sara. That her best friend hadn't met him first—not that he'd have probably noticed her—and face the fact that even if they'd met, Jess wasn't for her. He'd been meant for Sara.

But that didn't stop the longings he awoke in her. She wondered if she had been hiding from them all along, or if they were of a more recent vintage. Had she somehow been betraying Sara in her heart all these years?

The thought made her shudder. It wasn't an ugliness she wanted to find in herself. No, she argued, this had just started, just since she got here. It was simply sexual attraction to a very appealing man. Nothing she hadn't felt before, but nothing she could act on because of Sara.

But it hadn't been there before, when Jess and Sara were married. No way, because she wasn't that kind of person. It was like dealing with money, sometimes huge sums. The money in her bank account was real, because it belonged to her. The millions that floated through her computer accounting, the stacks of cash that had occasionally landed on her desk, they had never seemed real because they weren't hers.

Tainted money, someone had once called it. "'Tain't mine."

Well, she felt that way about men, too. No attraction she had ever felt had survived discovering a man was dating, engaged or married. Like flipping an internal switch. "'Tain't mine."

So no, she was sure she hadn't had these feelings when Sara was alive. And she shouldn't be having them now, because of Sara. Sara's death hadn't erased her loyalty to her friend, and she was sure it hadn't erased Jess's love for her.

Foolish thoughts, standing there in the bitter cold, and she was glad to be freed of them by the sound of Jess's returning steps.

"Everything okay?" she asked.

"Still forty degrees in there. Listen, if you want a walk, I can get a flashlight and we can try to walk down the drive to the road."

Belatedly, she thought of his leg. As he drew closer she could hear the unevenness of his step. "No, I don't think so," she said. "I'm starting to feel the cold a bit."

Which wasn't exactly a lie. However overheated she'd become getting dressed in all this stuff, it was gone. When she moved, she could tell her outerwear was getting colder.

"Okay." He took her hand again and they made their way alongside the house to the front porch.

Then everything inside her froze, even her breath. "Someone's parked out there."

He looked as she lifted an arm and pointed. Fear pierced her, but it didn't strike him the same way. "Maybe I should drive out there and see if someone's in trouble."

She hadn't even thought of that. A much more likely possibility, right?

The car was parked along the road. It could be someone having a breakdown. Getting cold, hoping for help. She felt small right then.

"I'll go with you."

They quickened their pace, but as they rounded the corner to the porch steps, the car pulled away, driving off east into the night.

"Guess not," Jess said. "Maybe someone pulled over to answer a phone call, or make one before he got out of cell range."

"Yeah." But she didn't believe it. Damn, sometimes she hated the mouse she had become. Absolutely hated it.

Bad enough to be naturally shy. Worse to be jumpy over everything.

Jess stood with her on the porch for a few minutes, but the wind started blowing harder, gusting stronger.

"A good night," he said, "for all wise mortals to be indoors."

Once inside, Jess watched with mild amusement as Lacy struggled out of her gear. For his own part, he was more interested in warming his leg again. He dumped his parka and gloves in the hallway and hobbled into the living room. The fire in the stove still burned brightly and after he stripped his snow pants he plopped into the rocking chair, waiting for the heat to hit his leg. Layers of clothing weren't total protection against cold like this, and there was no blood circulating through his lower leg to bring it warmth. He'd felt the joint stiffening a bit, too, defying the directions from the microprocessor that helped manage his leg's movements.

He shouldn't have gone out, except that he'd needed to, and he hated cutting himself unnecessary slack just because of his leg. Taking a walk had been essential to beat off the cabin fever, although you'd think being housebound with a gorgeous woman would fend that off well enough.

Except this was Sara's best friend. Off-limits. Don't even go there.

Finally she wrestled her way out of the unaccustomed winter gear and toppled into the sofa facing him. "What about you?" she asked bluntly before he could ask her.

"What about me?"

"I heard you limping. What's going on with your leg?"

"It's cold. Getting a little sticky, so the microprocessor isn't working as well. No big deal."

He watched her eyes widen and almost smiled.

"Microprocessor?" she repeated. "Really?"

"Really. It makes minor corrections, helps stabilize me when I walk. We've come a long way from the peg leg."

"I guess so! How does it work? How does it stay on? How do you keep from getting sore?"

Then he did smile as he watched her cheeks redden.

"Sorry," she said. "I don't mean to pry."

He shrugged. "It's okay. I have a vacuum socket, which means when I stand on it, it pumps out excess air. It'll adjust throughout the day if necessary, and if it should get too tight for some reason, I can let air in."

"And padding? It has padding?"

"I wear a silicone sock over the stump, which also creates the vacuum seal. It has some cushioning, and then I have a little extra in the socket because my leg has shrunk some. I can't explain how every part of it works, but I walk without problems most of the time. Next best thing to a real one."

"Sounds like it." But she caught on what was missing. "But no running?"

"I'd probably face-plant. In theory I could, but not very fast, and it's fatiguing because the leg is so heavy. I know amputees who have more than one leg for various purposes. I sometimes think about getting one for running because it would reduce the effort and fatigue by adding more spring to my step."

"You should."

"More money than I have right now. Nope." He patted the leg on the thigh socket. "I'm mostly content. This is a great leg." But nothing would make it sound or feel like the real thing. Or, come to that, behave like it.

She leaned forward, clasping her hands. "It must have been hard to learn to walk on it."

He nodded. "Different muscles need to be used, and even different motions. It took a while to get the hang of it and build them up. And since I was doing all this post-op, it took longer. No advance preparation."

She fell silent, apparently absorbing all that he'd said. Then he saw a new question occur to her and he waited for it.

"Microprocessor? So you have to plug your leg in?"

"Every couple of days."

"Wow," she breathed. "I know you must hate needing it, but it sounds like a marvel."

He looked toward the fire, not sure how much of the love-hate relationship he felt toward his mechanical leg he wanted to share. Yes, he hated needing it, but he was eternally grateful to everyone who'd made it possible, from the company that had designed it down to the physical therapist who had so patiently worked with him for six months, ignoring his occasional outbursts, his frustration, his anger and always reminding him he would walk again.

"I'm lucky," he said finally. "And grateful."

"Lucky?" She repeated the word dubiously, but didn't press him.

He wondered if she was thinking about Sara, whose loss had gutted him so much that at times after he'd been shipped home he just wished the damn explosion had ripped his head off instead of his leg. When he'd left for Afghanistan again after her funeral, he hadn't expected to come back. He hadn't wanted to come back.

Of course, the Navy and the Marines had considered that possibility and had run him past a psychologist until they were sure he wouldn't be a fool out there.

Well, of course he wouldn't. He might not want to come back, but he never, ever would have done a thing that might have caused harm to anyone in his unit. That was a whole different matter.

Never. No matter what.

He closed his eyes, remembering that day of his wounding again, but this time without the grip of a flashback. This time as if he were watching it rather than living it.

"Jess?"

"I'm still here, just thinking."

"I'm sorry. I guess I stirred things up."

He shook his head. "They never go entirely to sleep. It's okay." He popped his eyes open and looked at her again. He felt the unmistakable tug of desire for her, and wished she were any woman on the planet except his late wife's best friend, because right now he'd have loved to bury himself in that beautiful body and forget every other thing in the world. Sara was well past being hurt, but Lacy wasn't. He had no idea how she'd react given that they shared a past that included Sara.

But something else lay between them: his leg. Even without Sara's ghost in the room, he'd have been reluctant to show her that stump. How much less sexy could you get? A missing leg sewn together by docs who were more interested in saving his life than in cosmetics, then several more surgeries to get it in shape so that he *could* wear an artificial leg, and it was not a pretty patchwork. The years hadn't removed all the redness from the scars yet; the marks from the hundreds of stitches made him look like a movie version of Frankenstein. Sure, that would turn a woman on. Right.

Instant mood killer.

Crap, this whole situation was nuts. It had been quick and easy to say, "Come stay with me" when all he'd been concerned about was giving her a break from her constant edginess. A breather. He hadn't expected all these complications to get off the bus with her. A beautiful woman, being locked away together in a house with Sara's memory hanging around, and maybe some worse kind of threat right outside his door.

Why the hell would anyone be after him? Yeah, the CO had gotten a reprimand for going outside his orders and walking them straight into an ambush, but it wasn't as if anyone had reported him. Not as if the brass couldn't tell that orders hadn't been followed by the location they were at when they were attacked.

Twenty miles out of their way. Twenty miles into dangerous territory that had cost the unit, had cost a town, a whole lot of lives and futures. No, a simple map would have been enough to indict the man.

But of course he hadn't been indicted. Academy grads on the fast track didn't face court-martials. They just got reprimanded, and the track slowed down. Maybe.

So what could he have possibly done to have anyone after him, unless some Afghani with a serious grudge had tracked him down, and that was about as unlikely as you could get?

Other enemies? Oh, probably a few. And some he hadn't even known he'd made. Emotions ran high under those conditions, guys got angry and some had long memories. Things got said that shouldn't have been said. Punches got thrown that shouldn't have been. Even a poker game could cause trouble. Unit cohesion went just so far. Human nature triumphed in the end.

His mind trailed back to that car parked out front. It hadn't been there when they'd come outside, and it had driven off quickly as they came around the house. Perfectly innocent. It wasn't as if he lived along a rarely traveled road. It could have been any one of the ranchers from farther out, and probably was.

But he wasn't feeling quite so smug about how safe things were around here for either of them as he had been when Lacy arrived. His nerves were starting to hum with heightened awareness, a feeling he hadn't had since he last came home.

Trouble could have followed Lacy, or it could have followed him. He couldn't let his guard down until he was sure. That damn note. Totally cryptic. Maybe that bothered him more than anything else about it.

Rising, he went to the foyer window where he wouldn't be backlit, and looked out. It took a few minutes for his eyes to adapt, but at last he could see that against the faint sheen from the snow no one was on the road. Time to remember some old habits. Time to be on high alert. For both their sakes, regardless of what might be going on, he couldn't afford to relax completely.

"You're nervous."

He turned and saw Lacy standing in the door of the living room. "Fair to say I can't quite settle."

"I know that feeling." She wrapped her arms around herself. "I didn't want to bring trouble to you, Jess."

"First off, I'm not sure there's trouble. And as Gage made so clear today, I'm not sure that if there is trouble that it's because of you."

"Nice conundrum."

"Yeah." He looked out the window again, his eyes adapting more rapidly this time. The little bit of light coming from behind her in the living room hadn't been enough to fully kill his eyes' dark adaptation.

"Jess?"

"Yeah?"

"If this were a mission, what would we be doing?"

He stiffened and faced her, forgetting the road for the moment. "What?"

"Seriously. I know you were a medic, but we're both sitting here like cats on a hot stove, ready to jump at anything. So what precautions could we take? Assume someone is out there who wants one of us. Surely you learned enough in the military to know how we should get ready."

Something inside him stilled as he saw Lacy in a new light. She might be afraid, she might be shy, she might sometimes look at him with quickly shuttered need, but she was also brave as hell. Courageous.

"You want to prepare for a siege?"

"I don't know." She leaned against the doorjamb. "What I do know is I'm tired of waiting and then re-acting when the crap starts to fly. I've been doing that my whole life. For once I'd like to be ready before it hits the fan."

He almost smiled. This attitude surprised him, but he honestly didn't know why. This woman had taken on her bosses and some serious drug types. Maybe she thought that was simply reacting to what had landed in her lap, but he saw it differently. She'd made a brave decision. It may not have occurred to her that her life might be in danger, but she had certainly been aware there'd be a high price.

Then, even in the dim light, he saw uncertainty take over her pretty face. "Sorry," she said. "That might stir up things for you."

He stepped toward her, glad that his leg responded normally again. "Things are already stirred up. Might as well act. It's better than waiting."

Then against all reason and sense, he held out his arms. She astonished him by walking straight into them, and he wrapped her up tightly. It felt so good to hold her, made him feel more alive than he had in years. Her curves, usually concealed under loose clothing, fit him as if they'd been made for him, and once again awoke the man in him. He hoped she couldn't feel it, and shifted a little to put a distance between his hips and hers.

Of one thing he was certain: for the first time in a very long time, he felt he had something to truly fight for. Something good. A long impenetrable shell began to crack open, reminding him of reasons to live. Reminding him that running on automatic was no life at all.

He could almost feel Sara with them, slipping around on the drafts in the house. He felt no disapproval. None. But sooner or later, he and Lacy were going to have to deal with Sara. Really talk about her. Create a new place for her in their lives.

Because she was still very much alive in their memories.

Chapter 9

"Jess?"

"In my bedroom. Come on back."

Lacy had run upstairs to clean up a bit and returned downstairs to discover what Jess was planning.

She walked down the hallway toward the warm glow of light falling through an open door. When she stepped in, she caught her breath.

Jess had shed his pants and was sitting on the edge of the bed in a T-shirt and running shorts. For the first time she saw his artificial leg and the socket that ran up most of the way to his groin. It brought home the severity of his injury in a way that little else had, and filled her instantly with pain for him, and amazement that such a leg existed. Contradictory feelings that held her still while she absorbed them.

"Shocking?" he asked, a crooked smile on his mouth.

"No. Surprising. I've never seen a prosthetic before."

"Curious?"

"Very. Do you mind?" Of course she was curious. And now that he was willing to show her, she wanted to know everything about it and what it meant to him.

He shook his head. "If I was ever modest, life took it out of me. I was about to remove it for a while, let it charge. But I warn you, my stump isn't pretty."

"Well, at least something about you isn't. That's a relief." The tartness of her voice astonished her, but it drew a surprised laugh from him.

"So you think I'm pretty?" he asked, wiggling his eyebrows.

"More like gorgeous."

"Not nearly as gorgeous as you," he said frankly.

He might have pumped all the air out of the room. She froze, and he watched her with gentle amusement. "It's okay, Lacy. My pouncing days are over."

"Too bad," she muttered honestly, making him laugh again.

"Come sit beside me. You can see it all and satisfy your curiosity."

She felt a flicker of shame, as if she were prying into someone's extremely personal secrets, but noticed that he didn't seem disturbed. He'd called her back here, after all.

All of a sudden she was more curious about why he'd wanted her to see this. Three steps brought her to the bed, and she sat beside him.

"This is it," he said, rapping his fingers lightly on the black socket on his thigh, then holding his whole leg up. From the socket emerged the metal parts, a joint that appeared to be a knee. The whole ran down to an ankle with a metal band around it, then to a plastic foot.

"Okay," he said, pointing, "this is the socket that holds the whole thing on. The knee that usually bends just as I want it to now that I've learned to manipulate it. There's a shock absorber in the ankle along with the joint. That plastic foot is so that I can wear regular shoes and socks. It's not necessary, but people stare a whole lot less."

She looked openly because he seemed to want her to and strove for humor. "Not going for the Terminator effect, huh?"

He chuckled. "Well, I could. Who knows, it might wow the kids when they come to the clinic."

"You need a thicker accent."

"Maybe some racing stripes."

She turned her head more and looked right into his eyes and face. Was she imagining a bit of uncertainty there? If so, she wouldn't blame him. He must have been wondering how she would react.

"What about the cold?" she asked, resisting the urge to just lean over and be and touch him like a brazen hussy. "You said it stiffened."

"Sometimes when it gets really cold. There's obviously no circulation in it, so nothing to warm it up. Most of the time, not a big problem."

"But tonight it had you limping."

"Yeah. It wasn't as stable as usual. I think the microprocessor's okay because it seems fine now. I guess the joint just got a little cranky. Anyway."

He pointed to a white button on the inner side of the socket. "That's how I break the vacuum seal. I press that until the socket is loose enough to remove."

"That is quite a piece of engineering."

"And they're getting better all the time."

"Does it ever make you sore?"

He shook his head. "Not unless I don't fit it right, and with the vacuum setup, there's almost no chance of that. As time passes, the stump will shrink in size and layers of padding will be added until I need a new socket."

Risking the intimacy, she leaned closer, studying the assemblage. "Do they give you a personal fit?"

"That socket was molded right to my stump." He reached for the button. "Anyway, you might want to go have coffee right now. I need to recharge this, and when I take it off, I'm going to remove the sleeve for cleaning. It's not pretty."

"You mean your stump?"

"What else?"

All of a sudden her mouth went dry. He'd just shared an amazing intimacy with her, but he was giving her a chance to escape because he didn't think she could take the rest of it. Or maybe because he didn't want her to see it.

She looked around, taking in the room. He'd been Spartan in his furnishing choices, as if he felt the other rooms needed to come first. But then through a partially opened door she saw a shower that could have stepped out of a magazine. At once she saw he could walk into it, and it was big.

"Lacy?"

She licked her lips nervously. "Do you want me to go or are you afraid of my reaction?"

"It's not pretty. Considering I didn't lose the damn thing through a neat surgical procedure…"

She turned to him and rested her hand on his forearm. "It's okay, Jess." Their eyes met and his seemed to bore into her, as if gauging whether she really wanted to see or was just being nice.

If she was being nice, she'd have left the room. No, she sensed a hurdle here, one they needed to cross if ever…if ever what? She had no idea. They both needed to know something, for whatever reason. Her mouth remained dry, but she half suspected that by now her imaginings were far worse than reality.

He shook his head a little, released a sigh and then pushed the button on his socket several times. She could hear the faint sound of air escaping.

Then, with surprising ease, he pulled the leg off. He stretched a bit to lean it against the wall, while she took in the plastic gray sock that covered his stump nearly to the groin. She could see even through that how mis-shapen his thigh was. She could barely imagine what he must have gone through. *That* exceeded her imagination.

With one more glance at her, he reached for the top of the sock and began to ease it down, turning it inside out as he did so. "Isn't that hot?" she asked.

"Surprisingly not."

Then came the scars, still vivid, many of them. Some small, some big, some stitched as neatly as a seamstress might have done, others looking hurried and sloppy. Probably the first urgent ones meant to save his life. The neater ones had probably been from the surgeries to repair him enough to wear his prosthesis. There were occasional pits where she assumed flesh and muscle had vanished forever. She could definitely understand why he'd been concerned about her reaction, but all she could think about was the pain each of those scars represented.

She reached out and laid her hand on his thigh. "I'm so sorry, Jess. So sorry."

"I've got plenty of company," he said, clearly trying to sound light about it.

"I know you do." Then on an impulse she couldn't restrain, she twisted and bent over until she could press a kiss to those wounds.

He let out a sound like air escaping a tire. "Lacy…"

Arms closed around her and the next thing she knew they were lying across his bed, legs dangling but torsos pressed together. He lifted a hand, brushing hair back from her face. "You're amazing," he murmured.

"Why?" Truthfully, she didn't care. This close to him, looking into his beautiful eyes, everything else slipped away as if carried on the howling wind of need that swept through her. And just as powerfully, she felt as if she had found her fortress against the world.

He brushed her hair again, smiling slightly, but making no other move. "You were always pretty," he said. "But until you came here, I never noticed just how pretty."

Of course not, she thought with a sinking stomach. Sara. He'd probably been operating under the same "'tain't mine" rule that she always followed. Some feelings weren't worth the cost and had to be ignored.

You just couldn't afford them.

He leaned closer and pressed a kiss to her forehead. As if she were a child. A bubble of resentment grew in her, then popped almost as quickly. He would always be Sara's husband. They both knew that.

With clear reluctance, he urged them both into a sitting position. "I need to plug in," he said gruffly. "Get some warmer clothes on. You wanna make some coffee or something?"

He was sending her on her way. Wisely, even though she hated to admit it. For just an instant she could have sworn she saw a flicker of heat in his gaze. Had felt tendrils stretching out between them.

A dangerous thing.

"Sure," she managed to say brightly, and rose, walking away to the kitchen, her feet feeling like lead. Maybe it was time to address her own confused state.

Jess joined her a little while later as she was stirring cocoa on the stove. She heard him come down the hall and could tell from the sounds that he was using his crutch.

She turned as she heard him enter the kitchen behind her, a smile ready on her face. He stood there in kelly-green sweats with one pant leg pinned up so it wouldn't flop around.

"I smell cocoa," he said, returning her smile.

"Yes. I hope it was the right choice."

"Sounds good to me." He swung himself over to the table and sat. "We need to talk."

She turned back to the stove, her stomach fluttering nervously. "About what?" Sara? Why they had to ignore the attraction that seemed to be growing between them? Or the unknown threat that might be stalking one of them? None of those promised a quiet mind for the night.

"You asked me to make a plan," he reminded her.

"Oh." Now her stomach sank. For a little while she'd allowed fear to fade into the background, allowed blossoming desire to take its place, even though that promised no happy ending, either. Silly wishful thinking, of the kind she was usually too practical to allow herself. And all the worse because of Sara. *Don't hate me, Sara*, she thought silently. *Please don't hate me.*

"Planning," Jess said, "would be easier if we had any

idea who and what might be coming. Right now, I'm at a loss. The note seems ridiculous. Why warn us?"

"Pleasure," she answered slowly. "Letting one of us know what's coming so that we'll be miserable and afraid."

"That's a twisted mind."

She turned to look at him over her shoulder. "It would take a twisted mind to do any of this. So he's a sadist. Or she."

He nodded agreement. She poured the cocoa carefully into mugs and carried them to the table. "Sadist or not," he said as she sat near him, "he wanted us to guess that something was up. I half suspect he doesn't expect us to take any action."

"Why? Or better yet, how can we? We don't know that he intends to do anything. We don't know what it might be if he does, or which of us he's after."

"Which is exactly the problem I'm up against. The only thing I know for sure is that he can't get into this house without making some noise."

Startled, she creased her brow. "Why?"

"Because the windows won't open." He looked almost rueful. "I told you I hadn't gotten around to replacing them yet. Well, they have wooden frames, and they're old. Before I bought this place, they'd warped enough that no amount of effort will open most of them, and the few that will make a horrendous noise. As for the doors…deadbolts, no access from the outside. So he can't just waltz in here."

"Fair enough. But maybe he doesn't plan to."

"And that's where we start running into problems." He surprised her by reaching out and resting his hand on her forearm, giving her a gentle squeeze. "I can turn this house into a fortress against penetration. It's half-way there. I could put trip wires outside that would warn us if anyone approaches. So I could make us credibly safe in here."

She nodded as it sank in. Great. They could be safe as long as they didn't leave the house. How long would that be?

He sighed and ran his hand back and forth along her forearm. "All I wanted to do was help you feel safe. Instead I walked you into a situation where I don't even know the parameters."

"Quit blaming yourself. You didn't know this was going to happen. How could you? You're right, I probably didn't get followed all the way from Dallas, or I'd be dead right now. So how were you supposed to know that some weirdo might suddenly come after you? This hardly falls under the category of normal life events."

"I still feel badly."

"I'm sure you do. And you're pretty quick to blame yourself for things that aren't in your control."

Now it was his turn to look surprised. "What the hell do you mean?"

She couldn't even look at him. "You being home wouldn't have saved Sara's life, Jess. You need to accept that. Didn't you hear what the doctor said? It happened so fast probably the only thing she ever noticed was that she was getting a stomachache. If you'd been standing right beside her, it wouldn't have saved her."

"Lacy…"

"How many more things do you blame yourself for? I can only imagine. Lives you couldn't save because it wasn't possible under the circumstances? For failing to find some miraculous way to get that officer back in line when he changed the mission? Do you take everything on your shoulders?"

"You don't know what you're talking about."

"Maybe not," she admitted, but the words kept tumbling out of her anyway, driven by something deep inside. "But I've been listening to you for a long time, Jess. I know you feel responsible because you weren't there for Sara, even though nothing could have saved her. I hear it. And now you're apologizing because you somehow should have known that some lunatic would make an appearance right after I arrived here?"

"Lacy…"

"Let me finish, because this is ripping me up." And all of a sudden, it was, as if something locked deep away inside her had suddenly found voice and freedom, something she had hardly been aware of until right this moment. "Sara used to admire your sense of responsibility, but it worried her, too, Jess. Oh, she didn't share personal details about you and her with me, but sometimes things came through. Worries about you. She was worried that going to war was especially hard on you. You know what she said to me, Jess?"

His face had gone hard as stone. "Tell me," he said tautly.

"She said, 'Lace, I'm worried about him. It's all so personal, especially the civilians, the kids. I'm not sure he'll be able to deal with it.'"

"It's personal for everyone," he said harshly.

"Of course. And lots of people live with nightmares for a long time. I get it. But she was worried about you, and she told me why, and then over the time since her death I've felt it in you, Jess. I don't know how many faces you see when you close your eyes, but I know you're taking blame for at least one thing you couldn't have done anything about. And now you're doing it again."

Now that all that had burst out of her, she realized she was shaking and verging on tears. Grabbing her mug, she left him, tottering into the living room and collapsing on the couch.

Maybe she'd just been unbelievably cruel, but Sara's concern, expressed a couple of times, then pushed aside as something she chose not to discuss in depth, had taken root somewhere deep inside Lacy. To hear Jess blaming himself for drawing her into possible danger had broken the lock on secrets unshared. Not that she needed anyone to tell her that Jess felt guilty for being away when Sara died. Of course he did. That was a normal human response, probably aggravated by the fact he was a medic and would always wonder if he could have recognized the signs early enough to save her…despite what the doctor had said.

Sara wouldn't want that. Of that Lacy was certain. She wouldn't want Jess to always wonder if the doctor had simply given him a comforting lie, and she wouldn't want Jess to feel in any way responsible for a failure of her own body, an aneurysm that had probably been there all along until finally it ruptured early one morning.

But Lacy didn't want Jess feeling responsible for dragging her into trouble, either. She'd already been in trouble, looking over her shoulder constantly, worried about every face in the crowd, wondering if she was being followed. Wondering if someone out there wanted her dead and was trying to make it happen. Jess wasn't responsible for that. All he'd done was offer her a haven.

Not his fault the haven had a demon living in it.

* * *

"It's getting late." Half an hour later, Jess crutched into the living room and stood a few feet away. "Don't you want to sleep?"

Lacy shook her head. "I'm so wide awake I could probably run five miles and not even feel it."

"You need a hamster wheel."

She glanced at him and tried a small laugh, even though she didn't feel like it. Jess had offered her his home and his protection, and then she'd gone off on him like a shrew. She'd even analyzed him in a way she had no right to. She was no psychologist to begin with, and it was none of her business how he chose to grieve.

"I feel pretty much the same," he admitted. He swung by her and balanced himself on one leg and the crutch, while swinging open the stove door to throw another log inside. He let the influx of air cause the flames to leap all over it before he closed the door. At once the flames settled down to a friendlier glow.

Then he returned to his rocker. Quite amazing, really, how well he managed with or without his leg.

He rocked for a while, leaving her to wonder if he was giving her the silent treatment. Then he surprised her.

"You're right," he said. "I feel guilty that I wasn't there when Sara died. I'll always feel that way. She shouldn't have died alone, for one thing. For another… well, there's just no freaking way that I can escape the fact that I might have recognized what was happening quick enough to do something. Yeah, I have enough training to know how slim that possibility is, but it exists."

She hesitated then asked, "Most people don't survive that, do they?"

"An aortic rupture? Some do if they get a warning, but the rest rarely do. It's the biggest blood vessel in the body, and when it tears like that, your heart pumps the blood fast. She had a huge tear. So beyond all reason, I know that once it ruptured, probably nothing on earth could have saved her. But I'll always wonder if she might have been having some kind of symptom beforehand that I might have caught."

Lacy swallowed, feeling an upwelling of grief, for him, for her, for Sara. "She was young. Who'd be imagining a fatal problem from some relatively minor symptom? What would she have had? An occasional tummyache?"

"Maybe more."

"I know," she said finally. "I read up on it. She might have had no symptoms at all. She might have had symptoms so minor and infrequent that she never mentioned them. The thing is, Jess, Sara wasn't stupid. If she'd had severe pain, weakness, throbbing…any of the major symptoms that don't always occur, do you think she would have ignored them?"

He averted his face a moment. "Probably not," he said finally.

"Exactly. So if you'd been there when it happened, what? CPR and hope to get her to the hospital in time? The doctor told you it was a large rupture. That she wouldn't have made it. Are you thinking he lied to you to ease your mind?"

"No. Yes. Maybe."

She sighed and tucked her legs under her, propping her chin on her hand. "You're a caretaker by nature, Jess."

"Meaning?"

"You went to war as a medic. Now you've invited me

into your home because I was afraid. You want to make everything better. You know you can't always do that. It must be hard to live with."

He tilted his head to one side, studying her. "Why do I feel so damn naked right now?"

For some crazy reason, she could almost have laughed. Then he smiled, as if to let her know she hadn't offended him.

"Nice analysis of my character," he said. "Very flattering."

"It wasn't meant to be flattering. It's just true. You didn't go for the machismo of being a soldier, you chose to risk your neck to save lives. Says a whole lot to me."

There was a thud from the front porch just as the wind gusted. Both of them froze, then Jess said, "I wonder what just blew our way."

"I'll go look."

"Don't bother. Probably a dried-out piece of tree limb, or a plastic planter from someone's porch."

But she was already on her feet, determined to look anyway. She needed to, needed to prove to herself that she hadn't turned into a complete coward who wanted nothing but a safe hidey hole. Yeah, as if she could spend the rest of her life that way.

Time to start acting again, even if it was a minor thing like looking out the front door. She was getting fed up with *herself*.

She hurried, grabbing her jacket from the hook and stuffing her arms into it. She could hear Jess rising to follow, but this was something she needed to do for herself, alone, so she moved swiftly.

The front door lock gave easily and she swung it open, expecting to see some branch out there. Instead she saw a piece of plastic pipe with caps on both ends. And something stuck to its side.

She heard Jess only dimly as he cried, "Lacy, run to the back of the house. It's a bomb."

Well, she already guessed that, didn't she?

The next thing she knew she was lying on top of it, covering it with her body.

Chapter 10

Jess froze for an instant, just an instant, braced for what was to come. Lacy lay curled over that length of pipe, exposed to the elements and at any moment he expected her to vaporize.

"Get out of here, Jess."

Her voice sounded oddly calm. Steady. Determined.

"I'm not going anywhere."

"What's the point of both of us dying? It could go at any second. Get out of here!" At last her voice rose to a shriek that drowned out even the endless wind.

"I'm not leaving you."

But he couldn't exactly move her. The bomb hadn't gone off yet. Who knew what would trigger it? Moving it? Picking it up? A timer? He swore silently, every other word in his head a curse.

Nor could he leave her out there to freeze to death, waiting for the damn thing to do its ugly work. His cussing became audible as he grabbed for his jacket and cordless phone and worked his way back to his bedroom while dialing 9-1-1.

The sheriff's dispatcher answered. "This is Jess Mc-Gregor. I've got an unexploded pipe bomb on my front porch and my houseguest is lying on top of it. Get out here now."

He pulled the pin from his pants, yanking up the material until he could pull on the silicone sock and jam his stump into the socket of his artificial leg, and his feet into boots. Then he grabbed every blanket off his bed and out of his closet. Hobbling back to the door, he felt the cold sucking every bit of heat out of the house. He didn't care. Let it go. Let it all go.

"Jess, I told you to get out."

"What if it's a dud? I'm not letting you freeze to death."

He stood on the lintel and began to spread blankets all over her as best he could. By the time he was done, the cold had sliced through his sweats and all the way to his bones. He paused a moment to zip his jacket, knowing he'd be no good to anyone if he grew too hypothermic. "Don't move," he kept saying. "We don't know what will trigger it."

"Just get out of here."

Anger stirred in him as shock gave way. What the hell had this woman been thinking? She should have closed the door and yelled for them to go out the back. Anything but this.

Nightmares began crawling up from the depths of his being. He'd seen one of his buddies do exactly this to protect others. He'd hoped he'd never see it again. Nor did he need to see that damn thing go off to know what it could do. He'd seen that, too, and had relegated it to a locked place in his mind and heart.

Lacy was crazy. Suicidal? He wouldn't have thought so, but what did he know? People had done crazier things to protect others. But to protect *him*?

"Lacy, why?" he demanded, terrified sorrow filling his heart as he spread the last of the blankets.

"Too many movies?" she suggested, but if she meant to be funny it wasn't working. "Jess, what's the point if we both blow up? Back off."

He could hear her teeth starting to chatter. Over the wind he began to hear the wail of sirens. Help would be here soon, though what good they could do with Lacy lying on the bomb he couldn't imagine.

Dear God. He closed his eyes, and prayed harder than he had in a very long time. *Let her be all right.* Straightening, he leaned inside and grabbed his gloves. His hands would soon be useless, too, if he didn't keep them warm.

He squatted again, pulling a corner of the blanket up to cover her exposed cheek. "They'll be here soon," he said, trying to sound reassuring. Never mind that this county didn't have anything approaching a bomb squad. But he couldn't afford to think of that right now. "How you doing?"

"I'd be doing a whole lot better if you'd get out of here." Her chattering teeth made her almost unintelligible.

"And I'd be doing a whole lot better if you'd yelled *Bomb* instead of throwing yourself on it. So here we are, and you'd better hope I don't have to follow you to the gates of hell to find out why you did this."

Everything inside him felt as if it were shredding.

His mind kept skipping into the past, then back to the present. He'd been here before. He was here again. For the love of God, was there no end?

He wanted to grab her up in his arms and run with her, but knew better. Falling on that bomb may have started a trigger mechanism. Maybe it was a timer. If it wasn't motion-activated, then he could pull Lacy away. But if it was, who knew what triggered it? Pressure on it, rather than dropping? Release of pressure, like the spoon on a grenade? Turning it upright? Too many questions, and any one of the answers could kill her.

Her eyes were squeezed shut, and he saw a tear ease from one corner. He wiped it away, quickly, gently, so it wouldn't freeze. "Don't cry," he whispered. "God, woman…"

"Please go, Jess," she said almost as quietly. "You've been through enough."

"And losing you would be nothing? Why?"

She didn't answer. At least she wasn't shivering as hard, good if the bomb had some kind of motion trigger. But maybe she was getting that hypothermic. The medic in him kicked in, trying to judge her physical state. He'd worry about her mental state later…if she were around to worry about.

He stared toward the road, seeing flashing lights in the distance. The fire company as well as the sheriff. He hoped to God they had some capabilities beyond those he already knew.

"They'll be here in a minute."

"I can hear," she said, her voice now oddly steady. "I loved Sara, Jess."

"I know."

"That's why."

"Somehow I think she'd be cussing you out right now."

"Yeah. Like you will when this is over."

He glanced at his watch, surprised how much time had passed. Why hadn't the thing activated? It must be a timer, but timers could be unreliable. Or worse, the bomber had thought it would be in someone's hands when it went off. Or what about remote detonation?

Not likely, he decided. Any bomber who had planned that could see that his target, whichever of them it was, was out here now and vulnerable.

God, the sins of his past were rising like black bubbles from a tar pit, suggesting possible reasons anyone could be after him. Because he didn't believe this bomb was intended for Lacy. If someone wanted her, a bullet to the head would have been infinitely easier, and would probably have already happened, even in Dallas. No, this killer was after him, and he had to figure out who it was and why.

He'd have to wade into that tar pit, like it or not. Recall things he'd done his best to forget.

But first, most important, his entire focus returned to Lacy. The past could wait. The present held enough terrors to damn him a hundred times over.

"Lacy…"

A sense of clarity settled over him, a feeling of the universe stilling, quieting the roiling agony and terror inside him. He had to get her off that bomb, and he needed to run with her away from the house. With each step, the blast wave and possible shrapnel would dissipate.

He knew his own limitations when it came to running, but the chances were better than if he left her there and she took the full force of the explosion. Carrying her away would provide his back as protection, too.

"Hang on," he said, adjusting his position for better leverage.

"Jess, what…"

He closed his eyes for a split second, summoning every reserve of strength. Five feet. Ten feet. Then face down on the ground. It might save her.

Without warning her, he took one quick step, scooped her up into his arms and began running as fast as he could on a leg that felt as if it weighed a ton and didn't like being forced to this movement. Screw it. Screw it all.

He had to try to save Lacy.

She cried out a protest, but he scarcely heard her. He took the two steps in one leap, feeling the jolt all the way through his body, feeling his leg trying to lock up against the force. He refused to let it. Limping noticeably, he ran with the woman in his arms, blankets threatening to trip him. Each step meant another measure of safety.

And with each step he expected to hear the explosion, feel the shockwave knock them down. Just get away from it.

More steps, accumulating into ten feet, twenty feet. Then with sirens rolling closer, he dropped to the ground, covering Lacy with his body.

The explosion never came.

As trucks and cars rolled up his gravel drive, he touched her cheek.

"You should go," she begged again.

"No. If that thing goes off, you're not dying alone."

Atonement. He had so much to atone for. A fear he hadn't felt since Afghanistan, along with an ugly mire of guilt, filled him as he watched the fire truck pull up closest to the house, the fire rescue ambulance behind it. Police cars filled in a loose semicircle.

Not everyone climbed out. First came the fire chief, Wayne Camden, and the sheriff, Gage Dalton. Camden wore full gear, looking nearly twice as big as usual with it layered over cold weather clothing. Jess sat up, resting his butt on his heels, keeping his back to the house, cradling the blanket-wrapped Lacy against the frigid night.

"Where is it?" Camden asked Jess.

"On the porch. About six inches long, plus screw caps. About two inches wide."

"Did you see anything else?"

"Something was stuck to the side of it. Black. I couldn't make out details before Lacy fell on it."

The thud of his heart was nearly loud enough to drown out the rumble of the roaring diesel engine of the fire truck.

"And you yanked her off it?" Camden asked, sounding amazed.

"What the hell else was I going to do?"

"Good question," Gage said. He turned and started calling orders. A photographer began to take pictures through a long lens from a safe distance.

"Depending on the type of explosive," Camden said, "it's probably not a very big charge." He paused. "Not that that makes much difference under the circumstances."

No, thought Jess, shutting his eyes for a moment. With Lacy right on top of it, a small explosion would have been enough to kill her. Hell, it wouldn't have to be much more than a large firecracker.

"We don't have a bomb disposal unit," Gage said.

"So we're going to have to wing this. I've got a couple of guys coming who know something about explosives from their military experience. They should be here any second, okay?"

Jess simply nodded. "Lacy? You still with us?"

"Yes." She spoke between clenched teeth. "I'm cold, but I'm fine."

Jess doubted it, but there was no point in arguing.

"Thing is," Gage remarked, "most explosives have an aromatic signature. Wayne here has a chemical sniffing device. We just gotta figure out how to use it."

Jess managed a stiff nod. He held Lacy so tight his arms felt as if they would never unlock again. "But it's in a sealed pipe," he pointed out.

"Let's not hurry our fences," Gage said, as another car pulled up. "It could have left traces on the outside. Damn it, when are we going to get that K-9 they keep promising us? Look, let's get you two out of the cold and into one of the cars."

Jess didn't argue. He could feel the frigid cold seeping into his legs, and could feel Lacy shivering violently. "Someone's going to have to help me up."

At least they didn't try to take her from him. Obliging arms helped tug him to his feet, then a deputy guided them to a car far enough back from the porch, behind the protection of the massive fire truck.

Jess slid Lacy into the backseat of the patrol car, then just as he was trying to straighten and turn to ask for some hot beverage, a deputy handed him two disposable cups. "Straight from the bottle. Don't burn your tongues."

Coffee. He slid in beside Lacy, allowing the cop to

close the door and the car's heater to blast over them. "Can you drink?" he asked her.

"Carefully," she replied, her teeth still chattering.

"You heard him. I'll hold the cup but be very careful. You don't want to blister your lips and tongue."

She gave a jerky nod. He tested the coffee and realized it was already cooling down. Still hot, but not hot enough to burn. The trek bringing it over here must have cooled it considerably.

He held it to her mouth and noticed that dribbles escaped, as if she could barely control her lips. "We should get you checked out at the hospital."

"You can do it," she answered.

God, she could be stubborn. Even as the shackles of terror began to loosen, he felt a rising sense of frustration and helplessness. Why had she thrown herself on that thing? How the hell was he going to persuade her to leave so she could be safe? Toss her out? The thought of doing that clawed at his heart painfully. But clearly she was at risk here and the thing he wanted most was to keep her safe, whatever the cost.

They were going to have to talk, but later. He got the coffee into her, and the car heater began to do its work. Her shivering eased, and finally she worked her arm out of the blankets. He handed her his cup. "Here, I'll get more."

"Okay. Thanks."

He climbed out as quickly as he could, trying to limit her exposure to the biting cold. Pulling up the hood on his parka, he stuffed his hands in his pockets and went to join the men gathered a respectful distance from his porch. The sheriff and fire chief, of course, but three other men as well. Deputy Micah Parish, formerly special ops. And two former navy SEALs, Wade Kendrick and Seth Hardin. He barely knew them. They weren't the kind to show up in his clinic, and most of his friends came from the town's small medical community.

"If it's a bomb," Seth Hardin was saying, "it's not a very big one. It might have killed the woman because she was lying on it, maybe blown a hole in the porch floor, but few bombs that size have a wide damage radius. It's about the size of an antipersonnel weapon."

"Like a hand grenade?" Jess asked. Five faces turned toward him.

"Yeah, but no worse. At this point I'm beginning to wonder if it's a dud."

"The cold," Gage suggested.

"C-4 works to 40 below," Wade answered. "Unless the cold affected the trigger, why hasn't it detonated? It's been a half hour since you found it."

"Since it landed with a thud on my porch."

"Landed?" Micah, Seth and Wade all turned to look in that direction.

"Landed," Jess repeated. "I thought the wind had blown a loose limb. Lacy went to look and the rest you know."

"Okay, not a shock trigger," Seth muttered. "Lacy falling on it could have started something, but a half hour? I'm betting it's a dud."

"Remote control," argued Wade.

"If it is," said Micah, "then he had his chance when these two were right there. Something didn't work right. Or it's a dud. Wayne," he said, turning to the chief, "you have the chemical detector, right?"

"The best the Department of Defense could send me."

Apparently, Gage's mind was running on something

else as well. "I've got deputies looking around for foot-prints and tire tracks. We've got to find the perp."

As the wind gusted again, stirring up clouds of dry powdery snow, all Jess could say was, "Good luck with that."

"Go back to the car," Gage said firmly. "Get some more hot liquid in you and your friend. We'll keep you posted."

Feeling utterly useless at this point, Jess hobbled back to the car, picking up two more steaming cups of coffee on his way.

Damn, what the hell was going on? Vague worries had coalesced into an inescapable threat. He couldn't be sure which of them was being tormented, although he suspected it was him. And he couldn't figure out how the hell to get Lacy out of this mess because all he'd be doing would be leaving her alone with her fears again, fears that by now had probably grown to epic proportions.

As had his.

His own bravado rang hollow in his ears. He could turn this house into a fortress? Whoever was out there had just proved he couldn't do that. No way.

The last time he'd felt this exposed had been half a world away.

Lacy was so relieved when Jess returned to sit with her in the car. Her cheeks burned as they thawed out, thanks to the blasting heat, but her shivering had been reduced to occasional waves. She felt able to shrug both arms free of the blankets and accept the coffee he held out.

"Any news?" she asked.

"They're beginning to think it might be a dud, but

they're not counting on it. Regardless, if it's real, it's a small charge. Might blow a hole in the porch. Could have killed you because you were on it."

She felt criticism in the words and knew he was right. Instead of trying to read his inscrutable face in the near dark, she looked out the window. A moonless, dark night that tried to turn this car into a cave.

All the light came from the vehicles in front of them, and all of it was pointed toward the house and porch. Occasionally she caught sight of a flashlight as deputies fanned out over the surrounding area.

"Lacy…"

She stiffened, expecting him to jump all over her for her foolhardiness. She knew she'd done something stupid, and she didn't need him to tell her. But he'd better not ask why, because she would have found it impossible to explain her split-second decision to throw herself on that pipe. The very sight of it had awakened a sense of turmoil inside her that she was far from sorting through. That she might never sort out.

Instead, however, he astonished her by draping his arm around her shoulders and pulling her close to his side, taking care not to jostle her and spill her coffee. "Don't scare me like that again," he said quietly. "Please."

She looked up at him, reading the tension in his face, even as dim as the light was. "I'm sorry."

He shook his head. "I'm not looking for an apology. I can't even demand a promise. I'm just asking."

She managed a nod, not knowing what she could possibly say. Then, with each of them holding a cup of coffee, he bent his head until their mouths met. Cold lips, warm tongues, this was no brotherly kiss. It seemed to drive a shaft to her very center, as if a flag of possession had been planted on her being. It warmed her in ways she had never felt before.

"Please," he said again, as he broke the kiss. "Please. Now drink your coffee. This night's not over yet."

No, it wasn't over, and Lacy had plenty to think about, not the least the way Jess had risked his life to scoop her up off that bomb and carry her away, using his back like a shield. She was painfully aware that she'd forced him into that position because of her own action, one she couldn't begin to understand.

Throwing herself on top of a bomb? That might happen in movies, it might happen in combat, but it wasn't a sane thing to do and she knew it. Jess had been right to tell her to run for the back of the house. Instead she'd put them both in inescapable danger.

She'd acted on some instinct she couldn't explain even to herself, but as her shivering subsided and warmth began to reach deeper than her surface, it struck her that she must have opened up an entire chamber of horrors for Jess.

Not just her lying there on what might have been a bomb, but memories from the war. She might as well have taken a shovel and piled them all up near the surface again.

She tried to look at him, but he'd averted his face and was staring out the window. She could only imagine what he might be thinking, but she could feel the deepening tension in him, despite the layers of blankets and jackets between them. She didn't know if he was remembering, or if he wanted to be out there, part of the action.

You're not dying alone.

He'd spoken those words while she sprawled on those pipes and he covered her with blankets. They'd spoken about that very thing earlier tonight, when she'd pointed out that feeling guilty about Sara being alone when she died was pointless. Now he'd faced that again, and it was her fault.

Nor had she spared him anything except a journey into places he didn't want to go. The bomb hadn't exploded, and minute by minute, she wondered if it had just been a sick joke, although who would be out in this weather just to give someone a pointless fright, she couldn't imagine. What kind of mind?

She glanced at Jess again and figured he was probably trying to answer the same question. He wanted to know what was going on, what had just walked him through hell, yet he was sitting here in this car taking care of her.

Right then, she felt not only stupid, but very small and thoughtless. If Sara were here, she'd probably be yelling at Lacy for putting Jess through this, for casting him back into a place he'd been trying to forget. And she would be right.

But Sara wasn't here, not to soothe him or yell at her. Sara was gone and Lacy had reminded Jess of too many losses, too many horrors.

God, she hated herself.

"Jess?"

He turned his head. "More coffee?"

She shook her head and pulled away a little. "I'm fine and you want to be out there, don't you? Go ahead."

He hesitated but there wasn't a whole lot of light in the backseat of this patrol car for reading faces. "You okay?"

"Yeah. Really. I can feel my fingers again. Just go. I know you want to know what's happening."

He tilted his head a little and she thought she saw a glimpse of his teeth. A smile? "Don't you?"

"Well, of course, but I'm not sitting here on the edge of my seat. I can wait for my lecture."

At that a short, quiet laugh escaped him. "I bet you can."

Then he opened the door and slid out, slamming it quickly to keep the warmth inside. Alone, she sat holding a nearly empty cup of cold coffee and wondered what the hell was happening inside her.

Jess rounded the fire truck, and was astonished not to be ordered back. Camden was putting away equipment, and Gage was involved in deep conversation with his deputies and the two ex-SEALs.

"Well?" he asked as he limped up.

"Dud," came the succinct response from Micah. He was usually a man of few words.

Gage spoke. "What we can't figure out is why someone would take this kind of risk to leave a phony bomb on your doorstep. He could have been caught."

"No," said Micah.

At that Seth Hardin's head lifted. "No," he agreed. "We used that tactic, too."

Micah nodded, his Cherokee face solemn.

"What?" Jess demanded.

Seth answered. "Rigging a bomb so you can get well away before it goes off, an improvised kind of timer. You rig it somehow so that it doesn't go off until something particular happens. And you have to make sure it can't be found in the meantime."

"Like a car bomb?" Jess asked.

"Similar, but this is really improvised. Whoever did

this didn't care when it appeared because it's a dud. So he could have put it in your porch rafters where you'd be unlikely to see it, and the wind could have finally worked it loose. Or something shifted. After all, all you had to do was find it, and it didn't matter when."

"What kind of sense does that make?" Jess demanded. "A dud? Just to scare us?"

"I don't know about that," Gage said, and held out a plastic bag to Jess that contained what looked like business card stock. "This was what was on the side of it."

White block letters on black paper.

Your move.

From a safe distance away, atop a rocky hill that seemed to have been forgotten by some long-ago glacier, amid leafless trees that had caught a great deal of tumbleweed, the hunter watched. Clad all in winter camouflage, wearing night-vision goggles and heavy thermal layers on his body, he'd be invisible to infrared and, in the dark, pretty much invisible to anything else. At this distance, he'd look like a patch of snow beneath the trees.

And it was some distance. Alerted by the sounds of sirens, he'd left his shelter and ventured out. It didn't take him long to realize that his present had at last worked itself loose and landed on the porch.

But the magnification he was using cut him down to only narrow areas that he could see at one time. Enough for a sniper, maybe, but far from the whole picture.

He reminded himself that it didn't matter that he hadn't witnessed the discovery. The point was the message, not whether he got to enjoy the show.

It had certainly activated the fire department and police. He doubted they could have handled it if it hadn't been a dud, which was his whole point. Planting a dud made it unlikely that they'd call in experts from anywhere. What did they have except two notes that sounded as if someone was playing a game?

A nasty game, maybe, but not a real one. Because, in his brilliance, he'd intuited that he could play with his prey in such a way as to make McGregor uneasy, but not give anyone a reason to believe he was truly in jeopardy.

Yes, he thought, he was brilliant. Far more so than his superiors had realized. When he'd called in that air strike on the valley, it had taken out a lot of hostiles. Hostiles that had been unreachable until he'd sent his unit into that town.

Then they'd showed up to be barbecued while they shot from the cliffs.

As for his men...collateral damage. Most had died, then or later. But soldiers had to expect that, didn't they? That's what they were there for. Just another weapon in a war.

He should have gotten a medal. Instead the whole thing had been swept under the rug because there were three survivors who might come back to haunt him, and the big brass hadn't wanted to take the chance. He'd taken care of the other two already, but now he was going to have his fun with the last of them.

McGregor's day was coming. But not too quickly. He wanted every bit of it to go just right.

And maybe while he was at it, he could get that woman to leave town. Much as he might fantasize about having fun with her, she was just another complication in what ought to be a relatively straightforward action.

One always cleared the battlefield of as many complications as possible, especially unpredictable ones. That's why they had snipers and covert teams.

Clear the complications. That woman fit the description. She had to leave.

He could just make out her shadow in the back of the police car, not that it really mattered. Maybe he needed to find out something about her. She had to appear in McGregor's past somewhere. She didn't just materialize out of thin air.

Leaving the officials to their fruitless work, he made his way back across rocky terrain, hammered by the wind but turning occasionally to be certain his tracks vanished. They did.

So the law wouldn't be able to consider the dud a serious threat. What bomber warned his victims first? None. So they'd probably conclude it was some kind of game someone was playing, true insofar as it went, and wouldn't devote much in the way of resources to it.

But McGregor was apt to be more suspicious, not that it would save him. He might make the woman move on to protect her. Or she might bail after being so scared tonight.

He'd settle for either one. But just in case, he needed to be ready to deal with both of them, not that either was much of a threat.

He was patient, but his patience was starting to wear on him. The confrontation he'd wanted for so long was just beyond his reach.

But close, he reminded himself. Very close.

He'd figure it out. He was brilliant. Everyone had said so…until that last mission.

Chapter 11

The woodstove was roaring, its thermometer registering over five hundred degrees, flames leaping behind the window like a view on hell. The house was warming again, but slowly. At least the living room had gotten comfortable enough for everyone to doff their outer wear.

Lacy sat curled in a corner of the couch, a big mug of hot chocolate in her hands. Jess perched at the other end while the sheriff occupied the rocker.

The front door opened and two deputies came in bearing armloads of cut and split wood. "Where do you want it?" one asked.

Jess pointed to the wood box near the stove. "Anywhere over there. Thanks."

"Get some more, guys," Gage said absently.

Jess felt his face flush a little. He wasn't an invalid; he could take care of himself. But he understood, too, the impulse to do something to help, however minor.

Almost as if Gage heard his thoughts, he looked up from the notes he was scanning and remarked, "I don't want you going back outside tonight. I'm going to leave someone at the end of your drive, but there are a whole lot of other approaches to this place."

Jess nodded shortly.

When the last load of wood had been piled inside, the front door closed, leaving just the three of them.

"Now we talk," Gage said. "You heard what Seth and Micah said. This is an old special ops trick."

"How so?" Lacy asked.

Jess looked at her. "Place the bomb so it'll fall when the bomber is long gone, theoretically triggering it, I guess."

"Oh." She jerked as if slapped.

"Military background," Gage continued. "Which means next to nothing about who the target is, but in my experience, anyone associated with a drug gang who might be coming after Lacy wouldn't do something like this. It's too soon to hear back from my DEA contacts on her case, but judging by my own outdated experience, none of them would have wasted time on this. Or on sending cute little notes."

"Notes?" Lacy asked.

Gage held out the bag. Before Lacy could move, Jess rose and reached for it to show her.

"'Your move'?" She read the words aloud, incredulously. "Like this is some kind of game?"

"Someone's toying with one of you. I know that's not especially comforting, but it's inescapable."

Jess nodded, taking the bag from Lacy to look at the note again. "Looks like white marker on black card stock."

"Or a piece of poster board. We'll check it for cut marks and everything else, but frankly, I don't expect to find anything. Whoever did this has some training."

Lacy didn't miss the way Gage zeroed in on Jess as he spoke. So Gage believed Jess was the target, not she. For some reason, that didn't comfort her at all.

Gage rocked a little, reaching for his own cup of hot chocolate and taking a few long sips. "We're going to put our heads together, Jess, but a lot of this is going to depend on you. I hate to ask it."

Jess's face turned rigid. He gave the barest of nods. "I know."

Lacy pivoted her entire body, understanding. Gage was asking Jess to pry into his past, to go places he probably tried to avoid going in his memory. Things he undoubtedly wished he could erase forever.

"And," said Gage, after draining his mug, "I could take Lacy to stay with my family."

"No!" The word burst from her. "Absolutely not. I'm not leaving Jess alone with this creep. And besides, you can't be sure this guy isn't after me. I'm not exposing anyone else."

Gage smiled faintly. "Kinda reckoned," he drawled. "Okay, then. I'll keep you updated on what the team can figure out...which probably isn't going to be much without some input." Again a look at Jess. "I'll let myself out."

He paused and turned, giving Jess a card before he picked up the evidence bag. "That's my personal number. Use it."

Then, with a blast of icy air, he left the house.

Neither Jess nor Lacy spoke for a while. The only

sound was the ticking of hot metal from the stove. After a bit, Jess rose and adjusted the damper. The flames softened into a glow from the logs. When he finally spoke, he was standing with his back to the stove.

"I'm surprised you didn't get any frostbite."

"My blood was probably pumping too hard." She didn't want to look at him, fearing some justifiable anger from him, but unable to look away. God, he looked exhausted. This night had been endless. She felt her energy seeping away, except for a nagging nervousness and fright. They wouldn't quit.

"Lacy...why? Are you crazy? Suicidal? What?"

She resented the question, even though she knew he had every right to ask. She'd had plenty of time to contemplate her folly sitting in the car outside, and plenty of time to realize that she could have put Jess in a whole lot of danger, too. But an answer was beginning to form.

"I did it for the same reason you scooped me up and used your back to protect me."

He opened his mouth, then snapped it shut. When he spoke, his tone was even. "I took a calculated risk."

"Bull," she said. "It was about as calculated as what I did. No, I'm not suicidal. But I saw that thing and all I cared about was that it not hurt you."

"Running to the back..."

"Didn't occur to me. I didn't know how much damage it could do, or when it would go off. I did the only thing I could. It's irrelevant anyway. It was a dud."

She felt his gaze stapled to her, but she looked down at the blanket that still lay across her lap. Frustrated, truly upset at last, she tossed it aside. "I guess adrenaline wears off sooner or later."

"You're feeling it?" he asked.

"You better believe it. I don't get why anyone would do something like that. And what makes it worse, as far as I'm concerned, was if that bomb had been real and gone off, it would have created another horrific nightmare for you. I would have been past caring, but not you."

He made a muffled sound. At last he took a couple of steps and settled in the rocking chair, as far from her as he could get in this small room. That hurt.

Thoughts were crawling around in her mind, none settling, nothing she could truly get a grip on. Probably an aftereffect. Clarity had escaped her entirely, except for that one moment when she had thrown herself on that "bomb." Then there had been clarity so clear and pure that it would linger forever in her mind.

"I've seen it," Jess said heavily. "A guy in my unit. He did what you did. I don't want to ever see that again. Ever."

Her imagination tossed up enough images to make her stomach turn over. "I'm sorry."

"You did it for Sara, didn't you?"

At that she looked at him. "That's what you think? Well, I guess so, if that's what you want to believe. You sure picked me up and ran, saying I wasn't going to die alone."

The corners of his mouth drew down into a tight frown. "This is all about Sara?"

"No!" She'd had enough. "I loved Sara. You know that. But she's gone, Jess. Dead. Who would I be saving you for? A ghost?"

"Then what, damn it? For what?"

"For you," she said simply.

"I'm not worth that, Lacy."

"Then who is?" she demanded. "Just who the hell is? You've been hurt enough. Quite enough."

"And you haven't? We both lost Sara."

"So? She wasn't my wife. She wasn't my life and my future. No, I tossed that on the trash heap all by myself. God, I can just imagine her watching the two of us right now and wondering what the devil we're fighting about."

"You scared the hell out of me," he said tautly. "That's what we're fighting about. You say I've been hurt enough? Then don't add to it by risking yourself."

"I'm just someone you know because of Sara."

He rose from the rocker. "Is that what you think? Is that really what you think? That you're just a piece left over from my past like an old photograph?"

"Aren't I? You shut me out after you were wounded. I get it. But like you've said, we're strangers but not strangers. Occasional phone calls didn't make us more than that."

"I invited you into my home. I didn't do that because you were flotsam left over from Sara."

"No? Then what am I?"

He clenched and unclenched his hands, his jaw working. "I'm sorry I cut you off for a while. But I cut everyone off."

She knew that; he'd told her. She drew a long breath, trying to calm herself. She was acting a bit crazy, maybe because of what had happened this night, maybe because dawn was approaching and neither of them had slept. Or maybe it was something else. How would she know? She felt awash in thoughts and feelings that wouldn't connect in any sensible way, and she was picking a fight with a man she cared about. What in the world did she hope to accomplish with this?

"Sorry, Jess," she said finally.

"No." He shook his head. "No. Maybe I cut you off for a while, but that was because I was unfit to deal with anything but my anger, my guilt, my pain. But when we started talking again… Lacy, you became my lifeline."

Her head snapped up. "What?" she asked faintly.

"My lifeline," he repeated. "When you fall into a pit and there seems to be no way out, sometimes you don't care. And then, all of a sudden, there's a lifeline. Do you grab it?"

"Jess…" But she didn't know what to say. Her eyes suddenly felt hot, her chest tight.

"Your voice. Your calls. They came from outside that pit. They reminded me there was a world, a different world than the one I'd become trapped in. Not fair to you, maybe, but essential to me."

Her throat grew so tight it hurt. She had never dreamed that those simple phone calls might have meant so much. "I'm glad I helped," she said thickly.

"You did more than help. You were light in a tunnel when I couldn't see the end. What did I have to live for, anyway? Nothing. Sara was gone, my leg was gone… oh, I visited the utter depths of self-pity."

"Who could blame you?"

He looked away. "They almost didn't send me back to Afghanistan after Sara died. You wouldn't believe how many stamps they had to put on me, saying that I wasn't going to do something stupid. I never would have, Lacy, but it's God's honest truth that I hoped I wouldn't come back."

"Oh, Jess…" She ached so for him that everything inside her felt squeezed in a vise. It became painful to even breathe.

"I should have died, but I didn't. I think that was most of my anger. That I survived. I couldn't tell you that."

She nodded, saying nothing because nothing could possibly help. She stood there, buffeted by the storm of his anguish, and would have given anything to erase his suffering.

"Anyway, when I finally decided to take one of your calls, it was because I realized something. Like it or not, I was still here, and I had to make something of what was left. You were about the best thing that was left."

She grabbed the blanket and pulled it over her lap again, mainly because it gave her a way to occupy her hands. They knotted around it. "I was a link to Sara," she suggested finally when he fell quiet.

"No. I knew to the very depths of my being that Sara was gone, that she'd never be part of my life again. My God, how many deaths do you have to experience before you understand its finality? I'd seen plenty before, and plenty after."

She tried to swallow, waiting, afraid the tearing, squeezing pain inside her might emerge and cause him to fall silent. He was baring his soul to her, and she didn't want, in any way, to make him feel he must stop. He needed to let this out.

"No," he said presently. "You were a reminder that there was still a life out here. A reminder of good things. That not everything in this world is colored by pain and ugliness."

She drew a slow breath. "That's what you meant about innocence."

"Partly. I'll never be innocent again. I've seen too much. But I can appreciate yours. I did. I do. And I'm sorry as hell about tonight because it exposed you to my ugly world."

"How do you know it's your ugly world? And what makes you think I'm such an innocent? I dealt with some pretty ugly guys just recently. Ones who considered money more important than human life, frankly. Oh, they thought their hands were clean since they were just moving the money, but they were making those drug sales possible, making it possible for killers and criminals to enjoy it. That's pretty revolting. Just because I didn't see the blood didn't mean I didn't feel the crime. Those millions and millions of dollars represented wrecked lives and murdered people. And with every day I dug into it and began to understand what was going on, I felt as if my own hands were covered with blood. Drenched in it. Hell, these guys are fighting a war in Mexico that's killing thousands of innocent people. No way was handling that money clean."

He'd grown still. She couldn't tell if what she said had reached him or if it had turned him off like a tap. Desperation began to rise in her. "Jess?"

"I hear you. I'm thinking about what you just said, and you're right. I keep wanting to see you as a pristine daisy in the sunlight, but you've walked on the dark side, too."

"I wish I were pristine," she said, everything inside her wrenching, her voice drawn tight with pain. "I wish I'd never stumbled into that stuff, never realized what I learned while working with the forensic accountants. Do you think they spared me? Yeah, they were nice to me for coming to them, but they didn't hide me from all the hideous acts that generated that money."

"They should have."

"But why? Any time I seemed to be flagging or dubious, or question my own conclusions, I heard about the things the people who owned that money did to get it. About all the lives ruined and laid to waste to make some filthy scum into rich men. They tied it to the Mexican cartels, and before long I was doing my own research, educating myself. I'd had some idea, obviously, because it was the blood on that money, not just the illegality of the transactions, that sent me to the US Attorney. But, my God, Jess, I had no idea just *how* much blood was on it. Just numbers on my computer screen usually, with orders to disburse it among accounts. Occasionally to send it to the investment people. Once cash landed on my desk. A huge amount. I had to verify the amount, then have a courier take it. By then I'd begun to put the pieces together, and maybe it was that cash that pushed me over the edge. Blood money, that's how I saw it by then."

He sounded astonished. "They had you handling *cash*?

"Only once. I'm a CPA, not a teller."

He shook his head sharply. "I don't get it."

"I don't know why for sure, but I suspect it was actually an under-the-table payment to someone in my firm. But that's just an assumption. The money never went on the books, and I could never verify I'd seen it and counted it. It was there, I tallied it, then it was gone. Maybe they were testing me."

"My God, you *were* in it up to your neck. I never guessed."

Her eyes felt like hollow holes as she looked at him. "I'm not supposed to talk about this. You're the first person I ever told outside the investigation about that money. Sometimes I look back at that case full of cash and wonder if it was a test, not from my firm, but from the Feds. Maybe they were already watching us. They never told me. But right after that, I went to the US Attorney."

"Maybe they had someone on the inside," he mused, continuing to rock. "Maybe they needed an ally."

"I don't know. I'll never know. What I did learn as we investigated was that I was working on a separate set of books, not tied into the overall firm's accounting. If I hadn't made copies and smuggled them out, those books would probably have vanished. Someone was using me. At least one person, maybe more."

Jess shoved himself out of the rocker and came to sit beside her, wrapping her into his arms, against his side. "No wonder they wanted you dead. And maybe still do."

She lifted her eyes. "I'm not crazy?"

"Oh, Lacy, you were never crazy. Except possibly tonight. I never guessed from the news reports just how involved they'd gotten you. Maybe someone thought handling all that cash could be used to keep you in line. They underestimated your courage."

"Or overestimated my stupidity."

"Nothing about you is stupid."

She shook her head, glad of his embrace because right then she felt as if she could shatter into a million pieces. "I was stupid enough. The firm had lots of big clients, both corporate and private. People who moved millions around the globe all the time. As a CPA firm, we didn't handle much of the banking or investment part of it, but we kept the books on it. Made sure everything balanced, that all the moving money didn't disappear along the way. I thought we were a backup of sorts to the investment bankers. The ones who could prove every transaction was on the up-and-up. Little did I know."

"Then what happened?"

"I thought I told you. I got moved to a special group of accounts to handle all on my own. I watched the money transactions. I even ordered some of them when a client called. I made sure everything stayed in balance and that no tax laws were broken."

"Until the questions started arising."

"Yeah." She let go of her tension with a loud exhalation. "I can't explain all the details to you. Accounting at that level gets very complicated. I thought at the very most my bosses were tax advisers. The kind of people who know the tax codes of multiple countries, not just this one. That every time we moved money, it was legal and designed to be a tax advantage to the client. It was a long climb from where I'd started as a tax auditor for local governments. I'd reached the heights."

She turned her face into his shoulder and was astonished when he stroked her hair.

"Moving among the billionaires," he murmured.

"Not for long."

"You aren't responsible for what those cartels did."

"I know. Deep inside, I know. But that I helped them at all still sickens me. And the more I learned about them, the more afraid I became. They may have rolled up the operation that was involved with my company, but that doesn't mean others aren't out there who'd like to see me dead anyway. Unlikely, I agree. I've done all the damage I'll ever do to them."

"You know, don't you, that if the Feds thought you might still be at risk, they'd put you in witness protection for the rest of your life?"

"That's what they said."

He was trying to reassure her and she appreciated it. But coming on the heels of all that had happened this evening, she couldn't quite let go of her fears...for both of them.

She burrowed into his shoulder, feeling almost guilty for stealing comfort from him. Not only had he been through some bad experiences of his own tonight, but she felt as if she were taking something from Sara, a completely crazy thought. Maybe she was losing it. Sara had been gone for five years and there wasn't a thing anyone could take from her now, not Jess's love, not the life they had managed to share, however brief. Those things were cemented in time and unchangeable.

But she felt guilty anyway, almost as guilty as she would have felt had Sara still been with them. She wasn't entitled to anything that should have belonged to her best friend.

Nor did she want to try to step into Sara's shoes, amazing shoes to fill. She'd never measure up, and Jess would always be comparing them. *So don't be stupid again*, she warned herself. Not again.

Inevitably, she would be bound to Sara in Jess's mind, no matter what. Sara was how they had met. Sara had brought them together and made them friends. He could never see her apart from his late wife, nor could she, or should she, hope for that. Like vines, they were tangled forever.

Hopeless. But she couldn't bring herself to move out of his arms. Couldn't make herself cut these moments off. She'd been brutally honest about herself, and it hadn't been easy. Not until that cash landed on her desk had she finally faced up to her own responsibility for whatever was going on. Until then, she'd tried so hard to play mental games, to hang on to the brighter future she had been promised, even as questions had mounted in the back of her mind.

She was no caped avenger seeking justice. No, she'd become terrified of what she suspected until she couldn't bear it anymore. Until she feared she might be being set up to take a fall. Until she felt the blood on her own hands.

No heroism in that. None. Sometimes she despised herself. And more than once, she wondered what Sara would have thought of her.

Then tonight she had done something utterly stupid, throwing herself on what she believed to have been a bomb. An act of courage or an act of self-loathing? She didn't know. The decision had been made before her mind processed any thoughts about it. Instinct had ruled her, and she had no idea what it had been rooted in. Her own unworthiness? A desire to save Sara's husband? Genuine concern for Jess or simply an indifference to what became of her?

"You're tensing up," he remarked, disturbing her unhappy train of thought. He began rubbing her back with one hand. "Is it all getting to you again?"

"Yeah." Although, to be truthful, more than tonight was getting to her. The last few years of her life were gouging at her with questions she'd probably never be able to answer adequately. No way could she go back in time to the moment of decision that had taken her to the US Attorney.

She could remember the shock of all that money, could remember how odd she felt about counting it, then sending it off with a courier. But she couldn't remem-

ber exactly what thought had occurred as that courier
had walked from her office, couldn't remember why she
had started backing up the books at that moment, not
on the external drive that sat on her desk, but to her secure company email account. That was routine enough
that no one had thought to question her, and having it
sit there, unsent, rang no alarms. Clients often wanted
to see their data and from time to time it was sent by
encrypted email.

By the time she downloaded it all on a computer in
the US Attorney's office, it was too late.

Hindsight might be claimed to be twenty-twenty, but
she knew better. She could construct all kinds of reasons for what she had done, but reaching back in time
and actually *knowing* why she had decided? Impossible.

Like that bomb. A split-second decision without
thought. No reason. Just action.

"Jess, I'm sorry."

"Stop, Lacy. Just stop. Don't beat yourself up. We all
do things in a moment that we can't explain afterward.
Like you said, we're not numbers."

No, they were not numbers. But numbers were adding
up in her head suddenly. She pulled back a little, sharing a real sorrow. "I can't be Sara."

"What?" He sounded thunderstruck.

"I didn't think… I don't think often enough, I guess.
My being here, in a place you wanted to share with
Sara… I must remind you constantly. It must hurt." Her
voice broke. "I'm sorry…"

"Oh for the love of…" He tightened his arms around
her, holding her with a strength that allowed no escape,
so strongly he almost squeezed the breath from her.
"You're not Sara. I wouldn't want you to be her. There's

no confusion in my mind about that. And this wasn't a place I wanted to share with Sara. Never crossed my mind."

"But you said…"

"I know what I said about her wanting to have some space, but I wanted it, too. I needed it. And I chose this place for me. Do you honestly think I'm building a monument to Sara's memory? Because I'm not. This is purely selfish Jess taking care of Jess's needs, not Sara's long-lost wishes. You know I loved her. But she's gone, Lacy, and I've faced that as many times as I needed to. I've been moving on for a long time now. Have you?"

The question startled her. "I thought I had."

"Tell me you didn't talk to me all those times on the phone just because of Sara."

"Maybe at first," she acknowledged. "But not later." That was painfully true. Jess had become *her* friend.

"Sara may have brought us together, but she's not what's keeping us together. I like *you*. I worried about *you*. I didn't ask you to come here for her sake, or because I needed to be reminded of her, or because I thought you could replace her in some way. You have your very own place in my life."

She let his words settle into her heart, and hoped he wasn't just saying what he thought she needed to hear. "But Sara is still here," she whispered.

"Sara will always be part of us both. That's the thing. People live on in our memories and hearts. We keep them alive. But that doesn't mean there's no room for anyone else. Our capacity to care is infinite, Lacy. Infinite. Put that in your internal calculator."

He was trying to lighten the moment, she realized, to fend off the dark thoughts pursuing her. But the idea that she had her own place with him eased her trepidation. She didn't want to be merely a pale reflection of his memories of Sara, yet she knew she could never measure up to her friend in so many ways. Sara had been vivacious and outgoing, so full of life. These days, shy or not, Lacy seemed to have lost her vivacity and to judge by what she had done tonight, her taste for life.

"I need to get this leg off," he said. "Landing on it the way I did seems to be causing some swelling in my stump."

Reluctantly she pulled out of his embrace, the seeds of new feelings she feared to name fading rapidly. But then he held out his hand as he stood.

"Come with me."

Jess didn't know if he was losing his mind. Maybe this night had been so fraught with peril, terror and fatigue that he just didn't have any mind left. He intended to just remove his leg, then try to get some sleep with Lacy safely at his side.

His move? He couldn't yet imagine what move he needed to make, but knew that with morning's light he was going to have to face his demons, the buried pit of his memories, to try to figure out what was going on here.

But not tonight. The stalker, whoever he was, had sent his message. Whatever was coming wouldn't come this soon. Especially not since the message had clearly said it was Jess's—or Lacy's—move.

As if this was some kind of game. Sighing, he shook the thoughts away. He was too tired for this, and he was far too distracted. Tonight had taught him something about his feelings for Lacy. He truly cared about her and what happened to her. He wanted to see smiles light her face and erase the fear that rarely went entirely away. And right now, there seemed to be only one way to do that.

He wanted her. The wanting had become a constant background to every hour and second with her. He had no right; he feared taking advantage of her, feared rupturing their blossoming friendship. But he wanted her. He ached with it, a feeling he had almost forgotten.

Her connection to Sara had rapidly been replaced by a growing connection between them. He wondered if she felt the same but didn't know how to ask without possibly stepping into a big problem.

In the bedroom, he perched on the edge of the bed and pulled his pants leg up to remove his prosthesis. This time she didn't watch in fascination.

"Want me to go upstairs?" she asked.

"I'm not letting you out of my sight. Crawl under the blankets."

She surprised him by stripping out of her own outerwear, down to the silky thermal underwear. So revealing, so appealing. He dragged his gaze away and focused on his leg.

The leg came off easily once he released the vacuum. Lacy came to sit beside him as he examined his stump.

"How bad is it?" she asked.

He tested it with his fingers. "Not much. Just a little swelling. It'll be okay."

"You were really something, you know."

He turned his head, possibly the biggest mistake of the night, and met her blue eyes. The hum of desire awoke to a roar. "Naw," he said.

"Yes," she repeated. "The way you grabbed me and ran with me. I thought you couldn't run."

"Oh, I can run, just not very far. This leg feels like a weight hanging off me, and my stride's not the best. That's why I sometimes think about getting a lighter piece with more spring, so it'll work more like a leg really does when running. Less fatigue."

She nodded. "I hadn't thought about the springiness in a step."

"Especially when running." Was he imagining it, or were their faces coming closer together?

"Jess?"

"Yeah?"

"Would we be betraying Sara?"

The question hit him straight in the gut. He knew what she was asking, but he hadn't expected it. He'd seen the glimmer of desire in her eyes, then how quickly it vanished. What woman would want a man whose body was such a mess? He'd been avoiding taking advantage of her and had presumed she just didn't really want him. Maybe he'd been reading the signals all wrong.

But what if he was reading them wrong now? But as he stared into her eyes, he found that hard to believe. He could see her breasts rise and fall as her breathing accelerated. Hell, he could see her nipples pebbling beneath the silky thermal shirt. No bra. The realization socked him again.

Then he saw uncertainty begin to grow on her face. God, what had life put this woman through? He was going to find out, but not right now.

Absolutely not right now. Her growing uncertainty lit the fire in him, filled him with a determination not to leave her feeling unwanted and rejected. Lacy didn't deserve another wound, and certainly not one at his hands.

Reaching for her, he lifted her and swung them both around until they were lying on the bed together. Then he captured her body with his arms and her mouth with his in a kiss into which he poured every bit of passion he felt for her.

To hell with the madman outside; a different kind of madness consumed him now. He wanted to discover every inch of her, to dive into her until he felt they could never be pulled apart. The pounding that grew in his loins was nothing compared to the need he was feeling in his heart and mind.

Need. It had been a long time since he had allowed himself to need anything. Life and military-bred self-denial had taught him all the dangers of wanting anything more than life itself.

But he wanted this woman that way. Beyond reason, beyond thought, he needed Lacy.

He spared one brief thought for Sara, and a crazy smile filled his heart. Sara would cheer. The only thing she would wonder was what had taken him so long to see what was right in front of him. The woman long since engraved on his heart would have blessed this moment.

Lacy squirmed a bit, and he pulled back just a little to let her breathe. In the light from the bedside lamp, he watched her gasp and open her eyes, and for the first time he saw that blue completely freed of shadow. Bright, burning like flames, they were clear and unclouded.

Whatever happened, it would be worth it just to see that clarity in her eyes.

A smile chased across her face and she tugged at his sweatshirt. "Come on, Jess. Give."

"What's the rush?"

"Me."

He felt her hips rise against him, and a new tsunami of desire washed over him. Every cell in his body awoke, tingling and hungry. Anticipation nearly stole his breath. He hadn't expected such boldness from the frightened mouse who had arrived here, looking as if life and terror had completely wrung her dry.

Oh, she was very much alive right now. She tugged at his shirt and he rose up on one hand as she pulled it over his head.

"You're beautiful," she whispered, drinking in his arms and chest. In that moment he forgot about all the other scars that peppered his body. "Such shoulders... such arms..." She ran her hands over him, leaving a trail of fire behind her caresses.

"Compensation," he said by way of explanation, but his voice was thick and he wasn't sure she understood. Nor did he care at this point. All that mattered was that she liked what she saw and wanted to touch him.

He let her have her way, his breath catching as she rubbed her hands over his own small nipples, sending a shock all the way through him, tightening the coil of building passion. He shifted a little and soon he was lying between her legs, balanced on his one leg, pressing his stiffness against her. The sensation seemed to delight her. She gasped and rose to meet him.

"Yes," she whispered.

Then she reached for the hem of her shirt. Propped on his elbows, rocking as gently as he could against her, he watched as that silky fabric trailed up over her body, revealing inch by inch the beauty underneath. A little too thin, but there was nothing at all lacking when she revealed full, pink-tipped breasts to his gaze.

"Perfect," he managed to say gutturally, lowering his head to kiss then suck each nipple in turn. Her response caused her to arch almost violently against him.

Her reaction acted like a wind on the firestorm she awoke in him. Her breasts drew his attention like magnets, filling him with both wonder and yearning. Beautiful breasts, full, seeming to reach up for his mouth. He obliged again, reveling in her response as she lifted up toward him and moaned faintly, as her fingers dug into his shoulders.

Then her hands slid down his back. One heart-stopping moment as she felt the depression of a shrapnel scar and paused, but not long enough to drag him out of the cauldron she had put him in. Then her hands found the top of his sweatpants and tugged them down.

God, he was alive and alight, all at once. His pants came down, to below his buttocks, baring his butt to the cold air and his erection to her warmth. The thermal pants might as well not even have been there. He rocked against her, letting her feel how much he wanted her, craved her. His entire body knew exactly where it wanted to be.

A groan escaped him and he reared up, tugging at her pants. Somehow he got them down below her knees, exposing the blond thatch of hair at the junction of her thighs. He glanced up, and saw a sleepy, sexy smile dance over her face, then without any urging at all, she parted her knees, her calves still trapped in fabric, but in a way that exposed her most secret delights to him.

He stared for a moment, the beat of the drum inside him reaching deafening volume, then slid down a bit until he dove down with his head, kissing her secrets with his lips, his tongue, drawing a cry of ecstasy from her, feeling her grow rigid again and yet again. Teasing that engorged nub of nerves until she was clawing at his shoulders, crying his name.

When he slipped his tongue inside her, tasting her, he could feel the contractions rippling through her, so strongly that he knew she hovered on the precipice.

At long last, he could stand it no more. Moving up over her, he pawed at the night table until he found a condom. Inevitably, that meant pushing up off her, and for an instant, just an instant, he totally loathed the protection he owed her.

Her eyes fluttered open and saw what he was doing. A murmur escaped her and she brushed his hands away, rolling the condom on him herself, pushing him even closer to the edge. Feeling her small hand grasp him and stroke his length was probably the most fiendish torture ever devised.

Then she opened her arms, reaching for him, and he could no longer deny either of them, not for anything. She was so wet and ready that he slid into her easily, feeling her stretch around him, then enclose him like a hot satin glove.

She pulled him down until his face was buried against her breast. Her hands roamed his back, dragging her nails gently over his skin, almost tickling, always teasing. He latched on to her nipple and bit gently, drawing a cry from her and then all finesse was lost in the driving, thundering need. Like galloping horses, they ran hard, ever rising across the plain of passion toward the soaring mountains ahead.

To Jess, it felt like the explosion began in his toes. As

he jetted into her, his mind filled with a blinding light. He felt the woman beneath him come to a shuddering climax of her own, felt her stiffen and cry out, her cry joining the light in his head.

Everything else vanished.

Lacy didn't want to let go of Jess, even though she knew she had to. She could feel the quivering of his muscles; her own quivered as well, as if the journey they had just made had stolen her last bit of energy.

Reluctantly, her hands trailing over him, she let him roll to the side.

"Be right back," he murmured, dropping a kiss on her nose.

Through half-open eyes, she watched him crutch into the bathroom. Only then did she realize that neither of them had fully removed their pants. Feeling almost giddy, she smiled and rolled over a little to grab a pillow. It was a poor substitute for Jess.

"Here we go," he said, suddenly behind her. The next thing she knew, her pants went flying. Then he lifted her gently and pulled a quilt over her. A moment later, he was in the bed, holding her from behind, pressing every possible inch of his front to her back. His hand brushed her hair back; a kiss fell on the nape of her neck.

Jess had taken her to heights she had never visited before. She felt awake, and alive, and utterly loved. She would have cheerfully banished reality from that moment forward.

For a long time they cuddled in silence, but finally he said, "Wow…"

"Wow…" she whispered back. She didn't want to talk.

She didn't want anything to disturb the heavenly glow that filled her.

"Sleep," he murmured. "I'll be right here."

Sleep? It seemed impossible after this night, but it wasn't long before it caught her. She couldn't remember the last time she had felt so relaxed. So good.

And that relaxation finally carried her into dreams.

Chapter 12

After the night they had been through, Lacy would have expected them to sleep late. Apparently not. A string of kisses from her earlobe across her cheek to her lips awoke her, melting her until she felt she had no bones left.

"I hate to let go," Jess said, "but I've got to get up. Breakfast soon, if you want it, or sleep longer."

She rolled over to watch him pull on his leg and a fresh set of insulated underclothes, the leg of one of which had been cut off and hemmed. "Undies are okay," he said with a wink over his shoulder. "I'll feed the stove and we'll see what the day looks like…whenever you're ready to get up."

She glanced at the clock and could scarcely believe it was only shortly after seven. Her sleep had been so deep and dreamless it felt like it had lasted forever.

Gathering up her long underwear, she quickly pulled

it on and headed upstairs to freshen up and get clean ones to wear. Not quite as comfortable as he about running around in undergarments, however concealing, she pulled out a flannel shirt to wear over it, plus some thick socks, then hurried downstairs, following the aroma of bacon and coffee.

As she entered the kitchen, he looked up from the stove with a warm smile that leavened his whole face and made her feel as if she had been hugged. Helplessly, she smiled back. "What can I do?"

"Keep me company. Today calls for bacon, eggs and flapjacks."

"So much?"

"I'm starving. How about you?"

Almost in answer, she felt her stomach growl. "I guess so."

"Grab some coffee, or make espresso if you want."

She went for the regular coffee. The espresso machine still daunted her. But as soon as she sat at the table, he pulled the frying pan off the flame and came over to wrap his arms around her from behind and kiss the side of her neck and her cheek. "You look good enough to eat," he murmured.

Surprisingly, she blushed. In a flannel shirt and long johns? The man was losing his mind, but she liked it.

He went back to the stove to check the heat on the griddle with a sprinkle of water. "Ah, ready." He poured batter onto it, then started eggs in the bacon pan.

Pulling her knees up to her chin, hooking her heels over the edge of the chair, she watched him move easily, looking more comfortable than he had since she'd gotten off the bus. Last night had been wonderful for her, and now she suspected it had been for him, too. She glowed inside.

The glow didn't last long, however. He brought heaps of food to the table, got himself fresh coffee, then sat across from her. "I would love to spend today cherishing you in every inventive way I can imagine," he said, causing her to blush again. "Unfortunately, there's no vacation from the stalker."

Her heart jumped unpleasantly and her stomach sank. "Did he do something else?"

"Not yet. But he will."

He served her a fried egg, a couple of strips of bacon and a pancake on the side, nudging the maple syrup her way. "Now that you don't feel like it anymore, try to eat. Think of it as fortification."

Great start to breakfast, she thought as her stomach tried to knot up. Obediently, she reached for a strip of bacon and dipped it listlessly into egg yolk. Eat? He must be kidding.

But then she thought of where he'd been, and how many times he'd probably had to eat in dangerous circumstances just to keep his energy up. Hadn't she read somewhere that soldiers routinely lost weight in combat because they didn't eat enough?

Summoning some determination, she began to feed herself. He was right. They couldn't ignore what had happened, even if they wanted to.

"You have a plan?" she asked.

"Not yet. I've been racking my brains trying to come up with something, but it helps if you know your enemy. I know nothing about this one. Not one damn thing. I think it's time to look up some of the men I served with in my last action."

"You think they might know? And how are you going to look them up?"

"That's what they make computers for. Are you up to a trip to the library?"

"Sure." Anything had to be better than hanging around here, wondering what would happen next. "But you think it's tied to when you were wounded?"

"Up to that point, anybody who wanted to get rid of me would have found it extremely easy. But let's leave that for later."

She nodded and forced herself to continue eating, although she was past enjoying what must have been a delicious breakfast. Even the maple syrup tasted flat.

"I could put you on a bus this morning."

That did it. Something inside her snapped. "I'm not going anywhere," she said sharply.

"You'd be safer than here, evidently."

She glared at him. "That makes me feel better how? I just turn tail and leave you here to face this on your own? I'm supposed to live with that? And anyway, we still don't know it's not someone who's after me."

His face, bright and relaxed when she first saw him, had grown drawn. Right now, he looked almost old. "I think we do," he said quietly. "The sins of my past are somehow coming home to roost."

"What sins?" she demanded. "You were a medic and you did your job. A soldier, and you did your job. If you want anyone to feel guilty, it should be the country that sent you into that hellhole."

"Lacy, I don't…"

"There's some national guilt that ought to be going around, and don't you dare argue with me. I won't have it. You served honorably. Beginning, middle and end."

He surprised her by smiling faintly. "You're a fire-brand, you know."

She blinked. No one had ever called her that before.

"But I'd still like to get you out of here."

"I couldn't live with myself. Put the shoe on your remaining foot and imagine how you'd feel. Knowing I might have a killer on my tail, you invited me here. You think I'm somehow less of a man?"

The way the words came out startled them both. Then, in spite of herself, Lacy giggled. "I didn't mean that exactly."

His smile widened. "Correct meaning understood, ma'am. Okay, short of having someone abduct you, we're in this together. Will you, for the love of heaven, eat? I swear you've lost another pound just since you got here. Power up, lady, because things are about to get tougher."

"This isn't the best mealtime conversation," she pointed out.

"I know. My timing stinks. The soldier in me, I guess. Just eat."

So she ate. At least one thing had been cleared up: she was with him in this until it was over. "Dang," she said as she mopped the last of the syrup with the last mouthful of pancake.

"Hmm?"

"It feels good to be taking charge of something again. Standing up. Making a decision. I've been driftwood for too long."

"Driftwood?" He repeated the word with disbelief. "Anything but. Look how much you've done."

"Very little of it by my decision. Once I went into witness protection, I had no control over anything. After I got out, it was almost like I'd lost control over myself.

Yeah, I could take care of the basic decisions, but major ones seemed like too much. I sent out résumés, received rejections and basically became a hermit. I talked to a few friends on the phone, but I quit going out. A grocery trip felt like a trial by fire." She shook her head. "An overreaction, I guess."

"Conditioning," he said quietly. "First they made you afraid, and then they took everything out of your hands. I hadn't thought how debilitating that might be."

She shrugged. "Still, I wasn't a firebrand before. Maybe I'm overcompensating."

"I can still get you on that bus." She glared and he laughed. "Okay, okay."

Feeling inexplicably better about herself—evidently there was something to be said for facing the fear head-on instead of running—she reached for another pancake. Another thought occurred to her. "Maybe I should stay here while you go to the library."

"Why?"

"Do you really want to leave the house empty after last night?"

"You forget. The police are keeping an eye out. Unless I'm mistaken, there's still one parked at the end of my driveway. But I'll check with Gage if that'll make you feel better. Lacy, I don't want you out of my sight."

She could agree with that. She didn't want to stay here by herself, but more important, she didn't want to be away from Jess. Most especially after last night. This might not be a romantic breakfast by any means, but he'd awakened feelings in her last night when they made love, and those feelings weren't evaporating in the harsh light of reality.

But Sara. Always *but Sara*. Was she betraying her

friend? Logically, she knew that was impossible now, but conscience still niggled at her. Jess, however, had been her husband, and he didn't appear to be suffering any qualms. But would he tell her if he were? Probably not.

Glumly, she looked down at the remains of the extra pancake she'd taken, and forced herself to cut off another mouthful with her fork. And here she thought she'd learned about getting caught in tangled webs with the money laundering. Apparently, life offered plenty of other kinds of tangles.

She needed to get her mind off this. Sara wasn't here to ask, and all she could do was deal with the present moment. "Why would this guy be taunting you—or me—this way? It doesn't make sense. Did he want us on guard?"

"Apparently so." Jess sighed and rose, taking his plate to the sink to rinse it. He returned with yet more coffee. "Maybe he gets a kick out of thinking we're scared."

"Then I hope he's enjoying it, because he's succeeded."

She caught Jess's green gaze fixing on her, studying her. "Has he? The only one I'm scared for is you."

"Not for yourself? Now I'll ask you if you're crazy." Then something he'd said popped up in her mind. "Jess?"

"Yeah?"

"You said after…after Sara died, you didn't care if you came back from Afghanistan. Do you…still feel that way?" Her heart thundered at her temerity, but she needed to know. If life still meant nothing to him then… then what? She ought to pack her bags when this was over and get the hell out.

"I still miss her, Lacy. I always will. But it's not like it was at first. I learned to live with it. Haven't you?"

Yes, she had. Seeing Jess again had refreshed her memories of her best friend, but the tearing grief of the initial loss had quieted.

"There'll always be a hole in my life," he continued. "A Sara-sized hole. But she's gone, and in my deepest being, I understand that. I won't look up one day and see her walking through the door. For whatever reason, I'm still here and have to deal with life. I'm in no rush to cash in my chips."

She nodded, pushing her plate to one side. "I remember. I remember that every time the phone rang I expected to hear her voice again. For the longest time, it was hard to remember that I couldn't pick up the phone and call her. I hated myself for months that I'd deleted her last voice mail message."

He nodded. "What was it about?"

"Coming to visit you guys for Christmas. I called back the next day and...she was gone."

Jess surprised her with a faint smile. "Well, that tells me something."

"What?"

"What she was thinking about the night before she died. Christmas. I was due to be home a week before the holiday, and I guess she was making plans."

"She was. She sounded so exuberant." Lacy's throat tightened. "She was so happy you were going to be home, and you know what she said?"

"What?"

"That I had to be there because a happiness shared was a happiness multiplied."

He closed his eyes, nodding, as if taking it in. His smile grew a little sadder, but when he opened his eyes, they were bright and clear. "Whatever happens, Lacy, stay through the holidays. I think we have a Christmas to make up for."

She guessed they did. She didn't know about him, but she'd celebrated the holiday only mechanically at work, or with an obligatory dinner with friends. After Sara passed, she didn't have the heart for it anymore. "I think she'd like that."

"I know she'd like that," he answered firmly. "She always felt you were family."

But more than that? Lacy wondered as she took care of her own dishes and helped with the cleanup. Of course, no one could have guessed how things would play out.

Jess made a brief phone call, then told her, "The sheriff has the house covered for now. So, you still want to go with me?"

"To the library? Of course." She wondered what revelations this would bring as she headed upstairs to dress. She didn't like the idea of Jess forcing himself to look into a past he'd clearly tried to put behind him, but he evidently felt it was necessary.

The worst of the weather seemed to be over. As soon as they stepped outside, Lacy felt how the wind had softened and seemed to carry more warmth with it. The sun shone brilliantly and was even beginning to make a few small icicles as it melted the little bit of snow that had caught on the roof.

The snow had changed, too, no longer feeling like dust but actually crunching as they walked to the car. The brightness of the day nearly blinded her, and she quickly donned her sunglasses. "Why don't you have a computer at home?" she asked as they drove toward the road and the sheriff's car.

"For me, it's just easier to use the library. I don't have a whole lot of time to spend surfing the internet at home, and I can do everything I really want to from work or the library."

"So you're not connected?" she asked lightly.

"I told you that you'd be off the grid here. Do you miss it?"

"I haven't used it since the investigation began. It's a hard addiction to break, but it's broken."

They paused at the sheriff's car to say hi, and the young man inside assured them he'd let no one near the house. "There'll be a different deputy here when you come back, just so you know. We're working in four-hour shifts."

Jess thanked him, then turned onto the road. The wind had apparently swept it mostly free of snow, and now only a few patches remained here and there, surrounded by darker shapes as they melted under the strong sun.

"God, it's good to be out," Lacy said. "And it's such a beautiful day."

Jess surprised her by reaching over and clasping her hand. "More beautiful because of you."

Oh, wow. Astonished, she looked at him, but his gaze was fixed on the road. Before long, they reached the edge of town and the houses grew closer together. Lacy liked the sense of enduring age about the place. Older homes, none of the boxy structures that were springing up like weeds in so many areas around Dallas.

Jess spoke. "The librarian is Emmaline Dalton, but everyone calls her Miss Emma. I'm not sure why but it evidently began a very long time ago. Regardless, she's the sheriff's wife, and a lovely woman. And her assistant is Nora Madison, who's married to—you'll never guess—our chief of police."

Lacy had to laugh quietly. "That's a secure library."

He gave a rusty laugh of his own. "You'll like them both, I believe. Miss Emma's roots in this county stretch back to the very beginning of the town. Her father was a judge. And Nora…well, she grew up here, too. Her father's a lunatic fringe type, a preacher with his own fanatical following. How Nora escaped that, I'll never know."

"You're obviously too new here or you'd have all the dirt."

His smile widened as he pulled into the small library parking lot. "Apparently so. I get the surface of the old gossip."

"What about the new stuff?"

"Every juicy detail."

"You'll have to fill me in."

"Someday. Lacy."

She swiveled her head to look at him as he set the brake and pulled the keys out of the ignition. "What?"

"Stay in the car. Just for a minute. I want to do a quick look-see."

God, that sent ice rolling down her spine. At the moment, they were fairly well surrounded by buildings, near the heart of the small town. Nobody seemed to be about, hardly surprising on a weekday. What did he fear?

With fists clenched, she obediently waited while he climbed slowly out and began to turn a slow circle. Her nerves stretched, but she understood that he had a better background for identifying problems than she did. What looked unimportant to her might trip some alert in him.

They had to wrap this up, and soon. Somehow they

needed to escape this shadow of fear. Guilt pinched her because she had to acknowledge this all might be because of her, regardless of what he thought.

Then he came around to help her out, but there was no longer anything relaxed about him. His eyes moved ceaselessly as they walked around to the front and up the steps into the warmth of the old Carnegie library. The country was dotted with them. Not very big, but better than no library at all.

A middle-aged woman with graying reddish hair sat at the circular desk in the middle. She looked up with a warm smile. "Jess! How good to see you." Then her gaze trailed to Lacy. "And your friend?"

"Lacy Devane. We've known each other for years."

Emma slipped off her stool and leaned across the counter to offer her hand. "Emma Dalton. I hope you're enjoying our little town."

"I hope to see more of it," Lacy said truthfully. "I met your husband the other day. A very nice man."

Emma's smile broadened. "I won't disagree with that. So what's it to be today, Jess? The computer room or the books?"

"Computers again."

"We need to bring you into the twenty-first century."

"You can work on me after you get Gage there."

Emma laughed and picked up a ring of keys. She turned to Lacy as they walked toward the back. "I keep the computer room locked up. You'd be surprised what some of our middle-schoolers get up to if I'm not watching."

Lacy laughed.

"It's open to the public, of course, but someone has to know who's in there and that we need to check from time to time. After school, a lot of them like to play video games, which is fine, but two years ago I had a delegation of parents demanding we make sure the games are age-appropriate." Emma rolled her eyes. "Like they don't go over to a friend's house and do it anyway?"

Lacy definitely liked Emma Dalton.

Soon they were alone in the computer room, which boasted a surprising number of monitors and seats. How they were wired up Lacy had no idea, but it was probably far more advanced than her little laptop at home, more like the way she had worked at the firm.

She didn't miss the way Jess chose a machine that put his back to a wall. Instinct or concern? She almost asked, but figured this was going to be an unhappy enough event for him.

"My move," he muttered as he tapped at keys and brought up a search screen.

"What was bothering you outside?" she asked as she sat nearby. "Did you see something?"

He hesitated, his fingers freezing over the keyboard. "In my last action…" He paused again, then shook his head as if freeing something. "We were diverted from our original mission and sent into a small town. The place was surrounded by cliffs. Not exactly the kind of place you want to waltz into."

He fell silent, so she waited.

"I don't like being surrounded by high points."

"I see." Her stomach began to skitter nervously.

"Anyway, long story short, fire began to rain down on us from those cliffs. We were pinned down, civilians were getting killed as well, and there was one little girl…" He stopped abruptly, once again shaking his head. "Doesn't matter. We got pretty chewed up, and then got chewed up even more when air support arrived. Hellfire raining from heaven."

She couldn't imagine it. Her mouth turned dry. "Friendly fire? Did you need it?"

"I guess we must have. Never should have walked into the place to begin with, but my opinion didn't matter. Just a medic. But you'd have thought any fool could sense what a setup it might be."

He had gone perfectly still, staring into some place only he could see. Lacy waited, then began to wonder if she should say or do something. Another flashback? She had no idea how to deal with it.

But then he stirred again, releasing a long breath. "Anyway, I still get edgy when I'm surrounded by high vantage points. Sorry."

"No reason," she said swiftly. "You're talking to a woman who gets edgy going to the grocery."

He turned his head and blue eyes met green. She felt a flash, almost like an electric jolt, then a smile eased his expression. "We'll get out of this."

"So what are you looking for exactly?"

"Guys I know who survived that last mission. Like I said, if someone wanted me dead, they had plenty of opportunity before that. No, somehow it's linked to that last mission I was on. The CO was a jackass, but he's not the only one. Changed our orders, but I have no idea whether he was following orders when he did it. I just know that walking us into that narrow slit in the mountains seemed stupid before we took the first step. I have no idea what he hoped to accomplish, but I'm sure he had a reason. At the very least, the guy was a freaking glory hound."

"He risked you needlessly?"

"Sometimes it sure felt like it. But ours was not to reason why, as the poem goes."

Her fists were knotting again, and nameless, ugly emotions were awakening in her. "So, did he walk into that village with you?"

"He remained in the rear."

She hated to hear him say that as if it were normal. The guy should have been there with his men. But what did she know about all that? "What did he do there?"

"Command and control."

"You mean, like calling in the air strike?"

"Yeah. Among other things."

She supposed she could take an entire class in how the military worked before she truly understood, but the image appearing in her mind now was ugly to the extreme. So the guy sent them into a death trap and hung out behind, watching it all unfold? If that was standard procedure, she had a problem with it.

With difficulty, she asked no more questions, figuring that for now ignorance was preferable. Besides, she could see from the hardening of his face that Jess was approaching places he'd rather not go, but felt he had to. At this point, she wished the sheriff would walk in and say, "Yeah, the cartel is after Lacy." It might be easier than facing what Jess was about to face.

Hesitantly, she placed her hand on his arm. "Are you sure about this?"

"Unfortunately. Lacy…" He hesitated, then clasped her hand tightly. "The sheriff was right when he asked if I had any enemies. And the question flashed me back to that last action. Something is trying to hook up in my head. My memory of it all isn't the best. I think I told you, I don't remember much after I was wounded. I don't remember a whole lot about the weeks immediately after. But there's something there, and it isn't a Mexican cartel. They wouldn't pull crap like what happened last night. But I know some types who would."

"And you're looking for them?"

"Not exactly, but we'll see."

She hesitated. "Jess? Are you sure you should try to retrieve those memories?" Worry filled her, worry about him and what those memories might mean to him. He had enough horror in his past. How much more did he need to carry with him?

His mouth tightened. "It's my move, remember?"

"Who knows what that creep meant?"

"I think he wants me to remember. One thing I know for sure, Lacy, is that unless I remember something, I'm never going to figure out who he is. I don't have to tell you what it's like to be stalked forever."

His words slammed her because they were so true. She knew the feeling intimately and wouldn't wish it on anyone. "But why would he want you to figure it out?"

He shook his head grimly. "Torture, I suppose. He's furious about something and he wants me to know my part in it."

She felt unnerved by all of this. Unnerved to be sitting by a man who intended to discover something he'd done that might be bad enough to make someone want to torture him this way. To threaten him. Unnerved by what he might learn, unnerved by what it might do to him, unnerved by how it might make her feel about him.

Sara had been so proud that Jess was a medic, that he'd taken such risks to save lives. But what if it hadn't been like that at all? What if he'd been forced to do something terrible?

She wasn't naive enough to think that anyone could go to war and not do some awful things. But even in war, some things went beyond the pale. What if an event like that lurked in his buried memories? She didn't want him to remember it, and she didn't want to know it. Sometimes, no matter how much you cared for someone, a thing so horrific could happen that you would never feel the same again about that person.

She ought to know. Men she had respected for years could make her shudder now.

She felt as if she was walking on shifting sands again, the way she had felt almost since the moment she had suspected that her work was somehow illegal. All the norms had blown up quickly, leaving her panicked and feeling that quicksand held her in its grip. The more she had learned, the more she could feel it sucking her in, threatening to drown her.

For a while, working with the government's forensic accountants, she had felt a little more stable, as if planks had been laid over that sand, giving her a path to walk. But then, after the trial, those planks had been yanked away. She was once again on her own in a world that would never be the same. Never. The way she had felt after Sara died. Losses, first the loss of her best friend, then the loss of her innocence and faith in other people.

Now this. She wondered if she was about to lose the tattered remains of her innocence, if she was about to discover that even Jess was not the man he seemed.

No way could she prevent this, though. It was his move, and he was determined to make it, no matter what it revealed. He probably had a better idea of the nightmares he might dredge up than she.

Braced for the worst, hoping for the best, she sat be-

side him and waited, avoiding looking at the screen. This
time, she was prepared to accept only what she was told.

The hunter, feeling not much like a tiger at the moment, drove past the McGregor homestead and noted
the cop out front. Not that it was totally unexpected, but
since that damn bomb had been a dud, he thought they'd
probably dismiss it as a game. Apparently not.

Oh, well, he could get past a single armed sentry,
probably one who was bored to death and wishing he
were anywhere else, typical of sentries. One man would
be a mere speed bump.

In the distance, he saw McGregor and his friend heading to town. He hoped he was about to take the woman
to the bus station. When they got in among the houses,
he steadily closed the distance until they pulled into the
library parking lot.

He drove slowly past, wondering if that meant Mc-
Gregor was making his move, trying to find out what
was going on, or if the woman was simply bored and
wanted a book to read.

But after last night, he was fairly certain McGregor
was looking into the past, although he couldn't quite
figure why he'd need the library. The computers? Was
it possible the man didn't have one of his own?

Hell, nobody was that cut off anymore, not even the
military. Weird. He parked down the street, waiting and
bored. His patience was being tested to the max and he
didn't appreciate it.

The cops would pull off their watchdog in a day or
two, if he was willing to wait that long. Assigning men
to that kind of duty was expensive, not something such a
small department could support for long. Regardless, he

had no doubt he could get himself into that house today if he decided to. He could slip past the sentry, pick a lock and be hiding somewhere before McGregor came home.

As for the woman…well, she'd be an easy target. He'd only have to decide whether to take McGregor out first and then enjoy her, or the other way around. He kind of liked the idea of McGregor being forced to watch. The guy objected to it even when it was women he didn't know. How much better it would be to see it happen to one he cared about.

It only seemed fair, after what his mere existence had put the hunter through.

Finally, the wait grew too long. Someone would notice him. He decided to head for the truck stop, since he hadn't been there in a couple of days, and order up some lunch. Even if he didn't get to see the two depart the library, he'd be able to find out soon enough if the woman was still there.

Then, he started thinking about just what McGregor would find online. Wondering if he would put the pieces together. That train of thought amused him, and he was smiling as he entered the truck stop to order lunch.

Chapter 13

"You must be bored," Jess said. "I don't want you out of my sight, but you can use another computer. Sitting here just watching me has to be a yawner."

Far from it, Lacy thought. Staring at Jess was an enjoyable pastime, but it probably was making him feel awkward. So she summoned a smile, moved to the next computer on the table and woke up another machine. It immediately presented her with a menu of games and ebooks, as well as a web search engine. Beside the list of games was a warning: *headset must be used.*

Yeah, she could just imagine what this room would sound like with a bunch of games playing at top volume.

She had no idea what she wanted to do, however. Starting a book would be a waste of time since she wasn't likely to finish it, and she hadn't used her social media accounts in nearly two years. That left surfing the web with no real goal in mind.

She soon discovered some curiosity about how her case had been reported in the papers. At the time, she had viewed none of the news reports, either on TV or in the print media, because she was on the inside. There was nothing the news could tell her, and her keepers didn't seem to especially want her to know, anyway. It was better, they told her, if her testimony wasn't affected by what others might say.

After a while, she was glad she hadn't read about the case while it was ongoing. In fact, she hardly recognized it from the coverage, but wondered at times if she was reading about an entirely different case. She wasn't all that surprised to discover she had been cast in the role of villain in some pieces, but the innuendo that she'd done all of this because one of the partners had spurned her advances shocked her. Wasn't the news supposed to be factual?

She read enough to feel sickened, and wasn't all cheered by the articles that claimed she was some kind of hero and that she'd helped bring down a large drug operation. Straight from the US Attorney's mouth. Still... No wonder finding work in Dallas had been impossible. Not only had she ratted out her employer, but she sounded like a femme fatale everyone should avoid.

"Dang," she muttered. Hardly surprising the guys protecting her had kept such a tight news blackout. Had she read any of this before the trial, she doubted she'd have been as cool and collected during her testimony, but rather angry and spoiling for a fight. She might have inadvertently borne out everyone's suspicions about her motives. A personal vendetta?

Angrily, she punched a few keys and looked for animal pictures. Anything to get her away from that cesspool.

"What?" Jess asked.

"Apparently, I squealed on my bosses because one of them spurned me."

"I saw that. If it's any comfort, I didn't believe a word of it at the time, and not everyone took that tack."

"I know. But now I truly understand why I can't find work. It's not just that I revealed criminal activities. It's that I have no honor left. My reputation is ruined, completely."

He reached out and took her hand, pulling her close on her rolling chair. "Not with everyone."

She tried to smile, sensing she failed miserably. He wrapped his arm around her shoulders and drew her close to his side. "You did the right thing, Lacy. Unfortunately, sometimes there's a high price for that."

He would certainly know, she thought miserably. It felt nice to have his supportive hug, however, and the knot of anger inside her began to ease. "You know what they say about eavesdroppers."

"Of course."

"I think I just eavesdropped on my own life. I won't do that again." But that brought her right back around to what he was trying to do. "Jess? Are you having any luck? Should you keep this up?"

"Actually," he answered slowly, "I'm learning things all right. And I'm getting steadily uneasier."

She reached up to hold his hand where it rested on her shoulder. "Like what?"

"Only four other men in my unit survived the last action I was in. Two died before they could be gotten to advanced treatment centers. That left two plus me, and those two have died since."

Shocked, she twisted to look straight at him. "Combat?"

He shook his head. "One appears to have been a suicide. The other was a...hunting accident."

She noted the hesitation when he spoke. Her own uneasiness began to mount.

"I know the suicide rate is high among returning vets. Way too high. But it's almost as if anyone who remembers that action is being erased."

"So that just leaves you."

"So it appears."

"But you don't remember much about it!"

"Not really." He looked again at the computer screen. "There's got to be something. Oh, I know the odds are high that there's nothing suspicious about how those two men died, but..."

"But now you've been threatened."

He nodded slowly, not looking at her. "I wish I could get the after-action reports, but I don't know anyone anymore who might be able to access them for me."

"What about your CO?"

"Well..." Again the hesitation. "Not that bastard. Apparently, he's out there somewhere, but I can't find him. He'd be the last one I'd ask anyway."

"Why?"

"Because he ordered us into that village. And he called in the air strike."

She stiffened. "Jess..."

"I know. Believe me, I know. I'm thinking about him, and I'm not liking what I'm thinking."

"But why would he be killing the survivors? It doesn't make sense."

"You know, I assumed he walked away from that without a scratch on his career, even though he deserved one. But he was a ring knocker on the fast track."

"Ring knocker?"

"Academy graduate. Headed for the heights. Military family, married a general's daughter, did all the right things. I think he was in Afghanistan just to get his campaign ribbons. Career acceleration. Anyway..." He shook his head again. "That type usually gets wrapped in bubble wrap and the skids get greased for them. I just assumed that whatever happened on that operation, he'd skate through it."

She thought that over. "So it's not all merit?"

"It never has been, sweetheart. Never. Meritocracies exist in people's dreams. In reality, someone is always pulling the strings of power, and the chosen few go right to the top like cream. He was among the chosen, so whatever happened, I assumed he wouldn't get any trouble over it."

"But maybe he did?"

"I'm wondering."

"But to kill someone over that? Surely he can't undo it now." But even as she spoke, she knew this wouldn't be about undoing it. Only about revenge. "But you were a medic, Jess. How many times did you say you wouldn't know much about those issues? How could he hold you responsible?"

His voice turned to ice. "I may not remember a lot, Lacy, but I remember holding that glory hound accountable for walking us into that hell. And maybe when I was in the hospital, half gone on painkillers and meds— maybe I said so. Hell, maybe I ranted about it. God, this little girl—"

He'd mentioned the little girl before. Clearly, she was troubling him as much as anything, but she didn't know if she should even ask. Questioning him might only make it worse, but the gnawing ache in her heart for him was almost too much to bear.

But then he started talking. "We had this mission when we went into those remote villages. A second mission. We weren't just there to clear out Taliban, but to win hearts and minds. That's what they called it."

"I think I heard something about that."

"Yeah. Well, we'd help rebuild where we could, if they'd let us. One time I'll never forget, we were running around like lunatics, trying to help some guy round up his goats. They'd broken out of their pen and he was terrified they'd eat a neighbor's crop. So there we were, chasing them. Thanks goodness some of the guys actually had farm experience." He smiled faintly as he spoke, apparently enjoying the memory.

"Other times, we knew as soon as we walked in that the people were terrified. They'd hide in their houses and wouldn't come near us. It was a warning to clear out because the insurgents were there, so usually we cleared out. But other times...well, it was part of my job to provide medical care as I could to the civilians. Vaccinations, if I had the serum with me, wound treatment, antibiotics, that kind of thing. Most of the time, I wasn't allowed to treat the women, but little girls who were young enough, I could help, as long as their mothers or fathers were present."

"Okay," she said encouragingly. "I think that's wonderful."

"So anyway, we walked into that village. None of the usual warning signs to let us know they were afraid. I'm convinced they had no idea the insurgents were hanging around. But I'm wondering if *we* did."

Her heart quickened. "Why?"

"Because it was a detour from our planned mission. Somebody had gotten wind those guys were up on the mountains, on the cliffs overlooking us. Why else would we divert that way? But it makes even less sense that we walked into that valley, instead of coming from above. Unless…"

"Unless?" she prodded when he remained silent.

"Unless some glory hound thought he could take out a whole bunch of insurgents with an air strike. But he'd need a reason to call for one, since we evidently had no solid intel on them."

Horror gripped her. Her voice dropped to a whisper. "Would someone really do that?"

"Bait a trap with his own men? Hell, yeah." He fell silent and she let him be as she struggled to believe that anyone would do such a heartless thing.

"All those people," she whispered eventually.

"Exactly. All those people. Including a little girl of six or seven who had an infected gash on her arm that I was cleaning up when the shooting started. I know she got hit. What I'll never know is if she made it, because that's the last thing I remember except insanity."

Time crept slowly by, neither of them speaking. "Of course, there's another possibility," he finally said.

"Which is?"

"He's erasing any witnesses so it *won't* come back to haunt him."

She felt perilously close to vomiting. She thought she'd seen ugliness, but apparently she hadn't even scraped its surface. "Is there any way you can find out if he's still on the fast track?"

"I can't even find him on the internet. He's probably smart enough to stay off social media, because a wrong word or two could cost him. I have no idea where he's stationed, and getting a list of active service members is tough. I don't know how many congressional documents I'd have to pour through to find out if he's been promoted, and even then I couldn't be sure it's him, and wouldn't know how to find him. The world isn't exactly low on Samuel Johnsons."

Despite the roiling horror inside her, she could see a flicker of humor in that. "Sam Smith would have been worse."

"Barely." He rubbed his eyes. "I found those two others because their death notices were in the press. This guy is flying under most radars."

She pushed away the mental images he'd elicited in her and chewed that over for a few moments. "Is that usual, flying under the radar?"

"Yeah, if you want to stay on the fast track. Keep your nose clean is the first rule."

"And his nose could be dirtied by this."

"It may have already been. Or he might be trying to prevent it. Questions must certainly have arisen if he wasn't following orders when he sent us into that village. He might have provided a good explanation of some kind."

"If so, what would you know that would be a threat to him? I don't get this at all, Jess. You were a medic. You wouldn't know all those details."

"No." He leaned back and let the computer go to its screensaver. "No, but I do know that we walked in there unprepared, that even the villagers had no idea that insurgents were in the area. That could be enough to raise questions about what he did if, for example, he claimed that he had received intelligence in the field and acted on it for a good reason. Lots of ways to justify changing your orders at the last minute. A certain amount of individual agency is allowed to field officers." He shook his head. "Why now? It's been four years. It has to be revenge. Or he's nuts."

"But… I'm confused here. Say he *did* receive intelligence about those insurgents. Say he claimed that. You said yourself you should have gone in there differently."

"But who's left to say we didn't go in there combat-ready? Me. He could have said the insurgents were in town, according to his intel, and he sent us in to clear them out. There's nobody left to argue otherwise."

"What exactly did he say about the change in the mission?"

He shook his head a little. "That we were diverting to avoid a large group of insurgents. Look, I can't know what he was thinking. I do know that I thought he was a glory hound. The diversion from our original mission was supposed to put us in a better position. When those grenades started coming from the cliffs above, I had a split second to wonder if the guy had seriously miscalculated. In retrospect, I wonder if he got exactly the outcome he wanted. And I have no way to find out if he paid for that day or if he got a medal."

He pushed back from the table. "Let's go get something at the diner, then head home. I need to do some more thinking about all of this. It's a muddle, and not only in my own head."

He didn't say any more. He'd probably already said too much. He'd seen the looks flitting across Lacy's face and knew how much he'd disturbed her with his honesty. But she had insisted on staying, and since she was here she had a right to know what they might be up against. If he was even remotely right that it was his former CO.

But his conviction had grown from the deaths of the other two who had survived that battle. He'd known Johnson for only a few months, but the guy hadn't been a complete unknown. Stories had followed him from other postings, and while he wasn't supposed to be in Afghanistan for long, Jess had seen enough ring knockers move in and move out after spending just enough time to claim their campaign ribbons to know just how well their butts were protected by the higher-level brass.

They all knew the guy was being groomed. Officers like that made them all nervous, because some would make decisions with an eye to a star someday. More than one soldier had died as a result of some guy's ambition.

But could he be certain it was Johnson? And even if it was, did he know enough about the guy to defend against him? To guess what approach he might take?

Once again, the need to get Lacy out of here overwhelmed him, but he couldn't force her to get on a bus. He made up his mind that after they got a bite at the diner, they were going over to see the sheriff. Maybe if Gage had gotten sufficient reassurance that Lacy wasn't in danger, she would agree to leave. He could always argue that he could protect himself better if he didn't have someone else to worry about.

Nor would it be untrue. The thing was, he couldn't be absolutely certain yet that she was out of danger, and he'd never forgive himself if he sent her off and it turned out that all of this was about her, and not him at all.

Sitting across the table from her, he realized that he no longer expected to see Sara every time he heard Lacy speak, or listened to the approach of her steps. A link that he had believed unbreakable in his mind had broken. Lacy was part of *his* life now, not part of his relationship with his late wife.

That was a good thing, he supposed, especially given that they'd made love last night. He'd feared, for the briefest moment, that she might feel like a stand-in. If she ever asked, he'd be able to say truthfully that it wasn't so.

He ordered roast beef and mashed potatoes with gravy for himself, and Lacy settled on a potato and cheese casserole. She needed to pack those calories in.

He hadn't studied much in the way of tactics and strategy; that hadn't been his role. Oh, yeah, he'd been through combat training—every marine had, even the medics that came over from the Navy, because in the Corps everyone was expected to be a fighter when needed. But that wouldn't give him much of a leg up on a man who had actually studied tactics, maybe even planned some operations himself.

Except, like a great neon sign in his brain, were the words, *He sure screwed up that last one.* While he packed in his own lunch with little thought of niceties, he considered what he could remember of that horrible day. A change in orders. Diversion to a small town from which they were supposed to launch a surprise attack on the insurgents.

He was fairly sure he'd heard that right. The entire unit had gotten the impression that their original objective had been so overrun, they needed a new plan. They were to group in the village while gleaning more intel on the enemy.

Except none of it had worked that way. When the fire started raining down on them from above, he'd been convinced that Johnson had known who was in those cliffs, that it had nothing to do with their original objective being overrun, and that he'd set it up so they could call in an air strike, something they normally wouldn't have done so close to a friendly village.

But all of that had occurred to him in mere seconds, seconds that had seemed endless, but still only seconds before the girl he was trying to help fell, before the grenade had exploded and taken his leg.

How could he be sure, when things had happened so fast that he couldn't even throw himself over that girl to protect her, that his impressions had been right?

He raised his eyes from his plate and saw that Lacy appeared pinched around the eyes. Instantly, he felt bad. "I'm sorry. I'm eating like a pig at a trough and ignoring you."

"I'm fine and you're obviously thinking. What you told me… Jess, I'm sorry you have to rack your brains to remember something so awful."

"I should have racked my brains a long time ago."

She shook her head a little and scooped up another spoonful of her casserole. "How could you know? Anyway, we can't be sure it's this CO of yours. You know that."

"Of course I know that." Immediately he softened his tone. No need to bark at her because he was facing things he should have faced before. "We're going over to the sheriff after we're done and find out if he's learned anything. And then I'm going to have to think about things I haven't thought about in years, like how to make us safe, no matter who's pulling this stuff." He hesitated, then tried once again. "If the sheriff says there's no one coming after you, you could get out of here."

Something in her face stiffened. "Trying to get rid of me, Jess?"

Oh, hell, could he have said anything more stupid, especially after last night?

"I know I'm not Sara," she rushed on, "but…"

"I don't want you to be Sara." He spoke evenly, spacing the words for emphasis. "I never wanted that, and will never want that. When you first arrived, it brought back some memories, freshened the loss a bit, but I don't regret it. All I want you to be is Lacy. And I'm not trying to get rid of you. I'm trying to spare you from whatever is coming. Don't damn me for that."

Her face softened slightly, but she said in a voice like steel, "I'm not leaving you to face this creep alone."

"I might have more to worry about if you're in the picture."

That caused her to bite her lip and look down. Then she shook her head, raising her chin and staring back at him. "And you need someone to watch your back. Everyone does. Tell me what to do, what not to do, and I won't get in your way, I swear."

Okay, she wasn't going to go. That would complicate his planning, but he figured he could do it. But he also figured one more dash of icy reality might help. "Can you handle a gun?"

He expected her to hesitate, to say she'd never touched one, but she astonished him. "Dad taught me when I was a kid. Pirates were always a problem."

"Pirates!" That shook him out of his self-absorption.

"Yes. With a nice boat like that? It's always a possibility. He was concerned about drug runners, and his boat was fast, with a good-sized hold. Taking someone's boat in the middle of the sea is a great way to cover your tracks, I guess. It had happened to others, so he took what he thought were reasonable precautions."

"Pirates," he repeated. Live and learn. He knew about the piracy off the Somali coast, but in the Caribbean? But when he thought about it, he could see it. An awful lot of drugs came up that way from South America. "How'd that make you feel?"

She smiled humorlessly. "I was young. It made me feel like Annie Oakley after I passed all the training with a firearms instructor. Ready for anything."

He looked at her, seeing a new Lacy, not the somewhat shy woman who had giggled endlessly with Sara and had helped bring some light and joy into his own life. Annie Oakley? Um, wow.

"I hate guns," he admitted. "I hate what they can do. I have a shotgun at home, but that's it. If you're going to stay, then we'll need to go by the gun store and outfit you. But I have to know one thing."

"What's that?"

"Do you think you can actually pull the trigger? People are different from paper targets."

He watched her close her eyes, searching herself. "Yes," she said presently. "In self-defense, in defense of another, absolutely yes. While I hope I never have to, I believe I can. I faced that a long time ago."

"Be sure, Lacy. Be very sure. Because you can get yourself into a real heap of trouble if you wave a gun and can't use it."

Her answer was slow in coming, but he appreciated that she was thinking it through once more. No one could be absolutely certain that they could shoot a human being. Not even a trained soldier. But he wanted her to be as sure as she could be, because he wasn't kidding. Waving a gun you couldn't use, or wouldn't use, merely gave your enemy an added weapon.

"I do believe I can," she said finally. Her face had paled a little. "Like I said, I won't want to, but if it's the only choice? Yes."

With that he had to be content.

He'd finished his meal and she'd been reduced to picking little bits from her casserole. "Are you finished? We can take that casserole home."

She shook her head. "It's awfully rich. I'd like something lighter for supper."

"Fair enough. Let's go see the sheriff."

He paid the bill at the register and opted to walk the short distance to the sheriff. He was surprised to realize he was feeling exposed as he walked. He'd never felt that way before in this town, and he didn't like the sensation.

In an instant he was back in a mode he didn't want to ever live again: high-alert. Scanning vehicles, rooftops, windows for possible threats. His skin crawling. Ready to take action in an instant, ready to throw Lacy to the ground and spread himself over her if necessary.

If a car backfired, he'd react without thought, and then have a lot of explaining to do. Cussing silently, he marched them as quickly as he could to the safety of the sheriff's offices. It had been a long time since walking half a block had seemed like walking miles in slow motion.

But not long enough, evidently.

He heard the quick patter of Lacy's steps as she tried to keep up, and he knew he should slow down, but he held her hand tightly and kept her going. At last they reached the door and he pulled them inside. Only then did he spare a thought for the fact that it was getting colder outside again, much colder.

"Well, that was brisk," she said, breathing a little heavily.

"Sorry."

Before he could speak to the dispatcher, Lacy squeezed his hand. "I know how you're feeling, believe me. It's okay. I became a speed walker in Dallas."

He could well understand. The world outside, once a welcoming new life, was now shadowed like the mountains, valleys and plains of Afghanistan. If it was Johnson, the man was going to pay for stealing his hard-won peace of mind.

"He's in the back," Velma said in answer to his question. She puffed on one of her endless cigarettes. "Poor man is beginning to sound like our last sheriff. You know Nate Tate, right?"

Jess nodded. "Fine man."

"And a bellyacher about paperwork. Gage is bellyaching today. Go give him a break."

Still holding Lacy's hand, Jess walked them at a more reasonable pace back to the sheriff's office. His threat sense was easing up, allowing him to relax a little. Of course, there was still the walk back to the car, the drive out to his isolated little house, and all that might happen afterward.

Gage greeted them with a mixture of relief and a scowl. "Damn paperwork will swamp a man. And most of it isn't even important. If you haven't read it, check the *Police Blotter* column in the local paper sometime. Farcical. As is most of what's on my desk."

Jess nodded sympathetically. "Nobody likes paperwork."

"Except maybe accountants," Lacy said, injecting some much-needed humor into the moment. Jess released the last of his tension, pulled a chair over for her, and when she sat, he sat beside her. He hated letting go of her hand.

Gage held up his hand. "I know why you're here. I'm waiting for another call, but right now I'd have to say nobody is looking for Lacy. According to the people I've talked to so far, she's off the radar and has been since the trial. They did a pretty good roll-up on the operation, and whoever's left isn't feeling particularly vengeful. One more call and I'll be sure."

Lacy didn't know whether to be relieved or not. Part of her felt like a fool for not believing the Feds, part of her felt silly with the imagined terror she'd lived with for too long and another part of her was terrified for Jess. To think she'd come here looking for safety from him when he was the one at risk. The irony was too much.

"So," said Gage, leaning forward with a grimace, "I ask you again, Jess. Do you have any enemies?"

"I think I might," he said.

Lacy half anticipated that he might have a flashback, as he had last time Gage asked that question, but he didn't. He seemed to square himself and get ready to face it head-on. "I learned this morning that I'm the last survivor of my unit, other than the CO. We walked into an ambush. Five of us got out of there, three left the hospital alive and two died since. One was deemed a suicide, the other a hunting accident. Which leaves me."

Gage nodded slowly. "I assume this CO survived."

"He didn't enter the village."

Gage drummed his fingers. "Unusual?"

"Not always. Depends on the man. Staying at a safe distance to observe and keep up communications is one way to go."

"Evidently the way he chose."

"Yes."

"So what's he after, Jess?"

"Witnesses. At least that's all I can conclude. We know he changed our orders. We didn't know we were walking into an ambush. Maybe he did, maybe he didn't, and maybe he told a hell of a good story and doesn't want the truth coming out. It's the best I can come up with, but we all knew he was a glory hound and that he was headed to the top. Best I can guess is maybe one of the other guys started stirring the embers a bit and he got scared of what we might know. Or he's gone totally off his nut."

"Where is he now?"

"Damned if I know. I spent all morning at the library trying to find out something about Samuel Johnson. At the time, he was a first lieutenant with the Marines. By now, he'd be at least a captain, maybe a major. Anyway, nothing on the internet at all."

"Common name, but it's pretty weird he wouldn't have some kind of footprint."

"Let's just say it's not one I can identify. And all my friends from the military are civilians now."

"Nor can you just pick up a phone and call the Department of Defense, I imagine."

Jess shook his head. "That information is confidential. If you need to find a soldier, sailor or marine, the most anyone will do is pass along a message."

"Guess I can understand that."

Gage started rocking in his chair, and with each move it squeaked a little. He stared off into space.

Lacy sat waiting, wishing she had something to offer. Then a question occurred to her. "Why would you need to find him? What good will that do?"

"I was hoping to find out if he's still in uniform, still on the fast track or what."

"But in the end, what difference does it make? If he's after you because you said something—which you clearly don't remember at this point—or because he's afraid you might say something to damage him after all this time...what does that have to do with the fact that he's probably the one stalking you?"

"Knowing for sure would give me some idea what I'm dealing with."

"Yes, you did mention that." She sighed. "I'm sorry I can't be more helpful. But it seems to me that whatever his reason, this guy has slipped his rails. Playing games? Telling you it's your move? That doesn't sound sane to me. None of it sounds sane. He either made a stupid mistake and lost his entire unit, or set it up somehow to make himself look like some kind of hero... Either way, he's crazy now, and you can't predict crazy."

Gage and Jess exchanged looks. "She's right," Jess said.

Gage nodded. "Absolutely."

"For all we know," she continued, "he made a dumb mistake, was losing his unit, panicked, called in an air strike which unfortunately took out an entire village along with you guys, and remorse has been eating him until he snapped. Now he just wants to get rid of anyone else who remembers his shame. But what difference does it make? He's coming for Jess and he's clearly not playing by any known rules."

"Yeah," said Jess, "what rules include a bogus threat, accompanied by a note telling me it's my move? It sounds more like a video game than reality."

"So he's playing some kind of sick game in his own mind," Lacy said.

Gage surprised her with a smile. "I like the way you think. Reminds me of my undercover days. Okay, then, Jess, short of putting you two under full-time protection, which I'm sorry to say I don't have the resources to do, and short of sending you away to some far-off desert island, I guess we need to put our heads together on a plan of action."

Chapter 14

Jess made Lacy wait at the sheriff's while he picked up the car. She thought it was extreme for half a block, but judging by the way he had hurried them over here, she gathered he was feeling threatened. Well, she ought to understand that. As she'd told him, in Dallas she'd become something of a speed walker, eager to get out of open places as quickly as possible.

As soon as she stepped outside when he pulled up, however, she felt the bite of the bitter returning cold and was glad he'd decided to get the car first. When they'd left this morning, insulated snow pants hadn't seemed necessary. Now they were practically essential.

On the way home, they stopped at the gun store. Familiar smells of gun oil surrounded her, taking her back to happier times in her youth, oddly enough. Somehow, training to protect herself against pirates at sea had always seemed more like a movie than a possibility. This was very different, and even as she remembered how much she had enjoyed her weapons training, she felt her skin start to crawl. She may have thought it an over-board fantasy of her dad's then, and been more interested in learning to shoot and care for a gun, but now it was for real.

All she had to do was remember last night, that pipe on the porch, and her and Jess's reaction to it. All she had to do was look at Jess to realize that she'd do anything at all to protect him.

"We don't want to be counting on accuracy," Jess said as he approved her choice of a Mossberg shotgun. "Not for this."

She agreed. She'd learned to be a good marksman as a kid, but when it came to a situation like this—well, there was a reason so many police carried shotguns and not rifles.

They waved at the deputy sitting in the car at the end of the driveway. He waved back, lifting a plastic cup as if in toast. Once inside the house, Jess began to relax, but not completely.

He got his own shotgun out of a cabinet in his bedroom and loaded it with six newly purchased shells. Then he passed the ammunition to Lacy, and she followed suit, loading her own weapon easily. Apparently, it was like riding a bicycle to some extent, she thought as she popped the final shell into the chamber. They both kept the barrels pointed at the floor and well away from each other.

"Do you know how to protect someone's back?" he asked.

"You mean, like in the movies? You walk forward and I walk backward?"

"Yeah, like that. Let's check out the house and practice. Make sure your safety is on."

He gave her pointers as they moved through the downstairs, then up the stairs. "Keep the barrel moving and don't fix on anything. What you want to be alert for is movement, okay?"

"Got it."

It felt weird, but as they made their way through room after room, it began to feel more familiar. Her comfort level grew. She could do this.

"He might do something to force us outside," Jess said as they finished the sweep. "If he does, keep low, and if you move, move fast, but not in a straight line."

"Okay."

"Pretend you're a squirrel. Dart every which way, and freeze only when you feel covered. He's going to be alert for movement, too."

She nodded, realizing that her mouth was beginning to dry. She sensed the day was dying outside, but didn't want to pull a curtain back to look. Another night approached, and she couldn't imagine what the madman might try when darkness came.

"With the cop out front, he should try to come from the back," Jess said as he made a pot of coffee. He glanced at the clock on the microwave. "We don't have long."

With guns on the table beside them, they sat facing each other, drinking coffee and eating some stale rolls.

"I could get you out of here," he said again. "There's still time."

She looked at him, seeing the tension in his face, the distance in his eyes. This man, she realized, had gone back in time. His gaze was almost empty, focused on things she couldn't see. He was a long way away, locked inside himself.

This hurt, she realized. After what they had shared last night, she felt him pulling away, and she didn't want to lose him, not even for a few hours.

She had no idea what was going on, why anyone should want to hurt him after all this time. He'd paid an unimaginable price for what he'd been through. Wasn't that enough?

Yet here he was, a man who had devoted himself to saving lives, facing it all again because of a war in a faraway place. God, she felt more helpless than she ever had.

He carried his coffee to the front room and pulled the curtain back a bit. "Our new watchdogs have arrived."

Small comfort, she thought. Gage had sent two men, his best, and one would be walking a patrol, not sitting in the car. Would it be enough? And given how cold it was growing again, she pitied the man who had to walk the perimeter.

It didn't seem like much of a plan. But what else could they do? Gage and Jess had been right when they concluded that they could put an army around Jess's house, but they couldn't keep it there indefinitely. This madman could simply outwait them. Law enforcement had been alerted to keep an eye out for strangers in and around town, but hoping someone would notice this guy was like hoping to find a needle in a haystack. A lot of people passed through. Few stayed long. They'd have to stay a while to be noticed.

"Jess?" She decided that this was not the time to be shy, and there was something she desperately needed to say. Her heart was full of it, even though fear was beginning to edge it out.

"Yeah?" Briefly he focused on her.

"When this is over, can we go to bed together for a week?"

Slowly, a smile cracked his stern features. "I promise. Lacy, I…"

The phone rang, cutting him off. Twisting, he pulled the receiver off the wall. "McGregor."

He listened, his face changing to stone. "I'll check."

The voice on the other end of the line said something.

"No, Gage. If he's hurt, time might be of the essence."

Then he slammed the phone down and looked at Lacy. "The deputies aren't responding. I need to go out there."

"I'll get dressed."

"You stay here. Pointless to expose us both."

Did he really think she was going to let him go out there alone? With no one to watch his back?

He must have read something on her face because he grabbed her forearm. "Lacy, I'm trained for this."

She tugged her arm free. "This must be it, Jess. And I'm not staying here while he lures you outside. We go together, or I'll be pointing a gun at you."

His brows lifted. "No, you won't."

"Wanna bet?" She lifted her new shotgun and carried it into the foyer, where she began pulling on her winter gear. "Some camouflage would be nice right about now," she said, a weak attempt at humor.

The man stood there, looking like a thundercloud, but finally seemed to realize that if he went out alone, the only way he could keep her in here would be to tie her up.

Which was just about how she figured it.

At last he stirred, pulling on his own winter gear hurriedly. Then he opened a hall closet and pulled out a backpack with a red cross on it.

"What's that?" she asked as she zipped her parka.

"Medical supplies. I keep them on hand for search and rescue." He pulled one strap over his left shoulder. He flicked her hood. "No snorkel. It'll impede your vision." Instead he dug around in the closet and offered her a ski mask. He pulled one over his own head, then picked up both shotguns.

With his hand on the knob of the side door, he paused to look down at her. "He could be out there. He could be waiting in that police car. Hell, he could be almost anywhere. Keep low, move fast."

"Dart like a squirrel," she repeated.

"We're gonna take my car to the end of the drive, okay? You stay inside it while I check on the deputy. In fact, stay low so no one can see you're there."

She saw the wisdom of that immediately. If the guy thought only one of them was outside… "Okay." But he might see her as they slipped out the side door and climbed in.

Except that Jess had parked very close to the door, and as they stepped out he pushed her in through the driver's door. No walking around the vehicles. She twisted herself over to the passenger side and scrunched as much of herself as she could get down to the floorboards. He dumped his backpack on the seat beside her head, then stacked both shotguns between the seats. In the brief moments of her exposure, she saw that the snow was blowing again. Either they'd had a fresh fall, or the crust had dried out again. Mini tornadoes whirled around.

The engine roared to life, and they began to move.

"Is anyone coming?" she asked.

"Half the cavalry, probably," he answered. "I'm just worried about the cops in the car."

"Gage didn't want you to go out."

"No. But someone's life might be hanging by a thread."

This, she thought, was the man who had gone to war as a medic. Saving a life above all else. She closed her eyes a moment, feeling a tearing pain for him that he should be forced to face this again.

But an instant later, she steadied and ordered herself to focus. There was too much at stake right now to let feelings get in the way. She needed to be alert and ready.

Catching her by surprise, Sara burst into her memory, smiling, and Lacy felt a sudden sense of peace with her friend's loss. The first real peace she had felt. Sara was gone, but she was doing what Sara would want her to do. And she was glad that her best friend hadn't lived to see this.

But maybe Sara had always understood there would be no future for her and Jess. Maybe, on some level, she had known, and that's why she lived so much in the moment. Why she had never spoken of plans down the road beyond Jess's next return. It wasn't that she feared jinxing them, but rather that she sensed it would never be.

Regardless, peace filled Lacy, almost as if she could feel Sara with them. Maybe she was, letting them know she would always love them both, that she was watching over them. They could both use a guardian angel, that was certain.

The bumpy ride down the driveway began to slow. They must be reaching the police car. Jess spoke.

"When I open that police car door, the cabin lights

are going to be like a beacon. You stay down until I see what's going on. I don't want him to see you even in silhouette."

"Okay." But as her muscles began to tighten from her cramped position, she wondered if she'd be able to move swiftly if it became necessary. And why wasn't she hearing sirens? Shouldn't the cops be on their way?

"See any police lights?" she asked.

"Not yet. But they might be approaching cautiously. No need for a light show."

Good point. Why announce the reinforcements? On the other hand, maybe the guy hadn't done this to lure them outside. If he had, surely he'd be expecting deputies to descend. Maybe this was another move on the weird game board of his own designing. Would he assume that Gage would call to let them know the deputies weren't responding? But why should he?

She wanted to shake the swirling pointless questions out of her head. Now was not the time to wonder about unanswerable questions, but to just be ready to respond quickly to whatever happened next.

Jess brought the car to a stop. The first thing he did was turn off the dome light in his own car. "I'm leaving the headlights on," he told her. He reached for the bag of medical supplies, then laid her shotgun across the seat in front of her. She reached up and closed her hands around it.

Then he grabbed his own and the bag, and climbed out of his car. He was going to stand out in the light from his headlamps. Stand out against any light from inside the police car. A clear target.

He left the driver's door open, then pulled open the door of the police car. *Smart man*, she thought as he crouched in the space between the two doors. She could see an officer inside, his head tipped to one side. Jess reached for his neck.

"Alive. No evident injuries. Slow pulse, steady even breathing. Like he's sedated."

"Where's the other guy? The one who's supposed to be on patrol?"

No answer, of course. Neither of them had any knowledge of that. And how could this officer have become sedated?

Jess straightened a little, looking around through the two windows. "I don't see anyone, but that doesn't mean he isn't out there. Hang tight. There's no injury for me to treat that I can see. We'll just wait here for the deputies."

The balloon of tension eased a bit. Another inscrutable move? Maybe. A bomb that was a dud, and now a sedated police officer? None of this made any real sense.

She'd been prepared for a volley of gunfire, for something terrible to start the minute Jess got out of his SUV. But nothing. Nothing at all. Some kind of taunting and torture?

Was someone out there watching from a distance, getting his jollies? Probably.

Finally she heard the rumble of an approaching engine. The cavalry. *About damn time*, she thought. But of course they had no idea what they were getting into. Of course they'd be cautious.

Unlike Jess, who appeared willing to bet his life any time anyone needed help. Like her. What if some drug types had been coming for her? She could have brought a new hell down on his head, but he hadn't hesitated to take her in.

"You know, Jess, you've got to stop this."

"What?"

"Putting yourself in harm's way to save everyone else."

He snorted, surprising her. "It's no big deal."

No big deal. Just doing what he had to. The words of every hero, just as he'd once told her.

Then everything seemed to happen at once. A car rolled up, followed by another and yet another. Lights came on from every direction, and she dared to push herself up off the floorboards and look. Cops seemed to be everywhere, including the sheriff.

She heard Jess explaining what he'd found and that no, they had no idea where the other officer was. She heard Gage telling him to stay in the car with her. She watched as he climbed back in beside her and a loose cordon formed around both cars.

More cars lined the road. A fire rescue ambulance was pulling up. Whatever this was about, it was over for now.

Deeply disturbed, she tried to see past the lights, to look out over the plains and hills for any sign of movement. Impossible to see, except that men were fanning out, probably in a search pattern.

Then a helicopter arrived, floodlights turning night into day as they swept the area in ever-growing circles.

Jess sat behind the wheel, gripping it tightly and then astonished her by hammering his fist on it, just once. "I want this bastard."

She'd never heard that tone from him before. It dripped with threat and fury. It dripped with death.

He'd been forced back to a place he had never wanted to go again, and there wasn't a damn thing she could do about it. Not one damn thing.

She wanted the bastard, too.

* * *

Hours later, the night began to quiet down again. They'd found the officer walking patrol. He, too, had been sedated with a tranquilizer dart. He might have frozen to death out there, but they'd found him in time.

Both officers were carted off to the hospital. Several cops checked the house for them, and then they were back inside, in the kitchen with Gage. Coffee seemed essential, hot and good and full of caffeine. Lacy sat at the table, keeping her mouth shut while Gage and Jess talked, nursing a simmering anger.

"There was no sign out there that anyone approached the house, although the ground is so trampled now, who could be sure? And anyway, the snow is blowing around again," Gage told Jess. "The whole thing was like that bomb last night, pointless. Useless."

Jess was limping back and forth the length of the kitchen. Apparently the cold had affected his leg. "So. Try looking at it from another perspective."

Gage looked at him over his mug of coffee. "How so?"

"Intelligence gathering. He was able to put out two deputies. Probably pulled up out front and asked your man for directions, then darted him while they talked. He'd probably already gotten to your patroller, but he could do that from a distance. So no, he wouldn't leave any tracks. But he saw how we handled all of this. Your response time, the size of your response, all of that."

Gage nodded grimly. "A military man would do that. So what now? I have to tell you, Jess, I've dealt with a lot, but nothing like this before."

"You're not usually dealing with trained military

men. So he got his measure, if that's what he wanted. Now he knows how long he has when he acts."

"He might be in for a surprise. We came up slowly."

"I noticed."

Gage half smiled without humor. "Probably seemed like forever to you two. What he may not know is how many guys were already here by the time we pulled up. We have enough special-ops guys in this county to put together a good stealth team when we need them. You weren't alone even when it seemed like it. Micah Parish, for example, is a deadeye marksman at 1500 yards. He's not the only one."

Lacy stirred, finally speaking. "Someone was watching?"

"We were," Gage said. "You were never uncovered from the time we realized we couldn't raise our patrol."

"Then why did you call Jess? He went out there and could have been killed!" Anger hit an instant boil.

"I hadn't counted on that part. I was just trying to alert you to potential trouble," Gage admitted, then faced Jess. "Don't do it again. You two stay inside. We'll put another patrol out front again, but they're the face of the operation. This house is being watched full-time now, okay? I don't need you or want you racing out there and providing a target. If Micah and the others are good at 1500 yards, that doesn't mean they can shoot a bullet out of the air. Got it?"

Jess finally stopped pacing and pulled out a chair. "I get it. I exposed us."

Lacy reached out and gripped his forearm. "You were worried about the cops out there."

Gage refilled his coffee mug, then joined them at the

table. "I understand, Jess. I know your motives were the best. It's the kind of thing you do. I know how hard what I'm asking is for you. But if I call again with news like that, just remember I've got more people out there than you know about and we're here to keep you two safe. All I'm doing is alerting you to potential trouble. Keep that in mind."

He drained his mug in one draft, then put it down with a thud. "I don't like this. If there's a playbook for this one, I haven't seen it. Keep in mind that you haven't, either."

A few minutes later, he took his leave. The house seemed awfully silent as the last cars pulled away.

Lacy, her hand still on Jess's arm, squeezed it. "You okay?"

"Feeling like an idiot."

"Never that," she answered swiftly. "What you did was noble."

"Screw that. I raced out there and risked both of us. Gage is right. I should have listened to him. And you! You should have stayed here even more than me. What happened to the timid Lacy who arrived here?"

She hesitated, biting her lip, feeling his green eyes bore into her. Then she admitted, "You."

He grabbed her hand from his arm, twisted on his chair and lifted her onto his lap. "God, woman, you drive me nuts. I'm half crazed with wanting you, and I need to deal with this creep somehow, if for no other reason than I'd like to take you to bed again, and I can't do that when we're being stalked. You make me forget everything, and right now that's dangerous. I thought we were safe for a little while last night, and where did that get us? No, we have to fix this."

She felt her cheeks heat, loving what he was saying, wishing they could just tumble into bed, knowing he was right that it could be dangerous. The stalker was getting bolder. He'd attacked two cops tonight. But oh, how she wished…

Jess's mouth clamped over hers and he stole her breath with a kiss so deep it seemed to reach her soul. When he at last pulled back, she gasped for air and heard him say, "We'll get our chance, Lacy. I promise."

"I'll hold you to that." Then she stiffened. "Jess?" she whispered.

"I heard it," he whispered back. Moving slowly, he slid her from his lap back to her chair. When he reached for the shotgun he'd propped in the corner, she half rose and reached for her own. She glanced at him and saw his finger across his lips.

She nodded. The he pointed upward. She nodded again. A creak from upstairs. A settling house? Or had someone come inside during all the confusion? But the cops had checked the house. Or maybe they'd missed something?

Her heart began to pound, sounding loud in her ears. She wondered if Jess could hear it.

He leaned toward her, his lips to her ear. "If he's upstairs, we need to make him come down here. We'd be exposed on the stairs."

She nodded.

When he rose from the table, he slid the chair quietly. Then he astonished her by clattering the coffee pot. "You want some more?" he asked in a normal voice.

It took her a split second to realize he was trying to make it as if they suspected nothing. "Sure," she answered, horrified to hear her voice crack a bit.

He clattered the pot again, but didn't pour any coffee. He motioned to her and she followed him on tiptoes toward the mud porch. To her surprise, he opened a door there and realized it was a second entry to his bedroom. A door that she had thought led to a closet.

The room was dark, completely devoid of light thanks to the heavy curtains. He guided her through it to the corner farthest from the door. "Get down here in the corner behind the dresser," he whispered. "When he opens either door, you'll see him because of the light from the kitchen."

"Okay. What are you going to do?"

"Get his attention. Do you have your safety on?"

"No."

"Round in the chamber?"

"Yes."

"Don't make a sound. Just be ready."

She clung to that shotgun like a lifeline. From the faintest of sounds, she could tell Jess was slipping across the room. He couldn't get out of here now without letting light in here. What was he going to do?

Her heart racing, her mouth dry, she waited. Then she heard it again, a step overhead. Definitely not the house settling. Never had she thought she'd be glad for the creaky floors of an old house.

She shifted her position so that she was crouched and ready to spring. Then to her horror, she saw Jess open the door they had just come through, and step into the mud porch on the way to the kitchen. He was walking out there to meet this guy?

He partially closed the door behind him, leaving it open about an inch, allowing some light into the bedroom. Her eyes were beginning to adjust to the dark, and she wondered why he'd left the door open, then realized he didn't want her to be blinded by sudden bright light. The man thought of everything.

Except that he wasn't doing her heart any good by going back out there. Armed or not, this guy was coming, and she doubted Jess would just shoot him on sight. No, there had to be a real threat, and the possibility that it could backfire on Jess terrified her.

She adjusted her position carefully, desperately wanting to act but well aware she might make this whole mess worse. What did she know about dealing with stuff like this?

Waiting seemed to last forever. Her skin crawled, her muscles tensed, her stomach knotted and then flipped. She thought she heard almost inaudible steps on the stairway. Then she heard voices and understood another part of the reason that Jess had left the door open: so that she could hear.

"Where's the woman?" a nasal voice demanded.

"I told her to slip out the back," Jess answered. "What the hell's going on, Johnson? I never wanted to see your sorry face again."

"You know."

"That's just it. I don't know squat. All I know for sure is that you sent us into danger and that a little girl died because of that, and the next thing I knew I was in a hospital. What are you afraid of?"

"Nothing."

"Then this game is pointless," Jess said flatly. "Just get out of here and I'll forget I ever saw you."

"Right. Like Stoddard and Callins forgot."

A silence. Did she hear movement? Was Jess even holding his shotgun? Her mind drew a picture of two armed men in confrontation in the kitchen, but she had no way to know. Her heart crawled into her throat.

"So you killed them," Jess said finally. "I wondered."

"Just like I'm going to kill you and then your pretty little girlfriend. She won't get far."

"What's the point, Johnson? Why were you afraid of us?"

"Who said I was afraid? I just don't like witnesses."

"Ah," Jess said. He paused. "So what the hell exactly happened that day? Why'd you send us into a friendly town and get all those people killed?"

"How do you know they were friendly?" Johnson demanded. "Word was, they were in with the insurgents."

"You can tell yourself that, but all of us who were there know the signs. Those people weren't frightened of us. Not at all nervous. So what was really going on in your mind? I'm sure it involved a medal."

"The insurgents were moving in on them. You men were supposed to defend that town. You failed."

"No," Jess answered, "we didn't fail. You failed. If you knew where those insurgents were, you had no business sending us into that valley with them up above us."

"I wiped them out," Johnson insisted. "I got the insurgents."

"And lost your whole unit. And the town. You must feel pretty good about that."

"It was war, McGregor. Because of me, we won that one."

"Winning isn't counted in bodies and collateral damage."

"Count on a medic to think that way. Weaselly non-combatants, not even a true marine. Useless baggage."

"Really?" Jess sounded disgusted. "You don't know what courage is, you jackass. You sent good men to die and kept yourself clear of the action. How did you manage to explain that to anyone, including yourself?"

"I did what I had to do. We were there to stop the insurgents. I suppose you thought bandaging little kids and giving them shots qualified for that."

"It made our troops safer."

"Yeah, you sure proved that, didn't you? You weren't even ready to fight alongside the rest of the unit. You can blame yourself for what happened."

Lacy had to fight not to gasp at that. Blame Jess for what this guy had done? Fury began to replace fear.

"Is that how you salve your conscience? By blaming the people who died to make you look good?"

She heard movement but couldn't tell what it was. So far, nothing sounded violent. She moved her gun a little, pointing it toward the open door.

"I don't need to salve my conscience," Johnson retorted, sounding angry. "And anybody who thinks I do needs to die."

"So the casualty rate wasn't one hundred percent. Not high enough for you?"

"You son of a…"

She heard a chair being knocked over. A scuffle. They were fighting. Fighting! No guns. Was Jess at a disadvantage or advantage because of his leg? She had no way to know.

Defying his instructions, she straightened and crept toward the open door. She had to help somehow, if there was any way she could.

She peeked out, saw the door between the mudroom and kitchen stood wide open. She opened the door of the bedroom a little farther and stuck her head out.

My God, they were wrestling over a pistol. Jess was trying to disarm the guy and it was clear it wouldn't be easy. Johnson was a big man and looked to be at a physical peak. Jess might stay in shape, but he wasn't a soldier anymore.

It was clear to her who might have the advantage. With fear and anger speeding her heart to a dangerous rate, she tried to focus on the fight in front of her, to find a way to help.

But they were so close together, and the shotgun blast would scatter widely, hurting them both. And with each second she hesitated, there was a chance that pistol in Johnson's hand would fire and get Jess.

An instant of perfect clarity seized her, like the moment when she had thrown herself on the fake bomb. Whatever it cost, she had to help Jess.

Rising, aware the two men were so absorbed in their struggle they were probably oblivious to everything else, she walked through the kitchen door, shotgun at ready.

"Drop it," she shouted, aiming the shotgun.

The fight froze for an instant, but just an instant. Apparently Johnson judged that she wasn't likely to shoot when she might hit Jess, and he was right about that. But that pistol in his hand could at any moment end Jess's life. She needed to act before that happened.

Raising the shotgun, she pulled the trigger and blasted a hole in Jess's ceiling. Then she racked another shell and waited.

The wait wasn't long. Startled by the unexpected fire,

Johnson made his mistake. He wrenched his arm free of Jess's grip and pointed the pistol at Lacy.

Jess moved in a blur, chopping his hand downward on Johnson's forearm. The pistol fell and skittered across the floor. Jess kicked it away.

Lacy leveled her shotgun at Johnson as Jess stepped back a couple of feet. "You're next," she said in a voice so steely she hardly recognized it as her own. She took a move forward.

"You won't," Johnson said.

"Yes. I will. I've faced down tougher dudes, you worm. I'd love nothing better than to blow a hole in your center mass. Then maybe weaselly Jess can stuff your intestines back in you."

The strangest expression came over Johnson's face. It looked very much like terror. He started to turn away, poised to run, but Jess tackled him and dragged him to the ground. Johnson struggled wildly, but Jess hung on, then at last managed to press his artificial leg onto the middle of the guy's back.

"Pistol," he said.

She grabbed it from the floor and placed it in Jess's hand. A second later, it was pressed hard to Johnson's ear. She immediately moved forward and added her shotgun to the mix, trying to stay carefully out of the man's reach.

"Sheriff," Jess said, sounding a little breathless.

Keeping her shotgun at ready, Lacy grabbed the phone and dialed for help.

"He's in the house. Jess is holding him at gunpoint. Send in your men," she told the dispatcher.

"Men," Johnson gasped.

"That's right," Jess answered, pressing the pistol even harder against him. "You didn't think they all left, did you? But then you were never good at thinking."

Chapter 15

A warm spell had followed hard on the heels of the clipper. Every door in the house was open, letting in the sweet, fresh air, a gentle breeze that seemed to clear everything from the house.

Jess and Lacy sat at the breakfast table with coffee, toast and eggs. It had been a long night, and the beginning of the new day seemed to have come awfully early.

"Sorry about your ceiling," Lacy said.

Jess looked up and chuckled. "At least I hadn't covered it with copper. You know, I don't think I've ever seen a more beautiful hole."

She smiled over her coffee mug, but it wasn't easy. Last night's events were fresh in her mind, but worse, there was no reason for her to stay here any longer. No one was trying to kill her. She had no excuse to remain.

But she didn't want to leave. In a few short days, she felt she'd planted roots here, with Jess. Every time she looked at him, she craved him. She wanted to spend time with him in the sunlight and out of the shadows. Her old life no longer held any appeal.

But how could he ever look at her without seeing Sara? It would be impossible for them both. Sara had brought them together, and she remained in both their hearts.

"I hope you'll stick around," Jess said, surprising her. "At least for a while."

"But…"

He arched a brow. "But what? Are you in that much of a hurry to ditch me? I guess after last night, I could see why."

"Last night has nothing to do with it. And I don't want to ditch you. It's just that…" She hesitated.

"Sara," he said quietly.

"Sara," she agreed, her heart feeling like lead.

He reached across the table and took her hand, holding it tightly. "Can I be perfectly honest?"

Her heart skipped a few nervous beats, but she knew it was time, yet again, to face reality. "Yes."

"When I first saw that bus, the first day you were here, every time I caught sight of you or heard you, I half expected Sara to be there somewhere."

She compressed her lips and nodded. "I understand."

"Maybe. But then something else happened. In my mind, you stopped being an extension of Sara. Well, not only in my mind, in my heart, as well. All our phone conversations over the years, they helped. I had been getting to know you as an individual. As Lacy. A short time after you got here, I realized I had moved past that. You're a friend to me now, and Sara's no longer the only part of that. How about you?"

"I'll always miss her." She hesitated, wondering

where he was going, but he was waiting for her to speak. "I guess I reached the same point. We both loved Sara, but we have lives apart from her now."

He nodded. "Exactly. Nobody can replace her for either of us, but we'll always still love her. She holds a special place with both of us. But that doesn't mean we can't make new special places for other people."

She sighed, clinging to his hand. "Things get so confused sometimes."

"There's nothing confusing to me about this," he said firmly. "You, Lacy Devane, have come to matter as much to me as Sara ever did."

She caught her breath and dared to meet his gaze. His green eyes were filled with warmth and heat.

"I don't want a replacement," he said. "I want *you*."

All of a sudden she couldn't breathe. All she could do was stare at him and wonder if she was understanding correctly.

"I realize you may not be as certain. It's been a rough couple of days and we haven't had a whole lot of time to explore each other, but if there's one thing I know I want, it's to wake every morning to your sweet face and fall asleep beside you every single night. Until forever."

He moved, pulling his chair around until he was sitting right beside her, then reached out to hug her. "You brought the sunshine back. You, not anyone else. You gave me back joy, and the hope for more of it. You gave me everything I thought I'd never know again. You did that. Just tell me you'll give me a chance."

"A chance for what?" She felt hope rising in her, an emotion so rare over the past few years that she feared it. She didn't dare hope for anything.

"For a future with you. A life with you. If you think you can stand living in this tiny town with me."

"I like it here," she said weakly. God, he was over-whelming her, and she was trying to batter down the rising hope because she didn't dare believe and...

Then he kissed her, hard and deep, and it was as if he brought light and passion to the darkest, emptiest corners of her being.

"Lacy," he said when he moved away an inch, "I love you. I hope you'll give me a chance, that you might come to love me, too."

The hope leaped the last of her barriers, filling her with wonder, a sense of a new dawning to a beautiful life. Her heart, which had become such a pained, pinched lump in her chest, seemed to expand to embrace the whole world. Jess loved her. She couldn't doubt it as she looked into his eyes, his beautiful eyes.

"I love you," she admitted finally. "I felt so bad about it, but... I love you."

"Don't feel bad. We're still here, you know."

Which was the whole point. They were still here. And if Sara was around, Lacy knew her friend would be happy for them, because that was Sara. She could almost feel a blessing settle over them, along with a warmth that had nothing to do with the breeze blowing into the house, and everything to do with life moving forward, growing again, putting out new branches and leaves.

She leaned into Jess's embrace, and felt their heartbeats slowly synchronize. Who would have believed dreams could rise out of such ashes?

Inside her, the blossoming began. It became springtime in her heart. New life. New love.

* * *

They flew to France for Christmas to meet Jess's parents, who lived in the south of France on the Cote d'Azur. But Jess had promised her a few days in Paris proper, although he warned her it would probably be cold.

She was getting used to the cold and didn't believe she was going to mind one bit. Throughout the long flight, they had held hands and talked quietly, except for a couple of hours when she fell asleep with his arm around her and her head cradled on his shoulder.

They'd been married a week earlier in Conard City, a quiet ceremony attended by his friends and their families, but once they reached his parents, apparently a huge party had been arranged. She was a little nervous about it, and had sent Jess into gales of laughter as she tried to learn French.

"The effort will be appreciated," he told her with a twinkle in his gaze, "but believe me, most Europeans speak great English. Relax."

She'd used a computer program to practice, and figured she might successfully manage greetings and a few essential questions, like "Where is the toilet?" Beyond that, she was sure she'd amuse everyone.

But she was more excited than nervous. A whole new family, a whole new country and a future brighter than the City of Lights.

"So you still want two kids?" Jess asked quietly as she rested on his shoulder.

"Yes. You? Have you changed your mind?"

"No way. I am so, so grateful to be making plans with you. I just wondered if you had decided you wanted more."

"And we'll finish fixing up the house together first."

"Life has something to say about that," he said lightly. "But yes, we'll try."

She hadn't told him yet and had difficulty preventing her hand from settling protectively over her still-flat stomach. She'd tell him in Paris. Maybe at the Eiffel Tower. Maybe on the Left Bank. Maybe...

So many possibilities, and he was opening them all to her. She twisted and kissed his chin. "I love you so much. So much that I'm kinda glad I ran into a drug cartel."

That drew a laugh from him, causing heads to turn. Most of them smiled.

"Who'd ever have thought of them as matchmakers?" he asked, giving her another kiss. "Never leave my side, Lacy. Never."

"I won't. And you'd better not, either."

"I learned my lesson. Joined at the hip forever."

Wow, she liked the sound of that. Forever. Or at least as much of forever as life would grant them.

She sent a silent hug winging heavenward to her best friend, thinking, "Thank you, Sara."

Then she let go and looked forward to life with Jess.

* * * * *

MILLS & BOON®

INTRIGUE
Romantic Suspense

A SEDUCTIVE COMBINATION OF DANGER AND DESIRE

A sneak peek at next month's titles...

In stores from 18th December 2015:

'The perfect Christmas read!' - Julia Williams

Jewellery designer Skylar loves living London, but when a surprise proposal goes wrong, she finds herself fleeing home to remote Puffin Island.

Burned by a terrible divorce, TV historian Alec is dazzled by Sky's beauty and so cynical that he assumes that's a bad thing! Luckily she's on the verge of getting engaged to someone else, so she won't be a constant source of temptation... but this Christmas, can Alec and Sky realise that they are what each other was looking for all along?

Order yours today at
www.millsandboon.co.uk

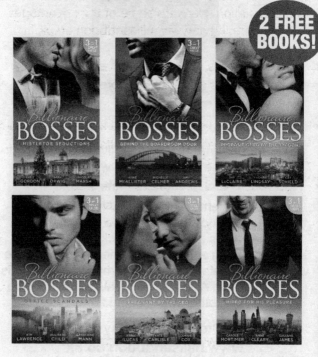

MILLS & BOON®

Why shop at millsandboon.co.uk?

Each year, thousands of romance readers find their perfect read at millsandboon.co.uk. That's because we're passionate about bringing you the very best romantic fiction. Here are some of the advantages of shopping at www.millsandboon.co.uk:

* **Get new books first**—you'll be able to buy your favourite books one month before they hit the shops

* **Get exclusive discounts**—you'll also be able to buy our specially created monthly collections, with up to 50% off the RRP

* **Find your favourite authors**—latest news, interviews and new releases for all your favourite authors and series on our website, plus ideas for what to try next

* **Join in**—once you've bought your favourite books, don't forget to register with us to rate, review and join in the discussions

Visit **www.millsandboon.co.uk**
for all this and more today!